THE HARP AND THE ROSE

THE QUEENSTOWN SERIES - BOOK 3

JEAN GRAINGER

To my mother, Hilda, with my love and gratitude, always and forever.

PROLOGUE

SHIMLA, INDIA, 1920

The rattan ceiling fan spun lazily, barely moving the humid heat of the Himalayan afternoon. A fly buzzed for a moment before it was swatted expertly by the young white-clad waiter who was standing by, at the ready to serve any one of the handful of guests. The card room of the Orchid Hotel was large, the baize tables scattered at a distance from each other for discretion's sake. On this Tuesday afternoon, the wheels of the Empire were being oiled in offices around the town by an army of British civil servants of varying ranks, and few had time to play cards. Apart from him and his companions, there were a table of ladies playing bridge in the corner, their pale skin glistening with perspiration despite their light, cool, pastel-coloured dresses, and a foursome of businessmen who sat near the bar, up to escape the stifling heat of Bombay; Ralph thought they were Dutch. They were playing pontoon, a childish game in his opinion, but judging by the laughter and the frequency of the waiter's visits with more gin and tonics and cold beers, they were not taking it too seriously.

Oliver Beckett languished in a cane chair, sipping a seltzer water, and Ralph sat opposite. Beckett was a tall, thin man in his late forties or early fifties. His salt-and-pepper hair was cut short in the military style, and his face, while not unhandsome, looked like it had been carved in granite. Beckett was as close to a perfect specimen of a high-ranking officer in the British army as could be achieved. He had piercing blue eyes and straight full brows. The only things amiss were his thin lips and slightly receding chin. His demeanour matched his appearance – sparse, nothing to spare. Though he had been there almost a year, nobody really knew him. He didn't drink alcohol and rarely socialised. He'd been married, it seemed – the mamas looking for potential suitors for their marriageable daughters had compiled a full dossier on him within hours of his arrival – but he remained aloof.

'So have you heard I'm being transferred to your neck of the woods, Devereaux?' Beckett's north-of-England accent belied his high rank. Generally the broad vowels of the north belonged on an NCO, but Beckett must have been something special to rise above his natural rank in life to the position he now enjoyed.

'Really?' Ralph had heard rumblings. Nothing was a secret for long in Shimla.

'Yes, Queenstown, in County Cork. You're from there, are you not?'

'Yes, that's right. My family have a house there, the Cliff House. I grew up there but then came out here as a young man. What's taking you there?'

Beckett gave a small sly smile. 'I seem to have a particular knack for managing insurgents. The powers that be reckon that if I can get the natives here back in line, I can apply the same techniques to the Irish, though they are considerably more pig-headed than our Indian subjects.'

Ralph nodded sagely. 'Yes, there's a certain mindset there, undoubtedly, a mulish ignorance, I think you'd call it. They make terrible servants, for example, most unbiddable.' He nodded at the young waiter with a white-toothed grin, who jumped to the command, and within a minute, another seltzer water and a gin and tonic appeared. 'A servant of ours, a woman, a devious, conniving creature, actually lives in my family home, I'm sorry to say. Her and her illegitimate child, allegedly the result of an affair between her and my brother, but I don't know about that. I've had all the devil of a job to remove them. To be honest, in the end I just gave up.'

'So have you been back there recently?' Beckett asked.

Ralph considered what to say. He'd kept more or less to the truth – it was the easiest way to not be caught out – but he was rarely drawn on the subject of his life before Shimla. 'Well, I went back after my brother died to confront her, but I'm ashamed to say, she saw the threat of my arrival to her newfound wealth and seduced me. I foolishly allowed it. The woman is a devil, I tell you. She lured me to her bed, and I was helpless to stop it. She is beautiful, I'll give her that, but the exact same methods she used to beguile my poor halfwit brother worked on me. I'm embarrassed about it now. She even forced an engagement on me, intimating that I had got her in trouble and that I had to do the honourable thing. Of course, against my better judgement, I did, but I soon learned that it was yet another of her lies, a ruse to trap me. Luckily I came to my senses and got out of there before the wedding.'

'Sounds like a lucky escape.' Beckett sipped his water.

'It was, most fortuitous. But my own fault. I was grieving for my brother, I suppose, and she saw that weakness. But if you're going there, keep an eye on her, and the daughter too. She's Rose Delaney and the daughter most unfortunately has our family name, Harp Devereaux. The mother knocks about with the local undertaker, a disreputable fellow called Matt Quinn, and to be honest, I've always had my doubts about him.'

'Why is that?' Beckett swatted a fly from his arm. He showed no sign that either the heat or the humidity perturbed him in any way. For some new arrivals, it was oppressive, and they were easily spotted, but Beckett seemed to adjust immediately.

He'd been sent from London last year to rout out any dissention among the natives employed by the Crown, the implication being that the viceroy was making a total dog's dinner of it, with the Ghadar Party having success in uniting the Indian Hindus, Sikhs and Muslims, when previously they'd remained conveniently at logger-heads. The Indian independence movement was gaining traction and getting support, not just in India but from all over the world, and the British were right to be alarmed. It was impossible to run the Empire without native help, but in doing so, the authorities ran the risk of allowing people who were disgruntled with the status quo right into the heart of the organisation.

Ralph took a sip of his drink. This was too good an opportunity for revenge to give up. 'Well, the last time I was there, I struck up a friendship with a Captain Pennington of the Royal Norfolk, a decent chap and a fine golfer. One night he simply vanished. There had been some argy-bargy the evening before with the daughter I mentioned, Harp. She's a chip off the old block, if you know what I mean. I went to bed and heard some kind of racket upstairs. I thought nothing of it. They live on the third floor, and who knows what visitors they have at night. Not my business. But then the next morning, Pennington was gone. Rose made up some story about him absconding without paying the bill or something, but I always felt there was more to it than that. And I saw Quinn lurking about that night too, so whatever happened, he's involved.'

'And did the army investigate?' Beckett asked.

Ralph sighed. 'It was 1916 and the war was raging – I think they had bigger problems. They sent a chap, all right, but he swallowed that devious cow's version. I'll tell you this – she will fool even the most astute of men into thinking she's a prim and proper lady. They had cooked up some story by then about Pennington going AWOL. Don't ask me the details now – I forget. But then a body was found near his parents' place in England, and they put two and two together and made five. Case closed. But I always knew there was more to that story.'

Before the conversation could go any further, Alfred Pascoe walked in, greeted them and sat down at the bar near them. 'Scotch, one lump of ice,' he demanded of the waiter.

'Ah, Alfie, how are you?' Ralph asked.

Pascoe turned. 'Hello, Ralph. Fine, thanks, and you?'

Alfred Pascoe was the only child of Isaac Pascoe, a wily old Cornish man who'd come out to the jewel in the British Empire's crown in the 1860s and made a fortune in tea. Isaac was a frugal, hard-working, sullen man, and he and his French wife had lived a righteous life, dominated by work and God. Alfred had been a miracle by all accounts, born as his mother turned forty-five years old. They spoiled the child, instilling in him none of the values they had hitherto espoused. The result was a paunchy middle-aged man with a florid complexion and a weak chin. *No wonder his wife seeks her pleasures elsewhere*, Ralph thought.

Ralph always made a point of being friendly to Pascoe. It gave him a thrill, knowing that Alfie was oblivious to the fact that Pamela Pascoe spent most afternoons entertaining Ralph in their marital bedroom.

'Marvellous.' Ralph smiled. 'You know Brigadier General Beckett, I trust?'

'Only by reputation.' Pascoe smiled as well. 'It's nice to make your acquaintance, sir. I haven't been spending much time up here of late – business in the city.'

Ralph suppressed a smile. *The business of losing his shirt in every casino in Delhi*, he thought. Pascoe was a gambling addict, and everyone knew the Pascoe fortune was in serious jeopardy. Luckily Pamela had independent means from her father, or Ralph would have to rethink his association there.

'A pleasure,' Beckett replied, but didn't get up.

Before the conversation could move on, a beautiful young woman arrived, followed by a young native laden down with shopping bags and boxes. 'Papa, so sorry I was delayed. How was your trip up? Frightful, I'd imagine, in this heat.' She kissed Pascoe's cheek as he embraced her. She didn't look at either Ralph or Beckett.

Marianne Pascoe was as perfect an example of an English rose as could be found. Slender and pale, with blond curls and a peaches-and-cream complexion, she had china-blue eyes and a kind of girlish innocence that endeared her to all who met her. She'd been at boarding school in England and then finishing school in Switzerland, and now that she was back, it seriously curtailed Ralph's afternoons with her mother. It was a bore to listen to Pamela drone on about how much she missed her daughter when she was away, but it was worse to have the airheaded young woman about.

'Oh, it was fine, darling. Worth it to see you again.' Alfie clearly adored her. 'Shall we dine? I booked a table on the terrace.'

'Marvellous.'

Alfie Pascoe drained his whiskey and bid the men a good day.

'She's a beauty,' Beckett remarked after they'd left. 'Is she spoken for?'

Ralph thought quickly. The officer was far too old for Marianne, but if he took a shine to her, it might be just the thing. If Ralph could engineer it, it would mean Marianne out of the way. But more importantly, Pamela would have a direct line to what was happening in Queenstown, and so, de facto, would he. Marianne didn't know him, but he knew her. 'No, she's just back from school,' he replied.

A silence hung between the two men, an unspoken conversation.

'Pascoe is up to his eyes in debt. He might be persuaded to offer her hand in exchange for a wager?'

'What makes you think I'd want to marry her? My intentions would be far less honourable.'

'Marry her and you can indulge whatever intentions you like, legally and forever.' Ralph smiled.

Beckett was clearly considering it. 'Possibly. What's his weakness?'

'Poker.'

Alfred Pascoe fancied himself a card shark, but Ralph wasn't fooled. The man was way out of his depth, and everyone knew it. Gambling wasn't a gentleman's pastime for him; it was a compulsion.

Poker was Ralph's main trickle of income these days, unfortunately, but he kept his winnings small and was confident that he was above suspicion. He was clever enough to play without losing his shirt, but he also ensured he made no enemies. No big sweeping of the board for him. A little win here and there, nothing to alert anyone's attention.

'Can you set it up?' Beckett asked, draining his glass and rising.

'Of course. I'll send word.'

Beckett nodded and placed his hat on his head before departing.

* * *

As Ralph had suspected, Pascoe jumped at the chance of a high-stakes game. And so the following evening, they convened again in the card room.

Pascoe was focused but exuded an air of desperation. Ralph caught the brigadier's eye, but they gave nothing away. Ralph knew that Beckett had at least a straight if not a full house. And Pascoe was in trouble.

'I'll fold,' Ralph said, knowing his hand was mediocre at best. Anyway he was more interested in watching the cat-and-mouse game between Beckett and Pascoe.

'I'll see you, and raise you twenty.' The brigadier threw another chip on the table with a cool self-assuredness, and Pascoe eyed the pile of chips in the middle of the table with ill-concealed greed.

On and on the game went, Pascoe clearly getting into deeper and deeper water as he saw and raised each move. But like all gamblers, he was sure his lucky break was just around the corner.

Beckett spoke quietly. 'How would you like an escape clause?'

'I beg your pardon?' Pascoe looked outraged to have the game interrupted like that; it was most irregular.

'Well, as I see it, you stand to lose a substantial amount. So I have a proposition.' Beckett's voice was barely audible, and Pascoe had to lean in to hear him.

Ralph remained impassive.

'Go on.' Pascoe clearly hated having to say it. Ralph noticed the bead of sweat that trickled down his pudgy neck into the collar of his shirt.

'Simply that if your hand wins, you take the pot, but if my hand wins, you get your money back in return for your daughter's hand in marriage.'

Pascoe swallowed. The pot was approximately 3,000 pounds. From what Pamela had said, it was money old Alfie definitely could not afford to lose. Ralph didn't want to see him bankrupted; Pamela would hate that and would end up having to dig into her own funds to save face, money Ralph saw as his. He needed Beckett to have a strong hand and for Pascoe to be as weak as he knew him to be. By the looks of things, Pascoe had a fairly good hand, not spectacular but good enough. Ralph hoped he was confident or cocky enough to think it was sufficient.

'But she's just a girl! She's only nineteen, and, sir, with all due respect, you're considerably older than that.' Pascoe reddened.

'Alfie, come now,' Ralph purred. 'Marianne is a lovely girl, and she would be taken care of very well by the brigadier. She would want for nothing and enjoy the life of the wife of a senior British officer. We know him to be a decent chap, and he would treat her well.'

'But she would never agree, and my wife...' Pascoe protested.

'Girls are silly – we know that. Marianne doesn't know what's best for her, but you as her father do. And *your* wife' – Ralph slightly emphasised the 'your' – 'will surely be guided by you as head of the family?'

Bingo. He knew from Pamela that she and Alfie had had an enormous bust-up recently and that he had threatened all sorts up to and including divorce if he wasn't given the respect he felt he was due. Pamela would hate the scandal of a divorce, and even though Alfie was frittering away the family fortune, the Pascoe name still meant something in India. Alfie's father, whom Alfie idolised, had ruled his family with an iron fist, and Alfie aspired, though failed, to attain such heights of control.

'So it comes to this, Pascoe. If you beat me, I walk away with nothing, but if my hand trumps yours, you walk out with your pockets full provided I have an undertaking from you that Marianne and I will wed within the month.'

Pascoe swallowed and looked around, and his eyes rested on Ralph's. *Help me*, his look said.

'It's a win-win, Alfie,' Ralph soothed reassuringly.

After an interminable minute, Pascoe showed his hand. A straight flush. He turned his cards up to reveal the nine, eight, seven, six and five of diamonds.

Pascoe looked slightly smug, and Ralph could tell by the gleam in his piggy eyes that the pile of chips would solve his immediate financial worries at least. Though undoubtedly he wouldn't use the money to pay his debts but would lose it all exactly as he'd won it.

Beckett's face was inscrutable. He made brief eye contact with Pascoe before revealing his hand. Ralph thought Pascoe would actually vomit. The colour drained from his face and the sweat formed on his brow almost instantly. He pulled back the hand that was poised to sweep up the chips and stared in disbelief.

A royal flush.

The brigadier calmly gathered the chips but then pushed them across the table to Pascoe. 'Thank you, gentlemen. Let me get you both a drink?'

There was a ruthlessness to the man Ralph identified. He recognised it because he too possessed that trait. 'Thank you.' Ralph smiled. 'And congratulations.'

The brigadier nodded, and they all watched as the waiter gathered the chips that would be taken to the manager, who would convert them to cash.

'A gin and tonic?' Beckett asked Ralph.

'Please.'

'And for you, Alfred?'

'The same please,' the other man managed, though his voice cracked and he mopped his brow with his handkerchief.

'Two gin and tonics and a seltzer water, lots of ice,' Beckett commanded the young Indian waiter. 'Now, gentlemen, thank you both for a very pleasant afternoon. I trust you will deliver the good news to Marianne this evening? I'll meet you both here tomorrow at four for afternoon tea to discuss everything.'

The drinks arrived and Pascoe downed his in one long draught, standing up immediately. 'I must get on,' he mumbled, and nodded his goodbye.

Ralph observed the brigadier over his glass. 'He was full sure he had you.' There was no pity or admonishment in his words; it was simply a statement of fact.

Beckett shrugged and changed the subject. 'Where'd you get that?' He nodded at Ralph's wooden leg beneath his cream linen trousers.

'An unfortunate bullet.' Ralph smiled. Everyone assumed his injury was earned in the war, and he never chose to disavow them of that assumption.

'Where?' Beckett was persistent.

'Below the knee,' Ralph replied, deliberately misunderstanding him.

CHAPTER 1

Twenty-year-old Harp Devereaux crossed over to the other side of the road and instinctively moved as the small group of Black and Tans made their way down Oliver Plunkett Street in Cork City. If her Cumann na mBan mentors, Liz and Cissy Devlin, had taught her anything, it was to stay out of their way inasmuch as was possible. The army and the navy were all right usually, but the Tans were a law unto themselves and terrifying. The women's wing of the republican movement were more at risk from sexual violence from them, and it was best not to give them cause to notice her.

Harp's classes at University College Cork were finished early that day, as it was the Easter holiday, and she was looking forward to the train journey home to Queenstown. She had set her heart on studying at Trinity College in Dublin, but the Devlins had mentioned how useful she would be to the movement if she stayed in Cork, and so she decided to attend U.C.C. She loved her studies there and had no regrets. She was thinking about her last lecture on Romance languages given by Professor Mary Ryan, the first female professor in the United Kingdom. It gave her a surge of pride and enthusiasm for the fight ahead to think that with each blow for freedom, they were striking a blow for women's rights too. Harp loved being at university – the reading, the learning, the sheer joy of it thrilled her – and for the first time in her education, she didn't feel like the odd one out.

Despite her good humour, however, the tension in the air was palpable. Since the first shots fired in the War of Independence the previous year, the IRA were gaining ground in every direction, and the result was that the ever-swelling numbers of Crown forces were on high alert and very trigger-happy. The success of the Irish Volunteers under General Michael Collins had even caused the smaller Royal Irish Constabulary barracks out in the country to close for fear of attack.

But the arrival the previous month of the Black and Tans – as the new recruits to the RIC were called – lent the entire conflict an air of savagery that had not previously been there, and everyone was on edge.

They jostled each other as they passed in their mismatched uniforms and almost knocked a toddler over, caring nothing for the population as usual. The supplementary police force, brought in to mercilessly quash the IRA and wreak havoc on the people of Ireland, were mostly demobilised soldiers from the Great War, damaged, drink-addicted, broken men who had left any shred of compassion or human dignity they might have once possessed in the trenches of Flanders and Ypres.

The killing of the Lord Mayor Tomás Mac Curtain the previous month, in front of his wife and children, had shaken the city to the core. Police, their faces blackened, had barged into his house and shot him, leaving him to die in his wife's arms. Cissy had been distraught – she knew his wife and was heartbroken for her – but Liz was different as usual. While the older woman felt all Irish losses keenly, Harp knew that Liz was aware that with each new outrage came more and more recruits to the IRA and Cumann na mBan. And goodness knew they needed more.

She wrapped her scarf more securely around her neck and tugged her knitted hat down. She had a handgun in the waistband of her skirt at the back, so she needed to bundle up. The gun had been used earlier in the day on a raid on the post office near the college; funds were always needed. The gunman had melted into the crowd, and the gun found its way to her as was arranged. Men were stopped all the time – JohnJoe joked that he wished that she was as familiar with the contours of his body as the British were – but they tended not to stop women, and girls clearly coming from their classes, large bags of books over their shoulders, were generally ignored.

She took to heart the instruction of Countess Markievicz, the women's army leader, when she said, 'Dress suitably in short skirts and strong boots, leave your jewels and gold bands in the bank, and buy a revolver.'

Weapons were critical, and the IRA sought to retrieve each and every one they could. Storing them was one of the biggest issues and one Matt and the Devlins were working on constantly.

There had been a raid on a loyal farmer's barn around Fota, and the IRA had lost a lot of weapons that night. Luckily no personnel were there, but that didn't stop Matt being furious. It was probably just a stroke of luck on the part of the RIC, but Matt was constantly warning them of the danger of informers. It had been, he was quick to point out, the reason each armed insurrection had failed in the past. And only by dealing swiftly and severely with anyone aiding and abetting the British could victory be achieved.

She exhaled as the Tans passed by and continued her journey. The city was busy, but she made her way to the station without a problem. Possession of a firearm meant execution, so it was no small thing to walk around with a gun in her skirt. But she felt strangely calm about it all. She wasn't particularly brave, she didn't think, but she believed the job had to be done and they had to be the ones to do it. She was reminded of the words of the Talmud, a Jewish holy book Henry had a copy of in his library. 'If not me, who? If not now, when?'

To her relief the train was full. It would be on Holy Thursday since the station would be closed the next day for Good Friday. Queenstown locals, children home from boarding school for the holidays,

British military and a handful of passengers for the port filled each carriage, mercifully necessitating that she stand. It was harder to find a reason to stand when the train was half empty, and it would be hard to sit with a gun in her back.

She found a corner of the carriage and leaned against the wall as the train pulled out of the station. She wished she could take out her book. She was engrossed in Edmund Spenser's *The Faerie Queene* and over the holiday was due to write an essay on the justification for its inclusion in the canon of works that constituted the literature of Western civilisation. That he wrote much of the text in Youghal, a seaside town just to the east of Queenstown, gave Harp an added level of interest. Reading would have passed the time nicely, but she dared not risk it; she needed to remain alert.

The train juddered as it rounded the bend in the tracks, and a fellow passenger fell against her. Instinctively Harp shielded herself, ensuring the girl crashed against her arms rather than her body.

'Oh, I'm terribly sorry,' the girl exclaimed in a British accent as she tried to right herself.

'Don't worry. It always happens on that bend.' Harp smiled. 'I think the train driver is in a rush to get home for his tea.'

The woman was around her own age, perhaps a little younger, and was remarkably pretty. Slight but shapely, she had that creamy complexion so admired in England, with innocent blue eyes and golden-blond curls piled under an extravagant hat.

'Well, I grew up in India, so these are very civilised trains compared to there. Indians think nothing of transporting livestock on the train, and the carriages can become awfully smelly. Even the first-class ones stink rather badly.' She made a face and giggled.

Up to the time she went to university, Harp would have cringed at the thought of a casual conversation with a stranger like this, but expanding her mind and education had given her confidence. Not feeling so odd all the time was refreshing, as she was now surrounded by people who were not only as well read or clever as she was but often remarkably more so. She loved it.

'Are you taking a ship somewhere?' Harp asked.

The girl shook her head sadly. 'No, I'm afraid not. My husband was recently posted here – he's a military man – and I've had to come with him. We just arrived three weeks ago. We live at a place called Peary Tower, an awful mausoleum of a house just outside of the town. It's honestly like a place one would go to be murdered!' She had a surprisingly deep laugh for a girl, an earthy chuckle that Harp found infectious.

'I know it.' Harp smiled. The other woman wasn't wrong in her assessment. It was a dark gothic mansion that had been owned once by some eccentric writer who never published anything. When he died without issue, the state took it over.

'Don't get me wrong – it's very pretty here and I love the cooler weather, but it's rather hard to fill the days. Oliver – that's my new husband – is out all the time, and I'm jolly lonely, I suppose. I'm used to living in Shimla, in the Himalayas – all the British live there once the city gets too warm – and there's always something to do or someone to see.'

'Well, you could play tennis perhaps. I think some of the British officers' wives do that?' Harp suggested, strangely warming to the girl though she was clearly the wife of the enemy. Perhaps a friendship with her could be of use. Matt was always saying that this was an information war; the more intelligence they could gather, the more targeted the attacks could be.

The girl grimaced. 'My husband took me to a sherry reception to meet the other wives when we first landed, but...' – she leaned in to whisper – 'they are all so old.'

Harp couldn't help but laugh.

'My name is Marianne.' She stuck out her hand and Harp took it.

'Harp.'

They chatted amicably about the possibility of interest or diversion in Queenstown such as might entertain young ladies, and Marianne described the move to Ireland from India in hilarious detail. She was such a live wire and seemed to have a turn of phrase that brought out the humour in everything. Harp found the arrival in the station came all too soon. Marianne was indiscreet certainly, revealing that her husband snored and that he insisted on sleeping with a window open even though she found it freezing at night.

As they alighted, Marianne fell easily into step beside her. 'So you have a boyfriend?' Marianne asked, gathering her bag and large hat box.

'Er…yes. He's American but he lives here now.'

'Ooh, an American! That's exotic.' Marianne giggled. 'There were a few of them in India. Everyone assumed they were filthy rich, and all the girls set their caps at them. Our own chaps would fume, but the Americans were so exotic compared with dull old George in his plus fours and Fair Isle jumper.' She did an impression of 'dull George' that made Harp laugh.

Harp noticed the checkpoint as Marianne carried on. Her heart thumped and she swallowed. There was not normally a checkpoint getting off the train. They would wave her on surely.

Straight ahead, at the ticket barrier, a soldier drew a middle-aged woman to the side and a female officer patted her down. Harp focused on her breath. She must not look guilty; they could spot that a mile away.

The crowd getting off the train slowed to a shuffle as each person was processed through the checkpoint.

Marianne chatted on, oblivious to Harp's disquiet, and soon they were at the barrier.

'Ah, Corporal Hastings, isn't it?' Marianne smiled, and the previously sullen soldier smiled back.

'Yes, Mrs Beckett, how nice to see you again.' He nodded.

'And you, how is that thumb now?' Marianne turned to Harp. 'The silly goose jammed it in a rather heavy trunk of mine as he helped us move into Dreary Towers.'

The man suppressed a grin; he was clearly charmed by her. 'I'm fine, Mrs Beckett, thank you.'

Marianne linked her arm with Harp's. 'This is my friend Harp.'

The corporal nodded pleasantly. 'Good afternoon, miss. Please, pass on.' He ushered them through the barrier and returned to his duties.

Harp tried to exhale slowly so as not to alert her new friend to her panic. Yes, developing Marianne's friendship was a good idea.

'He's rather a dish, isn't he?' Marianne asked conspiratorially as they walked out of the station into the late afternoon sunshine.

'Em...I suppose so.' Harp had no idea; all she ever saw was the uniform.

'I think so, anyway. I'd better head for Dreary Towers, I suppose. It was lovely meeting you, Harp. I hope we can meet up again?'

'I'm sure we will – Queenstown is a small place,' Harp replied. 'My mother owns the Cliff House guest house –'

'Oh, that beautiful white house overlooking the sea?' Marianne interrupted. 'I admire it every time I pass. You're so lucky to live there, and the gardens are spectacular, from down here anyway. I adore gardening. We had the most lovely gardens around our house in Shimla. Papa and I used to take care of them...' A dark cloud passed over her elfin face. 'Well, my father doesn't live there any more, but it used to be gorgeous.'

'My mother is a good gardener, but it's actually my boyfriend, JohnJoe, who has the green fingers. Come up and see the glasshouses and the gardens sometime if you would like?'

Marianne's face lit up with enthusiasm. 'Oh, I would love that. I'm sorry, I know I'm probably being frightfully pushy, but I have not a single friend and that awful house is truly driving me scatty. And the gardens out there, well, it's more like a tangle of wild wilderness really, all briars and thorns, so I don't even know where to start.'

'Could your husband get it cleared for you, and you could perhaps plant it then? Because of the Gulf Stream, the south coast of Ireland is actually more Mediterranean in terms of soil temperature, so we can grow things here that shouldn't flourish in our climate, or so JohnJoe tells me anyway. Apparently any involvement on my part with a plant is the kiss of death.' Harp wondered if she'd imagined the look of disappointment on Marianne's face.

'No, he said it's fine as it is – though the weeds and briars are taller than a man – so I doubt he would do that for me. But I'd love to come and see your garden.'

They walked along together until Harp was almost level with the Devlins' store. She would drop off the pistol there, and it would be collected by someone else later.

CHAPTER 2

The Devlins welcomed her as they always did, cheerfully and innocently. Never in a million years would anyone suspect them of being revolutionaries. They were, to everyone in Queenstown, just a pair of sweet old sisters who ran a shop. Neither Cissy nor Liz had ever married. Their parents had run the shop before them, and everyone knew them.

'Ah, Harp, 'tis yourself.' Cissy grinned as Harp entered the clean, bright shop.

Everything was where it was supposed to be, arranged neatly on the primrose-yellow painted shelves behind a large U-shaped counter in varnished pitch pine that ran around the interior of the premises. The Daz washing powder, Sunlight soap and Brasso occupied one section, and beside those were neatly stacked candles, matches, twine and other haberdashery. In the baking section, baking powder, flour, dried fruit and sugar in sparkling glass jars gleamed in the sun. The meat was all under the counter, stored in the cold meat safe, and the entire shop was always full of produce, biscuits, fancy jellies and sugared almonds. Harp's favourite section was to the far left. There Cissy had so many jars of black and white bullseyes, pink and white clove rocks, green and red apple drops, sugar-covered bonbons of pink and yellow, cinder toffee covered in chocolate, lollipops, liquorice and boiled sweets. In the summertime there were ice creams too, kept cold and sliced between sweet wafers in the icehouse out behind. Children gathered, usually on a Saturday, with their halfpennies or farthings, and Cissy never minded how long it took them to choose their favourites. She always added, with a conspiratorial wink, an extra sweet for luck.

Harp wondered if either sister had ever considered marriage. Cissy would have been a wonderful mother; she was so warm and loving. Liz probably would have been too, but she was by far the more reserved of the two.

The huge picture window overlooking the main street made the Devlins' shop so much brighter and sunnier than the huckster shops out towards the Holy Ground. Those places were a few pennies cheaper for bacon or candles undoubtedly, but the experience of shopping there was unpleasant. In the Devlins' shop, the smell was a combination of sweets, carbolic soap and fresh bread; it had never changed.

Liz was replacing the sheets of plain paper used to wrap purchases, dotted at intervals, on the countertop. There was a large scales over the meat safe with lead weights on one side; its blue enamel and steel gleamed. But the real centrepiece was the ornate brass cash register right in the middle of the counter that ran along the back of the shop. It had cost a fortune apparently, but Cissy had seen it in a catalogue of one of the wholesalers who visited twice a year and had convinced Liz that while the wooden box they kept behind the counter was adequate for their needs, this would be something they could admire for years to come. It was brass plated, with buttons denoting the different denominations; there was even a porcelain plate screwed to it to detect counterfeit coins. It was truly remarkable and the only one in the town like it. Cissy loved it. Liz had smiled one of her rare smiles at her sister's enthusiasm and had agreed to the extravagant purchase.

Nobody could accuse the Devlins of being spendthrifts. For as long as Harp had known them, which was all her life, they wore the same clothes: dark-brown day dresses, over which they each had a housecoat, one of pink, the other blue. They wore their grey hair tied back in neat buns, and neither wore any frivolities like jewellery or powder.

The new cash register had been the talk of the place the previous year. It was a peculiar and extravagant purchase for any business, but for the frugal Devlins, it was truly uncharacteristic.

'How are you, Misses Devlin?' Harp asked, addressing them normally. There were three people in the shop being served, so she stood and waited her turn. She used to enter their house by going around the back, but Matt felt to do so nowadays was to arouse unnecessary suspicion, whereas Harp had been going to the Devlins' shop all her life.

'Grand, love, grand altogether.' Cissy smiled at her but turned her attention to the man in the British uniform waiting to be served. 'Your usual, Sergeant Jennings?' She smiled sweetly.

'Yes please, Miss Devlin. Two ounces of Woodbine and a box of matches, and I'll take some of those Mint Imperials as well. I'm going dancing tonight – don't want some nice young lady to have to smell tobacco smoke off me.' He grinned and Cissy returned his warm smile.

'Indeed and you don't then,' she agreed sagely, pouring the sweets into a little paper bag. 'Where is the dance at all?'

'At the hotel in Rushbrooke. It's the local rugby club, I think. A few of the other chaps told me about it. But I think anyone can go.' He turned to Harp, who coloured under his admiring glance. 'It's Harp Devereaux, isn't it?' he asked.

How on earth did he know her name? Did he know something? She forced a smile, having trained herself not to panic in such situations. 'Yes, that's right,' she said pleasantly.

'I heard you play the harp in the cathedral last month, for the blessing of the boats. My dad was a fisherman, off Newquay. That's in England,' he added unnecessarily. 'But he was drowned when I was just a nipper. I heard the lovely music as I was passing and went in, and heard the confraternity band and then your solo. It was beautiful.'

'Oh, she's a rising star, our Harp, all right,' Liz chimed in, rescuing her.

'You must feel the cold, all wrapped up like that on such a fine day,' he carried on, determined to keep the conversation going.

'I'm just recovering from a flu. I wouldn't stand too close in case you catch it,' Harp said with a smile.

'Y'know, Miss Devereaux, a few days off lying in bed would be just the ticket. His Majesty doesn't believe in letting us laze about. Maybe you'll come to the dance with me and we can have a turn together and you can give me that flu.' He laughed, and she knew he was just flirting harmlessly.

'I'm sure she would love to, except that her mother was in here earlier, getting provisions for the guests coming this evening who are booked in for dinner as well, I believe?' Cissy said, keeping her tone light. 'And that new bobbin she ordered came in this morning, Harp, so I'll just get it for you. 'Tis still in the back – I didn't get a second all day to unpack the box, we're that busy.'

Liz was serving Mrs Grimes her daily two slices of bacon and a half dozen eggs for her Ernie's tea. The dour housewife paid and went on her way, and the man who just wanted the evening paper left the money on the counter and was gone.

'That's right, I'm afraid. My mother is a little like the king that way, no time for slackers.' Harp managed a little laugh.

'That's a real pity.' He looked genuinely crestfallen. 'Perhaps we can try another time?'

'I'm afraid she's spoken for.' The deep American-accented voice was unmistakable.

Harp's heart sank. It wasn't that she wasn't happy to see JohnJoe come through the door of the shop – of course she was – but the very sight of the British military seemed to rile him, and she worried that he was not as good as she or the Devlins at keeping his feelings in check. Matt had warned him on more than one occasion that he needed to be careful, but JohnJoe resented the presence of the British in a way that even the people of Queenstown didn't understand. To them, JohnJoe O'Dwyer was an American, and he both looked and sounded it. But what they failed to understand was that JohnJoe had lived in Ireland until he was fourteen, and then he'd been abandoned by his drunken father into the care of his uncle, Pat Rafferty of Boston. And the Rafferty name was synonymous with Irish republicanism in America. JohnJoe had been indoctrinated since he was a lad to fight for his country's freedom, to resent every seed, breed and generation of Englishman who put his treacherous and duplicitous foot on Irish soil.

JohnJoe was, far more than other young Irishmen, exposed to the outrages perpetrated on Ireland by their nearest deadly neighbour. He particularly liked the writings of Wolfe Tone, and Tone's immortal words were as familiar as nursery rhymes. JohnJoe often quoted him to Harp.

From my earliest youth I have regarded the connection between Ireland and Great Britain as the curse of the Irish nation, and felt convinced, that while it lasted, this country would never be free or happy.

Jennings spun around and took JohnJoe in. JohnJoe was taller and broader, and in his working clothes looked every inch the ruffian. His copper curls had grown now and were dusted in sawdust. A light golden stubble covered his jaw, and his green eyes glittered dangerously. Harp thought he had never looked more handsome.

'Oh, yes? By whom?' Jennings's tone had changed now, sounding much more belligerent.

'By me.' JohnJoe stepped closer to the sergeant, and despite the man's best efforts to hide it, the fact that he was intimidated could be seen in his eyes.

Harp shot JohnJoe a look, the one that said, *This is neither the time nor the place.* She had a pistol in her waistband, and a disgruntled servant of the king in their midst was the last thing they needed.

'Very well then.' Jennings smiled at her, ignoring JohnJoe. 'Forgive my impertinence, Miss Devereaux.' He nodded and, taking his tobacco and sweets, left the shop.

'Rein that temper in, lad, or you'll be neither use nor ornament to us,' Liz warned as she crossed to turn the sign to closed and drew the blinds down. 'Get in the back there, Harp, and, JohnJoe, let me leave you out there for fear he's loitering around outside and watching – you never know.' She opened the door and ushered JohnJoe out. 'Matt warned you, and he won't do it again. I know it galls you – it does us all – but getting your hackles up at them only puts them on their guard, and the element of surprise is all we have.'

'I know.' JohnJoe was immediately contrite. 'But I just thought he was –'

'I know, but as I say, rein it in, right?' Liz surreptitiously glanced up and down the street.

JohnJoe nodded and left.

Harp dropped the gun off and left to catch up to JohnJoe. He was in the workshop, on the main street opposite the White Star Line ticket office. The entire floor and walls of the shop were covered in coffins in various stages of construction.

'It's so good to see you,' she said, throwing her arms around him. She'd missed him. She stayed in digs off College Road with a very cranky woman in term time, but it was near the campus and cheap, and most importantly, the woman was a member of Cumann na mBan as well so didn't remark on Harp being out late or having messages or instructions delivered.

'Hello, beautiful!' He hugged her tightly and kissed her. 'Sorry about that. I shouldn't have…'

'It's all right. We forget sometimes how to be normal. I don't think I even know what that is any more.'

'Here, Aunt Kathy sent you some cookies.' He went to a box and extracted the tin of delicious chocolate chip cookies that Harp had enjoyed so much when she visited four years previously.

Boxes of treats for JohnJoe and Danny arrived weekly, as did funds for the Irish struggle and weapons too, all arranged by their uncle, Pat Rafferty in Boston. Danny and JohnJoe saw they reached the right hands but were extremely careful to avoid any obvious association with the Volunteers. They both worked for Matt in the undertaking business, making coffins, and as far as the authorities were concerned, they were just two Americans living in Queenstown, minding their own business. They put it about that they had come back to Ireland to avoid the draft for the Great War and had just stayed. There were some snide remarks about cowardice from time to time, but they didn't care in the slightest.

'My goodness, there must have been a lot of deaths in recent weeks.' Harp smiled and accepted the tin of biscuits.

Matt and the boys had come up with the ingenious idea of burying weapons and money in coffins in the graveyard. As undertakers, they were entitled to draw coffins about, and the IRA made sure there was a decent group of mourners each time. And even the British army would not demand the opening of a coffin. So the churchyard had become the biggest arms and cash dump in the town.

'Oh, a terrible outbreak of dying altogether.' JohnJoe winked and drew her in for another kiss.

'Hey, you two lovebirds better not get carried away among the caskets there…' Danny Coveney's voice interrupted their kiss.

'Hello, Danny!' Harp called as JohnJoe released her.

Danny looked as he'd always done, handsome and devilish. His dark eyes and wavy hair made him look more Italian than Irish, but it wasn't just his good looks that endeared him to everyone. Men liked him because he was a straight-talking, easygoing chap, and women were putty in his hands, a skill he used to its full advantage.

'Hello yourself, Miss Devereaux, and how are all the books treating you?'

'Oh, you know yourself, Danny, hard at it from dawn to dusk.' Harp sighed theatrically.

'Well, I'm glad you're back to put a smile on our kid's face. He's like a lovesick calf when you're gone.'

JohnJoe hurled a rag soaked in linseed oil at Danny.

'Well, I hope you've been behaving yourself. When I was home at Christmas, I seem to recall you'd caused quite a ruckus with the local girls, set them at each other's throats, according to Cissy.'

Danny held his hands up innocently. 'A misunderstanding, nothing more.'

'Hmm.' Harp raised a sceptical eyebrow.

'Look, Harp, the trouble is there's only one of me and not enough to go around, y'know?'

'Well, I'm not sure the world could cope with another Danny Coveney.' She smiled.

CHAPTER 3

're you seeing Matt this evening?' Harp asked Rose quietly as they cleared away the remains of the guests' dinner. They were a family of six visiting a sick relative nearby. There were very few holidaymakers round about these times; the air of tension and simmering violence was palpable.

'No, he's busy tonight,' Rose said as they scraped the scraps into the chickens' bucket.

Rose and Matt's relationship was a secret that only Harp knew. It was vital, Matt insisted, that nobody suspected an association. His position as commander of the IRA meant that if he was ever caught, his family would be at extreme risk, so to all intents and purposes, the undertaker lived alone, had one son in Dublin and was a widower. It hurt Rose to sneak around, Harp knew, but it was what had to be done.

'I miss Jane, she didn't mind dealing with the wretched chickens .' Harp sighed, eyeing the bucket balefully. JohnJoe's sister Kitty had been reunited with her fiancée, and they'd married and moved to Dublin and taken his younger sister, Jane, with them. The quiet presence of the child reminded Harp of herself at that age, and she was inordinately fond of both Kitty and Jane.

'You miss Jane? Well, I miss Kitty more, I can tell you. From the day that girl walked into this house, she was nothing short of a godsend. I was delighted for her of course that Seamus was released from prison, though to be honest, by the sounds of things, it's only a matter of time before he lands right back in there again, judging by his activities.'

Seamus O'Grady and his brothers, natives of Liverpool but with Irish parents, had come over in 1916 to join the Rising. They got incarcerated in a British jail for their trouble but seemed, if anything, to be delighted by it all. They were full members of the IRA. Seamus had befriended several leading lights of the cause in prison and was now high up in the organisation in Dublin. Kitty was in Cumann na mBan up there and kept in close contact with the Devlins and Harp and their branch of the women's organisation down in Queenstown.

Harp loved Seamus. He was full of fun and jokes, and she liked to listen to his Liverpudlian accent. He adored Kitty and she him, and the fact that she was raised to be a lady and he was a fishmonger was a source of amusement and fun to them both. Harp especially liked him because of how gentle he was with Jane. He knew and accepted that she and Kitty were a package and one didn't get either without the other. Rather like the Devlins.

Seamus and JohnJoe got on famously, and though JohnJoe would have rathered his sisters stayed in Cork, Seamus was determined to be in the thick of things in Dublin.

'Yes, well, we all have to take risks,' Harp replied quietly.

'I don't want to know,' Rose said darkly. She knew of Harp's involvement, but she wasn't in the women's army herself so had decided early on it was best if she wasn't party to details. She passed on any information that she thought might be useful, such as things she overheard from her military guests, but apart from that, she stayed out of it. If she knew Harp was, for example, chatting to officers' wives with a view to using them for information or being chatted up by a sergeant while a pistol was tucked into her skirt, Rose might have had a heart attack from the stress of it all.

'JohnJoe said he'd call later,' Harp said, changing the subject and wiping dry the plate her mother had washed in the sink and handed her.

Something about her tight lips or the strain in her face made Harp look at Rose keenly. 'What's wrong?' she asked.

Rose glanced around, though they were alone in the kitchen. They had hired new staff to replace Kitty, but the staff didn't live in. It was unusual for them to provide dinner for the guests, but this family were under such stress and had asked, so Rose had agreed.

'Matt is taking the lads out tonight.' The words dropped like stones.

The strikes against the Crown forces were coming hot and heavy now, all over the country but in Cork particularly, and though it was having the desired effect of making the enemy jumpy and prone to mistakes, each attack brought savage reprisals in its wake.

Last month they firebombed the RIC barracks in Gleann Rua. There were only five policemen there, and they were caught completely unawares. Once the building was on fire and the policemen were outside with their hands up, Matt and the boys went in and liberated several weapons and rounds of ammunition.

Up to the shooting of Lord Mayor Mac Curtain, the method was to damage property and steal weapons but not to kill personnel unnecessarily. But everything was different now.

The Black and Tans had arrived to the home of one of the Volunteers the next day. He'd been caught previously out past the curfew, so they were suspicious, and they'd been brutal. One of them punched the Volunteer's grandfather in the face, a man in his seventies, knocking him out cold. And when his sister screamed at them, one of them dragged her by the hair, flinging her away from the old man. They tore the house apart looking for the man, breaking the whole place up in the process. The Volunteer's mother begged the officer in charge to stop his men. But he'd just laughed and said she knew perfectly well how to make it stop, and that was to give him the whereabouts of her son and his comrades.

'*Ná habair faic!*' a younger daughter had shouted, clinging to her sister, entreating the family to remain silent, though on the ground her grandfather lay possibly dead and their house was being destroyed. She didn't need to remind her mother not to say anything – no matter what, she would never betray her son and his comrades. They were the only possible route out of this tyranny.

The use of Irish infuriated the British, as it was generally forbidden.

'What did you say?' the officer demanded, then grabbed the younger girl, no more than twelve.

This was all observed from a stand of trees behind the house, where Matt had had to physically restrain the lad from going down to defend his family.

'The barracks again?' Harp whispered.

Rose shook her head. 'No. You know that old house out past the old graveyard, Peary Tower?'

Harp swallowed and nodded. The image of Marianne Beckett came to her mind. The Devlins had seen her walking beside the girl from the station and told her she was the new Commanding Officer's wife.

'Well, a replacement for Potts has arrived. He was brought from India, I believe, because he did such a thorough job on quelling Indian resistance. Oliver Beckett is his name. A whole new level of authoritarian savagery, it seems. The Tan officer ordered the rounding up of all young men in the village of Gleann Rua last night and threatened to shoot every third one. Just like that. Cold as ice, he was, apparently. He said he didn't care if they were involved or not, he was going to rout out the IRA, and if that meant killing every man for a hundred miles aged between sixteen and sixty that he came across, then so be it.'

'Did he do it?' Harp asked.

'No, but he made them kneel all night in the street, and it was so cold. Eventually they got a tip-off – Matt doesn't know from who – and they arrested a few, but Matt said he was in no doubt Beckett would have done it if he'd not got the names. The poor lads he picked up are in custody now, so God knows what's happening to them.

'Mr Bridges down in the hotel and several others made a

complaint to Beckett about the behaviour of the Tans, not just that incident but the drinking and the looting and you know the way they go on, but Beckett refused to do anything about it. Mr Bridges is as loyal to the Crown as you can get – his wife is a sister of Brigadier Potts's wife, as you know – but even he's tired of the damage the Tans are doing to the town. When he heard about the threatened public executions, he spoke up and demanded Beckett rein them in, but Beckett said they had a job to do and he wouldn't stand in their way.'

Harp felt as if ice were churning in the pit of her stomach. It felt never-ending. Could the English not just leave, go back to England and leave Ireland in peace? There was no reason to stay. Their men were being killed; the RIC lived in fear in the barracks. But the British had controlled Ireland since 1169, and for some reason, they were not willing to let go.

'So are they going after this Beckett?' Harp knew that such an attack would bring about horrific backlash, but she was equally sure they were doing the right thing.

Rose just nodded.

'He'll be well guarded, though, won't he?'

Rose shrugged. 'He refused to be billeted at the barracks, nor would he stay at the hotel, insisting on getting a private house for himself and his wife. She's years younger than him, it seems, and they chose that awful old place. Nobody's lived there since Justin Pinkerton died, and that must be ten years ago. It's gone all over-grown and everything, but that was the place he chose. It tells you something about the man, doesn't it?'

Harp considered for a moment not telling her mother about her encounter on the train, and then immediately dismissed the idea. Though they were very close, she and her mother didn't see eye to eye on everything. 'I met his wife today,' she said, then sat at the kitchen table as Rose made them a cup of cocoa.

'Whose wife?'

'Beckett's.'

Rose stopped stirring the cocoa powder into the hot milk and stared. 'How? Where?'

Harp explained all about the train journey and the checkpoint.

'Well, thank goodness you did, because if they'd stopped you...' Rose swallowed. It wasn't necessary to say what they would have done if Harp had been caught.

'She wants to come up and see the garden. She sounded like she was having a very lonely time of it here. So I invited her.'

Rose looked wary. 'Well, I'm glad you were with her today, but I don't know about making any further contact. It can't end well, you know?'

'No, Mam, I have to befriend her. It's too good an opportunity to miss.'

'Harp, I don't know... He's a terrible man and...' Rose set the cup of cocoa down in front of Harp and took a seat opposite with her own. She sighed. 'That's the trouble with war, isn't it? I often think of those boys in the trenches, singing "Silent Night" in English and German and then going out into no man's land together on Christmas day, only to be back shooting at each other again the next day. The British soldiers they send over here to wreak havoc on us are just normal boys, but they have their orders, given by people like that Beckett, and war makes us all into people we don't recognise, people we never thought we could be.'

'But we are winning. We're getting somewhere. We just need to hold on, stay strong and resolute. They're cracking, I can feel it. We just have to push a bit harder.'

'I suppose so.' Her mother was clearly sad. 'But the cost is so high. And we have a long way to go yet. Sometimes I think it will all be for nothing.'

'This situation isn't easily resolved, Mam, you're right. And you know I'm not a political person, or at least I wasn't, but we can't live under their thumb – we just can't. In each generation we tried and failed, and perhaps we'll fail too, but we have to try.' Harp wished she could console her mother, but Rose was worried, and with good reason. Every day, Harp and Matt took chances that could have dire consequences.

'But this time *is* different,' Harp said. 'The tactics, the guerrilla war, with the use of civilians and the support of the population, we can do it. Collins has the right idea. For the first time we are making an impact, we're hurting the mighty British Empire because we know our country better than them, and we are sticking together. Every other time it was pitched battle in which we had no hope. Napoléon said, "You must not fight too often with your enemy, or he will learn your art of war." But what we're doing now, an army of shopkeepers, students, telegram boys and housewives, they've never encountered that here before and they don't know how to deal with it.' She took a sip of her drink. 'We have the people on our side. What can they do, murder every one of us?'

Rose smiled. 'You sound just like him.'

'Matt?'

Rose shook her head. 'No, Henry. He used to get so riled up on the subject too, just like you. It's hard to believe he's gone eight years, isn't it?'

Harp thought about it. 'Yes and no. Sometimes it feels like yesterday we were reading upstairs, the two of us, him telling me about the Oracle at Delphi or Frederick Douglass. But then so much has happened, so many people have come and gone in our lives that it feels like a very long time ago.'

'That's true.' Rose glanced at the clock.

Harp knew Matt gave Rose a signal that he was home safe each night he went out. He opened the gate from their garden onto the Smuggler's Stairs as he passed the Cliff House on the way to his own house. They kept it closed as a rule, so Rose could look out her bedroom window, and if the gate was open, Matt was home safe. If she was so worried she couldn't sleep, she'd get up and check and then she could relax.

'I still expect to see Ralph Devereaux walk in the door some days.'

Harp was surprised. They never mentioned him if they could help it. Ralph was gone, forever, and good riddance. She leaned across and laid her hand on her mother's. 'He's gone, never to come back. JohnJoe and Danny made sure of it. He can't hurt us any more.'

'I know, and I try to tell myself that, but...what if he does, Harp?

Especially now with all we're tied up in? And his cosy relationship with the British...'

'Danny and JohnJoe gave him a hiding he won't forget in a hurry, and we know he owes money left, right and centre here – and you know people have a long memory where that's concerned. And we're sure he's gone back to India because that awful woman who stayed here mentioned him – remember Mrs Monard or Monarch or something? Her husband was some big shot in a rubber company, and they knew each other in India?'

'You're right. I'm just being silly.' Rose glanced at the clock again.

'Watching it won't make it go faster.'

'I know.' Rose shook her head as if to dispel the dread and anxiety. 'So tell me about college. How's it all going?'

Harp was glad to change the subject. She was just as nervous as her mother was, but clock-watching wasn't going to help. 'I love it. I think of Henry so often when I'm there, how much he would have enjoyed it all. He wouldn't have enjoyed the socialising or any of that.' She grinned. Henry Devereaux liked only two people, Harp and Rose; everyone else was a nuisance as far as he was concerned. 'But the reading, the learning, the discussions are wonderful. Last week I was in a tutorial group discussing *Tess of the d'Urbervilles* by Thomas Hardy and someone said it challenged not just the ideas of Victorian feminism but also their beliefs about sexuality and purity. I added that I thought it displayed both the frailty and strength of a woman in that time and from that class so wonderfully, and nobody looked at me like I had ten heads.'

Rose pealed with laughter.

'Seriously, Mammy, you don't know how refreshing it is not to have to hide, to pretend like you don't know or have no opinions, like I had to do at school. University is a celebration of learning, and the whole place shares this insatiable thirst for knowledge and deeper understanding.'

'I'm glad. For you, of course, but also if you are a good student, then perhaps your other activities won't raise too many eyebrows.'

Harp knew her mother was resigned to her own involvement in

the freedom movement rather than an enthusiastic participant like the Devlins or Matt. Nobody would question Rose's loyalty, and she'd done everything that was asked of her without complaint, but Harp knew that Rose more than anyone longed for it to be over.

Harp smiled reassuringly. 'Lots of girls at college are in the *ciorcal cainte*. It's all quite innocent.'

Rose laughed. 'It is, in my eye, innocent. You might fool the British into thinking you are all sitting about discussing poetry in Irish, but are you really telling me everyone else is foolish enough to think that a bunch of young Irishwomen, who gather in a conversational Irish group once a week, aren't political?'

'They're not as smart as you give them credit for, Mammy.' Harp winked and went to the dresser, where a pile of letters was gathered.

Since they'd first opened the Cliff House guest house, Harp had asked the guests who were staying with them before emigrating to Canada, America or Australia to stay in touch, to let them know how they got on.

'Oh, look, this is a card from Ottawa, Canada, from that mother and daughter who were going out to her late husband's family – remember them?'

'I do. She was such a funny little girl, with that mop of curls that her mother couldn't touch because she screamed blue murder if she came within ten yards of her with a hairbrush. How did it work out for them?'

Harp scanned the postcard. On the front was a picture of a very straight Rideau Canal. 'She says they are having a wonderful time. Eloise is happy in school and speaking French fluently because her father's family there live on the Quebec border. Margaret, the mother, has her own little house attached to the family's, and they seem to have really settled in. She's working as a nurse in the local hospital.'

'Anything else?' Rose asked as Harp scanned.

Harp opened a letter postmarked Boston. It wasn't from the Raffertys; she knew Kathy's writing by now. The letter was headed with the crest of the Ursuline Order. Inside the folded sheet was another smaller one, which Harp absentmindedly placed on the table. She sat down as she read the short handwritten letter.

Dear Miss Devereaux,

I am writing to you with the sad news of the passing of our Sister in Christ, Angela. She had been ill for some time, as you know. She looked forward to receiving your many letters and asked that we make contact with you when she went home to God.

Angela, or Molly as you knew her, was a wonderful addition to our community and will be sorely missed by all who knew her.

Your mutual friends the Raffertys have been very kind, and Angela enjoyed their regular visits.

I know that you were aware of the troubled relationship she had with her family in Ireland, but she wanted you to know that they reconciled in the end. Her brother came to visit her and brought the best wishes of her parents and her other brothers. That gave her great comfort in her last days.

I enclose a note she wrote to you to be sent on the occasion of her death.

May God bless you and your family.

Sister Joan

Tears stung Harp's eyes. Molly O'Brien had been one of the very first guests at the Cliff House, and she was in many ways the reason Harp and JohnJoe were so close. Molly had been determined to join a convent, but her parents wanted her to marry a local farmer's son. She ran away and bought a ticket to sail to America, but before she could get on the ship, her father and fiancée turned up. A fight ensued, resulting in Danny being injured, which meant JohnJoe spent the entire summer with Harp and Rose while Danny recovered.

'I can't believe it,' Harp said, her voice choked with sadness.

'Poor Molly. God rest her soul. We'll have a Mass said for her.' Rose tried to comfort her. 'I know you and she wrote a lot.'

'I was to go and see her when I went to Boston, but with everything that happened and having to come back early, I never got to. I really wish I had now.'

Harp's visit to Boston in 1916 – when she met Chief O'Neill, the collector of Irish tunes, and brought back the proceeds of an enormous Irish American fundraiser for the cause, sewn into the lining of

Kathy's fur coat – seemed like a lifetime ago now. So much had happened.

'I feel guilty about that,' Rose said. 'You only came back to save me from having to marry Ralph.'

'Well, the only reason you agreed to marry him was to save me from swinging for the murder of Pennington, so it had to be done. But Molly was so nice. JohnJoe will be devastated. She loved him so much.'

'What does the other note say?' Rose picked up the note folded in four and handed it to Harp.

'"Dearest Harp, JohnJoe, Danny and Rose",' Harp read aloud. '"I know I'm gone if you're reading this, so I wanted to say goodbye. You all mean so much to me, and I pray for each of you every day that God keeps you safe and well."

'"I want to thank you for your friendship, and your love. It has made my life all the richer. I have never once looked back on my decisions and regretted anything. I followed my heart as Harp advised. Carpe diem! Thank you all."

'"As I write this, the lovely drawing you did for me, JohnJoe, of the cathedral in Queenstown is beside my bed. I wish you and Harp a lifetime of happiness together. No matter what the future holds, you two have a special relationship. And, Danny, you are a kind and good soul and there's a very special girl out there for you, I know it. Though that doesn't mean you need to dance with every single one on both sides of the Atlantic in the meantime!"

'"Rose, thank you for your hospitality and clear head that night. Though I only knew you for such a short time, I know you to be a wonderful mother, and I'm so glad that for all who spend their last night in Ireland in your lovely home, yours is one of the last Irish faces they see. Surely a comfort in the years of exile that follow."

'"My brother Pius came to see me, and he brought letters and presents from my parents and Billy and Kevin too. He even brought a card from Finbarr Clancy and his wife. He has three children now, and I'm sure he thanks his lucky stars every day that I left him on the quayside that morning in Queenstown."

"'I wrote to Eleanor as well. She's doing so well with her medical clinic and is hale and hearty, thanks be to God. If she hadn't given me her ticket that day, I don't know how my life would have turned out, but I do know it could not have been more fulfilled or happier than the years I've had here in Boston."

"'Harp, you are a special girl, with an incredible mind but an equally capable heart. Live well and be happy, my dear friend."

"'I wish I had more time, but the Lord is calling me home and so my work here is done. God bless you all. Molly".'

Harp went to bed with a heavy heart. She first ensured all candles were extinguished, as to do otherwise would be to arouse suspicion. That was the way they lived now, always thinking how any action would look to the authorities were they to barge in. The guests seemed genuine, but there were spies and informers everywhere, though less so now that the IRA were ruthless with anyone even suspected of working for the British.

Still, as Matt and the Devlins said insistently, they were to take no chances, give them no cause for a second glance, do everything in their power to act the lady and her daughter running a respectable guest house.

And they did. Rose was not just professional; she was friendly and warm to the British officers who stayed in the guest house, seemingly enjoying their charm and repartee with an attractive young widow, as they saw her. Never anything that could be considered flirting, of course not, but she was a welcoming face in a hostile world as far as they were concerned. The fact that her daughter, Harp, bore the surname of her father, one of the Devereauxes of Queenstown, a family notoriously loyal to the Crown, helped enormously, and nobody would ever suspect them of republican sympathies, which was a strength they had played to many times now.

The Cliff House had been used as a safe house so many times they'd lost count. IRA men who needed to be exited from the country for fear of execution had hidden in plain sight as travellers to America. Harp had even used her book of letters and cards as inspiration for their cover stories.

She lay in her bed, wide awake. It was a cloudy night, so no stars; even the moon was obscured. She could close the curtains and light a candle and read, but she never closed her curtains, preferring to see the stars and be woken by the dawn.

She stared at the ceiling as the clock ticked on her locker. All romantic notions of war in the wake of the Rising four years ago had long since dissipated. She was reminded of the remark by Erasmus that war was delightful to those with no experience of it. During the early days of the war, in the summer of 1919, just a short year ago, it was all glory and speeches. But since the Black and Tans' arrival, since the British felt cornered and that terrible combination of fear and bloodlust, since the Irish realised that there was no backing down from this fight now, irrespective of the outcome, it would now be to the death. Things had changed. People were dogged, determined, resolute, while simultaneously being so bone-weary of the whole bloody thing.

CHAPTER 4

*I*t was a cloudy, misty night. Matt Quinn gave the signal, and the first hand grenades were thrown through the open bedroom window. It was fortuitous that they didn't have to risk waking anyone by breaking glass. The blast was almost instantaneous, and flames sprung from the window within seconds.

Matt led the company of seven Volunteers, who surrounded the house, ensuring no escape for the inhabitants. Matt was a slight, agile man, dressed in black, his sandy hair covered under a black hat and his handsome face covered with a mask to prevent being recognised. When he was sure the dark, forbidding building was surrounded, he kicked in the front door and saw Beckett and his wife in their night-clothes, stumbling down the stairs, towels to their mouths to mitigate against the thick black smoke. Beckett was indiscriminately firing a pistol with one hand, and the other was covering his mouth.

Matt was just about to fire when shots rang out behind him. Suddenly the house was surrounded by soldiers. Whistles blew and he heard rounds of machine-gun fire. Before he had time to register that, a searing pain in his hand caused him to drop his weapon – he'd been hit. They'd walked into a trap. He cursed himself for assuming the six-foot-tall brambles and briars that surrounded the house would be empty. Beckett had clearly stationed troops there in the event of an attack.

The Volunteers knew the time had come to retreat. The enemy had clearly been lying in wait in the overgrown gardens. Matt had to protect his men at all costs, so he ignored the pain in his hand and retreated in the smoke and flames back to his position under some hedges behind a low wall fifteen yards from the house. He slid in beside the lad who had covered him as he'd entered the house.

'Pull everyone you can back. Nobody sleeps at home tonight. Scatter into the countryside.'

'Yes, sir.' The young man followed his orders without question.

Matt wondered if he should try to take a shot at Beckett, who was now standing outside the burning house. While it was tempting, it would alert the Crown forces to his position, and besides, he was surrounded and it was too risky. The wife too was an easy target, standing alone and apart from the others, and he took aim. But then she turned, tears streaming down her cheeks, and he saw how young she was, just a girl really, and lowered his weapon.

Matt watched as over to the right the Twomey brothers fought off three of them; they were managing well enough. The Twomeys were both wrestlers, as was their father before them, so they were more than a match for those pimply-faced recruits.

Beckett's wife was screaming, and the staff were running from the burning house. The butler was from Midleton, so Matt would ensure he resigned in the morning, along with all the others, for fear of being seen as collaborators.

The Twomeys, as he predicted, floored the soldiers and were gone away into the night. The house was well and truly unsalvageable now, flames licking from every window; the roof had caught on fire too. The sight of Beckett standing in his nightclothes and the whole staff huddled together gave him no pleasure, but it sent a strong message. At least they'd lost nobody.

He looked down, trying to see how damaged his hand was, but it was too dark. Blood oozed; it would be hard to conceal such an injury in the coming days.

Keeping to the back roads and lanes he knew so well around the town, he finally reached the Smuggler's Stairs. He couldn't dress his own right hand, so he had to go to Rose. Luckily there were no officers staying right now, just a family, so he could sneak in unnoticed. He used his key and crept up the back stairs to her bedroom, where he found her awake.

'Oh, thank God you're all right.' Rose leapt from the bed and stepped forward. Her long dark hair was loose, and her cream nightdress was almost translucent in the dark. She had the heavy drapes drawn and so risked a small candle. As the candle threw some light, she saw his bloody hand wrapped in his pullover. 'Oh, Lord, let me see that.'

She took Matt's hand gently, unwrapped the pullover and tried to assess the damage. 'It's gone right through, the bullet. We need Doctor Lane.'

'No, we can't trust him,' Matt said quickly. 'I'll be fine. Can you just bandage it up, Rose, and I'll get myself home to bed. I need to be there if they come looking. And I'll say I jammed this hand in the lathe making the coffin for Neilus Callaghan today in case anyone asks. Can you get Harp to tell Danny and JohnJoe so they'll corroborate it?' Beads of sweat had formed on his forehead from the pain.

'All right, I'll do my best,' Rose agreed. 'But what if you're seen going home? They'll be out and about by now surely. Maybe it would be best if you stayed here?'

'I'll go up through the gardens. I'll be grand.' With his good hand, he tucked a stray hair behind Rose's ear. 'Brian left me some morphine – I have it above in the house. He guessed I'd need it, I suppose. I'll take some and get into bed. I have to be there if they come looking, Rose, you know that. That Beckett won't leave a stone unturned now. He's a bad piece of work – we need to give him nothing.'

Matt's son, who had served as a medic in the Great War and was now working in a hospital in Dublin, had at one time been sweet on Harp. Rose knew Matt missed him. She pulled out a first-aid box and began to wrap the wound as Matt told her what happened.

'Are you sure they didn't see your face?' Rose asked.

'Positive. We had our faces covered the whole time, and we never spoke. They won't know who they're looking for. I had his wife in my sights, Rose, and I should have shot her, but she turned and she was just a girl, no older than Harp. And I... Well, it was him we were after.' Matt tried to remain stoic, but the sight of that girl had really shaken him. He'd seen and participated in so much violence in the last year, he'd thought himself hardened to it all, but she had caused him to pause. She was someone's child, just like Harp or Brian, and it all seemed so hard.

'Harp met her on the train down from Cork.' Rose filled him in on the meeting and the checkpoint.

'Well, that was a stroke of luck.' He exhaled. 'It might be a good thing for her to get to know that girl – she might be useful.'

'That's what Harp said,' Rose replied resignedly. 'I won't pretend I like it, though, getting close to his wife.'

Matt sighed and stood up, placing his good hand and his bandaged one on her shoulders. 'I know, love, it's all so nerve-racking. But they'll be like wasps from tomorrow now, so we need to be extremely careful, do literally nothing out of the ordinary and behave normally.' Matt made for the door, wincing as he went.

'I-is there a chance they'll come asking questions here?' Rose asked.

'They'll search everywhere. Just say nothing. You know nothing, saw nothing, heard nothing – you know, the usual.' He winked at her and gave her a one-armed squeeze. 'I'll have to have a good excuse for my hand if Danny and JohnJoe can back me up.'

'I can't believe they've never made the connection between the boys and Pat Rafferty.'

'I know. We've been lucky so far that nobody's copped on to that, but if they do figure it out, then we'll just have to brazen it out, Rose. There's no other way. Any bit of digging at all and they'll learn who their family are, and once the name Pat Rafferty comes into the conversation, they'll be on high alert. They're monitoring any support from America. They know there's money and weapons coming from there. But the lads' association with you is a good thing. Play on the Devereaux connection, loyal British subjects and all the rest of it.'

'Maybe they won't bother questioning us. As you say, we've never given them cause. I wish you could stay,' she whispered.

'I'd love nothing more. Well, actually I'd love a big dose of morphine first and then a night in your bed, Mrs Delaney, but better safe than sorry.' He kissed her and was gone into the night.

CHAPTER 5

The following morning, the town was on edge. Word of the attack spread like wildfire, but people were even afraid to be heard discussing it for fear it implicated them in some way. It was a complicated situation in Queenstown. Between the army barracks on Spike Island and the naval base on Haulbowline Island, the British military were the town's biggest employers. Almost every man and boy in the town served his time as an apprentice carpenter, block layer or plasterer, and almost every bit of food that passed the lips of the townspeople was paid for by earnings from the Crown. Up to the time of the execution of the leaders of the Rising, the drilling of the Volunteers around the town was seen as foolish at best, treasonous at worst, but everything was different now.

The installation of the Scots regiment, the Cameron Highlanders at the barracks at the top of the town, and the Tans in the RIC barracks in the square had galvanised the people's support for the rebels. Every weapon they had was pilfered or bought from the less-scrupulous Tommies, who were happy to lose their weapon for the price of a few pints.

The men who came off the various military bases located on islands in the harbour every evening were searched, of course, but nobody bothered with the apprentices. They were just lads, so they came ashore every day with ammunition, weapons, anything they could find. The result meant the IRA had more than enough for their own manoeuvres, but also the Queenstown Volunteers could supply neighbouring sections as well. Matt as the commander of that brigade was known as a calm and rational man, and he and the whole town were such an asset to the movement nationally.

It was through Queenstown that men were smuggled. They'd even gone so far as to dig a tunnel from a safe house all the way down to the dock so fugitives and incomers could be moved under the noses of the British.

Rose and Harp went down to the town early, ostensibly to go shopping but in reality to tell the boys about Matt's hand and to call on the Devlins, who were the eyes and ears of the whole area. They passed Danny and JohnJoe, who were busy loading timber from a delivery into the yard. Harp crossed the road and went into the undertaker's office, where JohnJoe was checking the delivery off in a journal.

'Matt got his hand caught in the lathe yesterday, and it's injured. It happened at five o'clock, so he went home and bandaged it himself. You and Danny were out the back cutting timber and didn't see it happen, but he called to you that he cut himself and was going home.'

JohnJoe nodded. 'Is it bad?' he asked.

'I don't know,' Harp replied, but she stopped talking quickly when Willie Mullen from the pub came in looking to borrow a hammer. 'Hello, Mr Mullen,' she said, and left promptly.

Matt was coming up the street on the other side. He never acknowledged them. Cissy Devlin was sweeping the footpath in front of the shop and beamed broadly as they approached. 'Ah, Mrs Delaney and Harp, isn't it a beautiful morning? You can really feel the spring in the air now, can't you? Though the nights are cold enough still.'

'It is indeed, Miss Devlin, but you're right – we have the range going every night despite the sunshine during the day.' Rose tried not to stare as several Black and Tans alighted from a Crossley Tender and spilled onto the street.

Brigadier General Beckett appeared on the street too from the hotel and spoke quietly and quickly to the commanding officer of the Tans. Within seconds one of the Tans began shouting. 'Return to your homes! Everyone off the street immediately!' a small puce-faced Scotsman yelled.

Mick Daly, who'd just set up his stall selling vegetables, began to object and was suddenly surrounded by three of them.

'Are you questioning my orders, Paddy?' The Scotsman sneered.

'Well, I have a permit to sell my vegeta –' His sentence was stopped by a savage uppercut to the jaw, sending the old man reeling. As he tried to get up, another of the Tans kicked him violently in the ribs.

His wife, in her sixties, screamed at them to stop and went to her husband but was flung away. She stumbled backwards and landed hard on her coccyx on the footpath. Beckett stood by, his face inscrutable; he did nothing to rein in the brutish behaviour of his subordinates.

Several people went to Peggy Daly's aid, but Mick was still lying in the street.

'Are you people deaf?' the small Scotsman yelled again. 'Get off the street!'

'Ladies, please, come inside.' Mr Bridges, the owner and manager of the Queen's Hotel, appeared at Rose's elbow, ushering her and Harp inside as Cissy withdrew and closed the door to her shop behind her.

Matt was abreast of the hotel now, and Rose could see him weighing up the situation. He could go back down to his office, but that would mean passing a second newly arrived military vehicle, which was disgorging the black-bonneted Tans at the other end of the town. Whatever was intended, it was a comprehensive action. People scattered in every direction, knowing that the shooting would come next. They were used to patrols, three or four soldiers at a time, but there were easily forty of them swarming around the streets now.

Rose glanced up at Mr Bridges. He was a decent man and had been very supportive of her over the years as a fellow businessperson in the town. She weighed that up against the fact that he was married to Angelica Hargreaves, whose sister, Emily, was married to Brigadier

General Potts, the man who preceded Beckett. Bridges was an astute businessman and careful to maintain a discreet distance from anything political, but he'd been vocal of late on the damage to property done during the drunken rampages of the Black and Tans. He made clear that all gentlemen and ladies were welcome at the Queen's Hotel regardless of their political or religious persuasion.

'Can you call Matt Quinn too, please, Mr Bridges?' Harp murmured in his ear.

A slight incline of the head was the only indication he gave that he had heard her. Beckett was just feet away, patiently tapping his baton on the gleaming top of his leather boot.

'Mr Quinn, could you come in, please,' Mr Bridges called across the street. 'There's something I need your opinion on with the cornicing in the ballroom.' He smiled at Beckett. 'And I believe Brigadier General Beckett has some work to do, so we might as well avail of the time and let them to it, shall we?'

Bridges's easy smile was met with a frosty nod. Matt walked casually across the road, his injured hand in his trouser pocket.

'Halt.' Beckett stood before him, his baton barring Matt's way. 'Name?'

'Matt Quinn, Brigadier General,' Matt replied neutrally.

'Hmm, I see. And your occupation?' He raised an eyebrow. His penetrating gaze was fixed on Matt.

'The local undertaker.'

'Take your hand out of your pocket.'

Rose's fingernails were digging into Harp's arm.

Matt removed his injured hand, holding it up.

'What happened?' Beckett asked.

'I got it nicked in the lathe yesterday evening. It could have been worse, just lost concentration for a minute.' Matt gave a self-deprecating laugh, and Rose was impressed at how calm he was. 'I often got much worse on the football pitch as a young fella.'

'And witnesses to this incident?' Beckett asked.

'Well, the two lads that work for me, they were out the back but they heard me tell them what happened. Danny Coveney and JohnJoe

O'Dwyer. You'll find them in my yard, or at least you should, if they're not skiving.' He smiled again.

'And what do you know about the disappearance of Captain Robert Pennington in 1916?'

Harp felt the colour drain from her face and her mother's fingers grip her even tighter.

'Pennington?' Matt looked perplexed. 'Oh, isn't he the man that went off, leaving a big bill above at the Cliff House? He was AWOL from the front I heard or something? To be honest, I don't remember that much about it.'

Beckett nodded, his face giving nothing away. 'Yes, that's the story I heard too.'

Harp swallowed. Heard? Who could he have heard it from? A sudden chilling thought occurred to her. Could he know Ralph? A sickening realisation lurched in the pit of her stomach. They were both in India, and though it was a huge country, she suspected people like Beckett and Ralph moved in the same circles. Maybe she could find out from Marianne. If Ralph had some contact back in Queenstown, she was sure it wasn't a coincidence. She fought the rising dread. They didn't know anything for sure yet, so no point in panicking unnecessarily.

Matt nodded and moved to the doorway of the hotel as Beckett strode down the street to where the Black and Tans were shouting and harassing the remaining public.

Bridges turned and went back into his hotel, Matt, Rose and Harp behind him. The lobby was busy. People who had intended to leave were deciding what to do now, and the staff were run off their feet as the breakfast rush was just finishing.

'Well, it looks like we are all to be discommoded once again,' Mr Bridges said in frustration. 'Could I offer you some tea or coffee while we wait this out?' His countenance indicated he was furious with what was going on. Gunshots rang from outside, and they all winced at the sound of breaking glass coming from the street.

'Thank you, Mr Bridges, tea would be very nice,' Harp replied, wondering what was going on. Bridges was a nice man, but they were not social friends. Why was he offering them personal hospitality?

He led them to his office off the lobby and instructed a young waitress to bring them morning tea. Rose and Harp took a seat on the overstuffed sofa opposite his large oak desk, behind which was an ornate office chair and a hat stand. Matt stood, his back to the room, observing the activity out on the street. There was no time for them to speak. Something was going on, but they had no idea what it might be.

Mr Bridges closed the door and took his seat behind his desk, his jaw tightening at the continued gunshots coming from the street outside. 'This really is too much.' His accent was clipped and as British as the officers he served. 'I'm quite frankly weary of the entire business.'

Bridges was on close personal terms with the British. His wife was from Surrey, his father-in-law was a conservative MP, they were wealthy Protestants... Everything about him reeked of the enemy, yet he'd always been good and decent to the people of Queenstown, a fair and kind employer and a great supporter of any commercial enterprise that enhanced the town. He had called them for a reason, and that reason terrified Harp.

'Look, based on who I am, I'm sure you might find my stance in this situation a little perplexing, but I want you to know that up to very recently, I did not hold with violence and I thought the rebels were mere troublemakers, creating unnecessary hardship. Life was fine, people were relatively prosperous compared with more recent times, and I thought it would be best if the Irish question was left well enough alone. But since the execution of the leaders of the Easter Rising, then the savagery with which actions to continue the fight have been met, well, it's escalating out of all control. And to be truthful, I'm appalled at the way the Black and Tans are permitted to behave, with no sanction or control from the upper ranks of the army. It's intolerable.'

As if to illustrate his point, another volley of gunshots, followed by more screaming and shouting, rent the air.

'This simply cannot go on, and the treatment of decent law-abiding people in this manner should offend everyone. So I have come around to the belief that there is only one way to ensure it ends, and that is with the departure of the British from this country for once and for all. I am reminded of the words of Charles Stewart Parnell, a man of my own class and faith, and I find myself in agreement when he said, "No man has a right to fix the boundary of the march of a nation; no man has a right to say to his country – thus far shalt thou go and no further."'

He smiled at the looks of incredulity on their faces. 'I know. I sound British, my wife is British, I was educated there, and we move in those circles, but I was born in Cork City.' He paused and fixed each of them with a look. 'And I consider myself an Irishman.'

Harp said nothing but watched him closely.

'Surely that is not such a hard leap for you to make, especially given the late Mr Devereaux and I would have been of the same mind?'

'Did you speak to him about that?' Harp asked.

Bridges shook his head. 'Henry was not inclined to talk, as you know, but his brother, Ralph, apprised me of his opinions. Of course Ralph thought him an idiot for thinking that way, but I did not then and I certainly do not now.'

'But your wife…' Rose began.

'Angelica is an Englishwoman through and through, but she is also a decent human being. She abhors this behaviour' – he gestured towards the window – 'as much as anyone. A Tan policeman tried to make an indecent assault on one of our kitchen staff last week, and only that my wife came upon the scene, the consequences for the poor girl could have been catastrophic. So she and I are of one mind on this, I can assure you.

'I don't expect or want you to tell me anything – I'm better off not knowing – but I have a proposal. I have an opening here in the evenings for a barmaid, and I thought it might be a good job for someone you might know. Perhaps you could recommend someone? As you know, the officers socialise here quite a bit, and a lot of conversations that might be of interest happen here, and given that alcohol has a way of loosening the tongue, perhaps it would be helpful.'

Matt caught Rose's eye. She gave him a slight nod. She had just the girl, a maid at the Cliff House whose brothers were Volunteers.

'Thank you, Mr Bridges. I'd be happy to recommend someone.'

'Very well. Have her drop in, and we can have a conversation.'

There was a knock on the door and a waitress appeared with some tea and pastries.

'Jolly good. Now if you'll excuse me, I have some matters to attend to, but please, stay here and enjoy the refreshments. That cabinet there' – he nodded at a large dark filing cabinet – 'has the check-in details of all the guests. The ones billed to the British army are in the blue folder. They contain dates of arrival and departure, and they have booked quite a few in advance. It also lists home addresses and things of that nature. I won't be back for quite some time, and you won't be disturbed.'

Before Matt or the women had a chance to say anything else, he was gone.

CHAPTER 6

'Matt' – Harp turned towards the cabinet, ignoring the tea – 'lean against the door. Mam, watch the street in case anyone comes in from out there.'

She opened the top drawer and extracted the blue folder. 'Names, dates of arrival, home addresses in England. This is useful, I suppose, but I'm not sure how… Hold on… There's a group arriving next week, no rank listed, but booked by the army. That means only one thing – G-men.'

The potential arrival of the feared special detectives from Dublin Castle, recruited for their ability to infiltrate Republican circles by any means necessary was a new and dark development.

Rose turned and gazed at her. 'But they were all up in Dublin?'

Matt nodded slowly from where he leaned on the door. 'They are usually, and they are ruthless up there, no rules of conduct whatsoever. There were rumblings that they might send a bunch of them down here to try to rout us out.'

Harp ran her finger down the list, memorising the details. Her ability to read and memorise text easily without having to write it down had proven an invaluable skill in recent months as she delivered notes and messages. She'd even invented a cipher using the first lines of famous poems for others to use, making the transfer of details much easier and less likely to be wrong or intercepted.

'Can you remember them, Harp?' Matt asked.

'I can,' she said, running her eyes over the list once more.

'That's why Bridges wanted us to see this. They'll arrive at all different times, seem to just be hotel guests, but all the while they'll be spying. They must know something to say they are going to this much trouble.'

'So what do we do now?' Rose asked Matt.

He moved away from the door as soon as Harp had replaced the folder and closed the cabinet once more. 'I'll have to take this higher, but there are four of them, and the first one doesn't arrive until?' He turned to Harp.

'The sixteenth, a week away. A Laurie Campton. And then on the eighteenth, Phillip Beasley and Edward Delahunt, and then on the nineteenth, Frederick Marlow.'

'This is invaluable.' He poured a cup of tea from the pot. There was no possibility of getting back out onto the street now, as the whole place was cleared of people and the Tans were conducting a house-to-house search.

'I hope Danny and JohnJoe will be all right,' Harp said.

'They'll be fine. There's nothing in the yard at the moment.' A shadow crossed Matt's face. 'There are a few pistols in the meat safe at the Devlins'. Danny was to collect them for burial with a load off an American boat the day after tomorrow.'

The Devlins' shop was normally the safest place for interim storage, lots of people coming and going all the time so no arousing suspicion, and the storage for the shop area was large, with lots of nooks and crannies. Up to now it had been an ideal place – nobody would suspect spinster sisters – but as the Tans shouted and brutalised their way through the town, they fought the urge to panic. The shop was on the corner, but from the window, they couldn't see it.

'Do Liz and Cissy know they're there?' Harp asked.

Matt nodded.

'Oh, no.' Rose swallowed, her beautiful face pale. 'We have to do something, Matt.'

'I could go out the back, cut through the barrel store of the pub and get over the wall into their back yard without being seen, but the trouble is the weapons are actually in the shop, not the store out the back.'

'We have to warn them.' Harp felt nauseous.

Matt shook his head. 'Too dangerous. They have Tans on all the steps around the town, and they'll have hidden more in houses and gardens. Beckett will know that as soon as they started the house-to-house searches, people would try to get away, and they'll have made sure every rat run in the town is covered. Cissy and Liz will brazen it out. The space under the meat safe is under a board – I made it myself – so unless they knew exactly where to look, they'd never find it.'

Harp hoped he was right. She'd seen what Matt had made. The metal meat safe was a ventilated cube with a door that rested on bricks under the counter. Matt had removed one section of brick, clad the whole base in timber and created a sliding door at the back, so a person would have to climb under the counter, get around the back of the safe and know exactly where to press to release the catch on the sliding door. He was right; it was close to impossible that they'd find it.

They stood and crowded around the window, trying to see what was going on outside. Luckily Mr Bridges's office had heavy lace curtains that allowed them to see out, but the soldiers didn't know they were being observed. Just outside, a soldier was pasting a notice to the wall of the pub.

'What does it say?' Rose squinted to read it from such a distance. Several other soldiers were doing the same, and soon the posters were on every surface.

'I can't read it from here,' Harp replied.

'We'll know soon enough,' Matt said darkly. 'Oh, look...' He pointed to the other side of the street, where several young men were being lined up outside the White Star ticket office. From all areas of the town, local lads were being pushed and jostled along, most late teens or early twenties but some younger and a few older.

'Ollie and Johnny Buckley, and the young O'Halloran lad, and Tom Sweeney, Boxer Healy, Vincent Lynch, Donal Coakley. I don't know who that is beside him – is it one of the Cantillons?' Rose counted them off as they stood in a terrified row.

'That's Eamonn Foley. He was in my class at school. And Richard Greene and Sean Murphy with him. And look who's rounding them up – Emmet Kelly.' Harp was incredulous.

The schoolyard bully had joined the Royal Irish Constabulary when all members of the Crown police force were issued with IRA warnings to leave their posts or be considered traitors and reap the consequences. It had been a very difficult time when those warnings went out around the country. So many of the police were just Irishmen doing a job to support their families, but Michael Collins was adamant. If someone wasn't with them, they were against them and had to be dealt with, no exceptions.

Harp remembered the conflict when Andy Keane, a very popular man and the local RIC sergeant, who was only a year from retirement and his pension, had to resign for fear of IRA reprisals. As he explained to Matt, all he did was keep the peace, breaking up brawls and dealing with petty criminals, and he had no British sympathies, but Matt had explained that it was the only way. Where possible, though, those who left the RIC were given help to find jobs, local people knowing the situation. Emmet Kelly, however, refused to leave, but because he was young and a local, he was given a beating as an indication that the IRA meant business. He disappeared soon after, but now here he was again, this time in the uniform of the Black and Tans.

'We should have put a bullet in him when we had the chance,' Matt whispered. 'He'll be getting one shortly, though, I can guarantee that.'

Outside, the brigadier was pacing slowly up and down in front of the row of fifteen men. All in working clothes, they were in equal measure defiant and petrified.

Matt eased the window up the sash slightly to better hear what was going on.

Though the street was deserted apart from the men and the Tans, Harp knew every window was in use as people watched the horrific events unfolding. How had their beautiful, idyllic town come to this? It should be bustling with people on Easter holidays, the shops all open, traders on the streets, the azure Atlantic twinkling out to Roches Point and the fishing boats bobbing about happily in the harbour. The green park beside the port, complete with ornate Victorian bandstand, would normally be full of people enjoying the sun, children playing and licking ices. Harp felt a profound sadness overwhelm her outrage.

Bad enough they had to endure the war years, the harbour filled to capacity with dreadnought battleships, the twin forts of Camden and Mitchell menacing as their guns faced the Atlantic and the German U-boats for four long years. The Great War might be over, but this one was raging, and it was every bit as bad, worse probably. At least in the Great War, civilians were not involved to the same extent.

'Name,' Beckett asked calmly of a young man Harp didn't recognise.

His answer was inaudible.

'Address?'

They just caught what he said, Rushbrooke. The next town up towards the city.

'Step forward,' Beckett said, never changing his tone. He passed two men, one of them the boy from Harp's class, Richard Greene, and stopped at the next one. 'Name?'

'Seán O'Murchú,' he replied in Irish. He was an apprentice midshipman in the British navy but loyal in his heart to the republican cause.

Matt exhaled. 'No, not now, Seanie, don't do it.'

'What?' Rose asked.

'He wants to join us, but I told him he was too young. He's only sixteen, and his mother would murder me if I got him killed. He's her only child. He said he'd refuse to answer any of them in English if they asked him anything.'

'Speak properly. Name and address.' Beckett enunciated clearly, but his voice betrayed no impatience.

'*Seán O'Murchú is anim dom. Is as an Árd Sráid mé.*'

Beckett nodded to the Black and Tan sergeant, the one who'd been shouting earlier. He swung his rifle and hit Sean on the temple, knocking him out cold. A trickle of blood ran down his head where the rifle butt had made contact.

Without another word Beckett moved on to the next man, and the next, instructing every third one to step forward until six men stood apart from the others.

'Kneel,' he ordered.

The selected men did as they were told, and at Beckett's nod, a Black and Tan stood behind each one, his pistol trained on his prisoner's head.

Beckett then raised his voice. 'An attack was made on my house last night by a criminal fringe. I will find those responsible and bring them to justice. Somebody in this town knows who these persons are. You have until' – he checked his watch – '4 p.m. to report to me.' Then he stalked off back to his office, leaving the men kneeling in the street, a pistol to each head, not knowing what their fate might be.

CHAPTER 7

The remaining Tans left to go back to the barracks, or most likely to the pub. They were drunk a lot of the time. Luckily the house next door to their favourite watering hole was the home of Nellie Burke, another loyal Cumann na mBan member.

Matt had drilled several holes in the dividing wall, with the assistance of the publican, who placed some prints over them to cover up the holes, and Nellie's parlour was where a lot of intelligence was gathered as beer and whiskey loosened the tongues of the rough men.

Gingerly, people began to emerge onto the street once more. The six men still knelt on the street, their guards steely-eyed.

Harp and Rose parted from Matt in Bridges's office and made their way to the Devlins' shop. The scene that greeted them broke their hearts. Liz was stony-faced, sweeping up the glass from their front window that had been smashed, the shelves ransacked, provisions all over the floor. But it was poor Cissy who made Harp so upset. They had destroyed her precious cash register, and it was now in several pieces on the counter, the old woman pointlessly trying to reassemble it. Harp knew how they had deliberated for so long over such an extravagance and the joy it brought them both, but Cissy in particular.

'Oh, Cissy.' Harp ran to her and saw the brightness in her eyes, but Cissy refused to let the tears fall.

Rose immediately began trying to straighten the shelves, the stocks of tobacco and whiskey were gone. Harp bent to pick up another piece of the cash register, the beautiful porcelain plate that had been screwed to the drawer.

'They never found a blessed bit,' Cissy said sadly. 'At least that, I suppose. They didn't even think we had anything, just came in and destroyed the place because they could.'

It was a relief, but Harp already knew that. If they'd found the pistols, the Devlin sisters would have been marched out to the barracks right away.

They spent the remainder of the morning trying to get the shop back into some kind of order. Danny came with a large sheet of timber to put in the window, plunging the normally bright shop into darkness.

Cissy had gathered all the pieces of her beloved cash register in a hessian sack. 'Would you and Danny get rid of the rubbish for us?' she asked JohnJoe, who willingly removed all the splintered shelves and broken glass.

Eventually, when they could do no more, Harp and Rose left the shop. Harp had not had an opportunity to speak to her mother about Ralph; it had been a horrible day and she needed to pick her moment. Danny, Matt and JohnJoe were in much demand around the town, making repairs on the worst of the damage.

Mother and daughter trudged up the steps and let themselves in through the garden gate. They would not have seen her but that she called out.

'Harp?'

They both spun around to find Marianne Beckett sitting on the stone bench inside the garden wall. The girl looked much more dishevelled than when Harp had last seen her, and she was wearing a black dress and gunmetal-grey coat. Under her hat, her hair stuck out at angles, and her eyes looked puffy.

'Marianne.' Harp gasped. 'I... What are you doing here?' Harp crossed to where Marianne stood, looking much more uncertain than the confident young woman she was on the train.

Rose followed and waited for Harp to introduce her.

'Ah...Marianne Beckett, this is my mother, Mrs Rose Delaney. I met Marianne on the train, remember, I mentioned?' Harp tried to keep her voice conversational and light and to not think about the fact that not only had Matt just attempted to kill her but also that her husband had six men awaiting their same fate on their knees down the town.

Rose took Harp's lead. 'Ah, yes, indeed. I remember. Won't you come in? Have a cup of tea?'

'Oh, would you mind?' Marianne's blue eyes lit up, and Harp saw the relief there that she was not to be shunned. 'Oliver, my husband, told me to stay in the hotel bedroom, but I...I needed to get out. It's been such a dreadful day, and I was so upset about everything. He'll be frightfully cross, I'm sure, but he has a lot of business to attend to today, so maybe he won't notice.'

Business indeed, Harp thought. 'Rebellion to tyrants is obedience to God,' said Benjamin Franklin, and Harp agreed. If she was ever in any doubt as to the moral imperative in the Irish struggle, the events of that morning had dispelled them. Beckett was a tyrant, representing a tyrannical regime, and the Irish were justified in any and all measures taken to repel them. Looking at the face of Marianne now, delighted at the prospect of a cup of tea, it was hard to see her as anything but the enemy.

'Oh, your escallonia is magnificent.' Marianne stopped at a large show of delicate pink flowers with small, dark, shiny leaves forming the hedge. 'Zackie Pascoe – my grandfather's name was Isaac, but we all called him Zackie – planted our entire perimeter in Shimla with devil's backbone, which looks all right but has rather a boring colour. So one summer when I was eleven, I reset the entire boundary with bougainvillea. It looks glorious now when it blooms. But the best was our rose garden. Roses are my very favourite. My grandmother has two named for her in the Royal Society.' She sighed. 'When I got married, I insisted only roses were used in the bouquets, though I doubt if Oliver would have noticed if we used thistles.'

'We have someone come in to do the garden, though. Neither Harp nor I have green fingers, I'm afraid. I can manage some things, but Harp kills everything she touches.' Rose smiled.

'Marianne, would you rather take tea in the garden?' Harp suggested. She wanted to talk to her uninterrupted, and there were staff and guests inside.

'That would be lovely, thank you.' Marianne smiled as Rose retreated, then turned to admire the border of cowslips, bluebells and primroses that snaked around the house. 'I really think your garden is the nicest I've seen since coming over here. Back at home, things look so different, you see, lots more colour and very different blooms. It's so much hotter and more humid, I suppose.'

They walked around the garden, Marianne knowing the names of flowers and shrubs that Harp had no idea about nor interest in, but the girl seemed not to mind. Daffodils were merrily dancing in the breeze. Marianne fingered the delicate petals of this plant and that, bending to inhale the faint fragrances. 'It needs to be warmer to release the oils and really get the scent, but the delicate fragrance of the simple primrose is heavenly, is it not?' She turned to Harp, who was listening keenly for more gunshots or signs that anything was happening downtown.

'Yes, lovely,' she replied.

Harp invited her guest to sit and joined her at the white wrought iron table they used for outdoor dining. 'Do you miss it a lot?' Harp asked. 'India?'

'Very much.' Marianne nodded.

'Tell me, did you ever know a man called Ralph Devereaux?' Harp kept her voice light. 'A distant relation of mine. I was just wondering.'

Marianne wrinkled her brow. 'There was a Devereaux, I think, but I'm not sure of his first name. He came after I was sent away to school, so I was only ever there on the holidays after that. I seem to recall Papa mentioning that name, but more than that, I've no idea.'

'Doesn't matter. I barely know him myself.' Harp brushed it off. 'So I expect you miss your family? Everything here must be so different.'

Marianne nodded slowly, and to Harp's horror, a small tear formed and slid down her pretty face.

'Oh, Marianne, I'm sorry. I shouldn't have...'

'No, it's all right. It's very sweet of you to ask. Nobody else does.'

Though the words could be interpreted as petulant, Harp knew she was simply stating the truth.

'I'm sorry for just barging in on you like this, but I have not one friend or even acquaintance on whom I could call, and after the frightening experience last night, I couldn't bear to be alone. I'm in a strange country where the locals appear to hate us, though why, I've not the faintest idea – something similar to India, I would imagine – and I feel so isolated and alone.'

'I heard about what happened last night,' Harp said tentatively, surmising that not mentioning it was even more suspicious than saying something.

Marianne shook her head. 'It was horrible. I knew we should not have taken that dreadful house. It was terrifying before the rebels ever got there, but last night, I thought they would kill us, but when they didn't... They couldn't, as Oliver had guards all over the overgrown grounds – that's why he wanted that house, I think. And with everything that happened next, the shooting and everything, I almost didn't notice that the place was up in flames. I lost everything, of course, all of my clothes, my personal things, family keepsakes, everything...' Her voice broke off in a tiny sob.

'I'm so sorry.' Harp wasn't, of course, sorry for the attack, not one bit, especially having seen the kind of person Oliver Beckett was, but she was sorry for this girl, so far from home and caught up in something she had no reason to be involved with.

'I don't care about the stupid house. I'm glad if anything. Detestable old mausoleum, good riddance to it, burned to the ground. But my things, things my parents gave me...' She was crying again.

'Well, perhaps you can write and they can send you more?'

Marianne looked at her. 'I can't. I had a photograph, taken the summer before last at the Viscount's Ball, of Mama and Papa and me. We had it taken on the steps leading up to the orangery, and the light and everything were perfect. Mama was laughing at something Papa said – he was very funny, my papa – and Mama and I had new dresses, mine pink and hers blue. He always used to call me his English rose. It was perfect.'

'Well, maybe you'll go back for a visit and you can recreate the scene and –'

'Papa is dead, Harp...' Her voice broke.

'I'm sorry. It must be very lonely being away from your mother now if she's all you have...'

'Mama and I were always very close, but we had a falling out. I didn't want to marry Oliver, and she thought I should. We've sort of patched it up now, by letter, but that's not the same...'

'Oh.' Harp had nothing to add. It all seemed impossibly complicated, and Marianne was unlike anyone she'd ever known. 'And was your father ill?' she asked, steering the conversation into safer waters.

'No, he shot himself.'

Harp was so uncomfortable; she wished her mother would reappear with the tea. 'Oh, I didn't mean to pry...' Harp searched to find some topic that wasn't contentious.

'It's all right. At home everyone knew – it's not like it's a big secret. Papa was a gambler, and his gambling led him to do something he couldn't live with, so he put a revolver in his mouth.'

Harp was astonished at the story, but also at the delivery. Marianne, she realised, was a complex young woman capable of lightness and fun, but that masked an inner darkness.

Rose arrived with the tea and began placing cups and saucers on the table.

'Oh, you serve your own tea?' Marianne asked, perplexed.

'Indeed we do, and do our own laundry and cut our own grass and scrub our own floors.' Rose took any sting out of the words with a smile.

'How modern of you.' Marianne poured tea and took a bite of the coffee cake Rose had baked the day before. 'I wish I could do that, but

Oliver employed these old people to work in that place, and there were soldiers too, but they all ignored me, so I had no opportunity for activity at all.'

'Could your husband not entertain you?' Rose asked, joining them.

'My husband, Mrs Delaney, cares nothing for my happiness or lack thereof,' Marianne said matter-of-factly.

'I'm sure that's not true. You can't be married long – you're not much older than Harp. You should be in the first flush of wedded bliss.' Rose chatted on.

When Marianne spoke, all the gaiety and joy Harp had heard on the train were gone. 'In polite society, at this juncture I would say something admiring about my husband. I would titter and smile coquettishly. But the truth is, my husband won me in a game of cards. My father gambled all of our money, and when that was all gone, he gambled all he had left, and that was me.'

CHAPTER 8

*P*amela Pascoe stirred as he gently turned the ivory handle of the door.

'It's not time to go yet?' she murmured sleepily.

'It is for me.' Ralph turned and smiled. He knew the sight of his leg revolted her, though she never said, so he tried to be dressed before she woke. The stump where what was left of his leg ended, four inches below his knee, was a daily reminder of all he had lost. He didn't need her pity or disgust as well.

'But the solicitor isn't due until this afternoon,' she complained.

She really was a dreary companion these days, so needy and clingy since old Alfie topped himself; he needed to limit his exposure to her to endure it at all. Besides, he had to get back to Sarita. The last thing he needed was her smelling a rat, or worse, smelling the once-pretty, now-pudgy wife of that pathetic loser. She was a looker as a girl, he was sure, but time had done its work on her face and body and she looked every day of her forty-five years. He envied Beckett the daughter in his bed every night. Marianne was blond and blue-eyed, but Pamela was dark. She was still passably pretty, but the grey roots could be seen if she was slow in getting to the hairdresser's and the crow's feet were deepening around her brown eyes.

66

Even Sarita had her limits, it seemed, and it had cost him dearly that last time she had to use a chunk of her inheritance to pay off his debt. It wasn't his fault, he'd tried to explain. The man was a shyster and a charlatan, and Ralph wasn't the only one he ripped off. Of course there was no confidence trickster, and if there had been, she should credit him with a little more intelligence than to fall for it, but he'd developed a rather expensive little habit with cocaine and Sarita was largely funding it.

She'd been so furious with him that she threw him out of her house and refused to see him, so he'd had to make the ultimate sacrifice to get back in her good books and take her to the Penraven Ball. Lady Penraven nearly choked when he arrived with a native. Poor old Sarita had done her very best, no sari or that silly make-up, and she dressed as an English lady should. Her manners were impeccable, he would say that for her, and her English only slightly accented. It had been enough to appease her. It was all she wanted, to be accepted by them.

She was a moron if she thought it would ever happen, of course; they saw native and nothing more. But she'd been so grateful to him that she brought him back to her house and her bed once more. And so his lifestyle could continue. But he was on thin ice and he knew it.

Things were still a little sketchy with Pamela's personal wealth now that Alfie was gone, and he needed to hedge his bets as it were until he knew more. If Pamela's money was safe from Pascoe's debtors, he might even marry her, secure his feet under the table, but he'd have to wait and see. Meanwhile he would keep Sarita on the go just in case.

He had to listen to Pamela drone on about Marianne. Should she have pressed the wedding; should she not? The woman was such a bore. Ralph had convinced her that Beckett was as good a match as Marianne was likely to make now, given the shame and everything, so he'd encouraged her – no, urged her – to press for the match to go ahead. Now Marianne was over there, whining and complaining in every letter how much she hated it, hated Beckett, hated the house, and Pamela was distraught with guilt. It was all very tiresome.

He tried to distract her with seduction. The sex was boring and perfunctory, but at least it shut her up. Nothing like with Sarita, actually, who was a tigress in the bedroom.

But now everything had changed. Marianne Beckett was his way back in, his eyes and ears in Queenstown, and she wrote weekly. All he had to do was make sure Pamela kept her money, and then he could use them both to exact his cold revenge on that devious witch Rose and her daughter.

He wanted to quiz Pamela about her daughter's letters, but it would make her suspicious – she was remarkably astute, actually – so he had to listen to boring drivel about the house that Beckett rented and how poor Marianne hated it. He remembered going to birthday parties at Peary Tower as a child; the boy was called Roderick. He was killed in a horse-riding accident aged sixteen, and his parents sold up and went back to Buckinghamshire, selling the place to some old recluse. Yet another beautiful old house given over to an oddball. Just as his own home was lost, first to his peculiar brother and now to his brother's bastard brat of a daughter, Harp. The very name, the very thought of her, made his blood boil.

If she'd not come back from Boston that time in 1916, he would have married Rose and would now be happily installed as the master of the Cliff House; he would be where he belonged. But because of the meddling of his socially awkward, odd-looking niece, he was back here, living on the grace and favour of a native and warming this spongy woman's bed for titbits of information. He so nearly had Harp too. She and Rose had bumped off Pennington. Sure, he had no actual proof, but he knew enough to rattle them; their guilty faces told him the rest. He could have dangled that threat over them forever, over that sly undertaker as well – he was somehow connected – but Harp had to come back and bring her two American oafs with her and ruin everything.

There was a knock on the door, and a maid came in bearing a letter on a silver tray.

'Ooh, it's from Marianne.' Pamela sat up, ripping it open enthusiastically.

'Read it to me,' he purred. She loved it when he cared, and maybe it contained something useful. Sarita could wait. 'I worry about her over there.'

'Oh, Ralph darling, you are kind. She will love you as I do when she finally gets to meet you.'

He sat on the bed beside her. 'I'm sure we'll get along famously, but let's not say anything for now. It's still early days after poor Alfie's passing.'

She leaned over and kissed him.

He suppressed a wince at her foul morning breath. Too many cigarettes and too much gin last night.

'You're so considerate.' She sat up properly. The skin between her breasts was getting crêpey, he noticed. She had enough money to make a reasonable stab at halting the march of time, but without the powders, potions and constricting undergarments, she looked distinctly middle-aged. The Indian sun was hard on British skin.

'I just care about you, my love, and Marianne too, because if you love her, then so do I.' He smiled and found he was enjoying the experience of her pathetic slavish adoration. He could play cat and mouse with her; it would be a diversion, he supposed. If she cut him off, he would hear no more of Marianne and Queenstown.

"'Dear Mama. At last some good news – I've made a friend. She's really lovely, and her name is impossibly romantic – wait till you hear – Harp Devereaux.'"

Pamela paused. 'No relation surely?' She knew he was originally from Ireland.

Ralph thought quickly. 'She could well be – there are lots of branches of the family.' He lied easily. 'Go on.'

"'She and her mother run a charming hotel, and it's so beautiful. The gardens are simply a delight, and though Harp can't tell a dahlia from a daffodil, she doesn't mind me pottering about. She's a student at the university here in Cork, imagine that, and she has an American boyfriend, so it's all very exciting.'"

"'I told you last time about that dreadful attack, and while I'm simply bereft about my precious things, it does mean we don't need to live in that dreadful tomb any more. In fact, I'm trying to arrange it that we move into the Cliff House. Oliver doesn't like to mix with his brother officers, so he refused married quarters at the base."

"'I know you said I should make the best of things, and I am trying, Mama, I promise, but he's not very nice. There, I've said it. He's quite rough, and very insistent on the subject of his marital rights, and he tries to control everything about me. He comments on my clothes, my hair. He even told me I looked a little thicker round the middle and to stop eating cakes and sweet things. He tells me to play bridge with the boring old women married to other officers, and we never have any fun at all. I said I might join the local croquet club, but he refused. Just like that. It's awful, Mama, truly. If it weren't for Harp, I swear I might go mad."

"'I wish more than anything that I was at home, with you and Papa, and none of this had ever happened. Your loving daughter, Marianne".'

Pamela looked up. 'Oh, Ralph, my poor girl! I knew it was a mistake. I should have never agreed. I told her she could marry but not necessarily restrict herself to him, that marriages among our kind were often more business transactions than love affairs, so long as she was discreet. I think she was a little shocked, but she agreed. But now it seems he won't let her out of his sight.'

Ralph was more absorbed in the news that Marianne had befriended his niece. Was this good or bad? Good, surely. It gave him access to Harp, and that had to be an advantage.

'Ralph?' Pamela's face was tear-stained. 'Don't you have anything to say?'

'Oh, darling, I'm sorry. I'm just so cross. Please don't upset yourself. I'm shocked that Beckett could treat a girl in that way. If I were closer, I would be having a word, man to man, let me assure you. Write to Marianne, reassure her. I'm sure she longs for your letters, my darling.'

'I could invite her home? I don't know if Beckett would allow it, but we would have such a marvellous time, us three. It would be like the old days, and I'm sure she'd love you as much as Alfie once she got to know you.'

Ralph hated it when she put him in the same age bracket as her pathetic failure of a husband. It was true that he was close in age to Alfie Pascoe, but he looked much younger. 'I doubt he would, and, Pam darling, be sure you never mention me in your letters to her, won't you?' he said silkily.

'I never do.' She pouted. 'You've told me not to about a hundred times.'

'I'll tell you what – why don't you suggest we all meet in London? You were saying you need to go over and check on your situation legally now that poor Alfie is gone, and we could meet Marianne and Beckett at the same time. You could go shopping with her. She'll have lost everything in the attack on the house, so she'll need new things.'

'Really, we can go to London?' she asked, her eyes lighting up. 'You and I, together?'

You'll be paying for it, you dozy cow, he thought to himself but smiled. 'If it would make you happy, my love, then, yes, of course. Write and suggest it to Marianne. I'll write to Beckett myself, have a word about how he treats her.'

She stroked her hair, crispy from all the lacquer she'd put in it the previous night. 'You take such care of me, and even though you don't know Marianne, I can tell you'll be a better father to her than Alfie ever was.' Her bitterness was palpable.

'I'll do my best.' He smiled.

'You do love me, don't you, Ralphie?' she asked with what she clearly thought was an impish smile but looked more like wretched beseeching.

'You know perfectly well how I feel.' He winked and pecked her cheek. 'Now I must be off. See you at the Orchid later.'

He let himself out, checking that the diamond bracelet Alfie had given Pamela for her birthday was safely in his pocket. Sarita would love it, and it would cement his position back in her favour. There was no possibility Pamela would see it on her. They'd never be in the same places. Luckily she'd asked him to tighten the clasp on it last night, so if she mentioned it, he'd just say it must have slipped off in the club; everyone there was notoriously sticky-fingered. They had been very drunk last night, so she wouldn't question it.

He would most likely get rid of Sarita – she was probably surplus to requirements – but just in case there was any problem with Pamela's money, he'd better not burn that bridge too hastily. She ran her father's textile business now, and made a decent job of it by all accounts, and she was by far the smartest woman he knew. She genuinely seemed to love him, and at least a man could have a proper conversation with her – she was no airhead – but she was Indian and he would never stoop so low as to publicly declare he was going native.

He called a rickshaw and got in. The stupid thing was garish and festooned with ribbons and images of their cartoon-like gods. Irritated, he pulled several of the wretched things down that were dangling from the hood over his head and threw them in the street.

'Gurdwara,' he snapped at the stricken boy pulling it.

'Sahib, my things.' The boy pointed to the ribbons and rubbish Ralph had just discarded. He rushed around, gathering them from the dusty ground and stuffing them in his pockets.

'Gurdwara,' Ralph barked again, and they were off.

He saw nothing as they travelled. He was deep in thought. He had spent the last four years ruminating on how he would destroy every single last one of them, but in his own time and in his own way. Matt Quinn, the two American thugs she got to kill him, Rose Delaney. And last, and only when she had lost everyone she loved, he would slowly twist the knife and make Harp Devereaux suffer.

CHAPTER 9

A week later, Harp saw Marianne before Marianne saw her. She just couldn't face her, so, feeling bad, she slipped down the kitchen steps, out into the yard and up to the outbuildings. Since that day she'd arrived unexpectedly, Marianne had taken to calling almost every day. Harp knew she was lonely and felt vulnerable, and her information was useful, but today Harp wished she'd chosen someone else to befriend.

The irony that she was turning away a friendship wasn't lost on her. For so long she'd have loved a friend, but this situation was just too precarious. Marianne, regardless of how nice or how lonely she was, was the wife of that murdering fiend Beckett. Harp liked her but was using her – some of her throwaway remarks had proved useful to the organisation when Harp passed them on to Matt – and she was conflicted. Duplicity didn't come naturally to her, and while she was totally committed to the cause, she wished she didn't have to use Marianne so callously to achieve that end.

The town was still reeling from the death of Seanie. He'd suffered a brain injury as a result of the blow from the Black and Tan officer, and his poor mother was distraught. She went to Beckett, demanding he press charges or call the man responsible to account for what he did, but Beckett dismissed her without even sympathising with her loss. The men he'd selected had been kept kneeling in the street all that day, without food or water. That night they were taken into custody, and nobody knew where they were being held. Undoubtedly they'd be roughed up and thrown out into the street somewhere in the coming days.

Apparently the day they cleared the streets, after the attack on Peary Tower, Beckett had set up a room in the Queen's Hotel and sat there all afternoon with the door open, calmly doing paperwork and waiting for informers. As Matt rightly pointed out, it was heartening that nobody took the bait, but they weren't likely to in all conscience, considering the eyes of the town were on them. Even if someone had wanted to inform, they knew it would be the last thing they ever did.

The IRA had made contact with the families of the men now in custody, offering whatever help they needed. In the case of all but one, they held no grudge against the rebels. One, Maurice Galvin's wife, a woman pregnant with her third child, cursed the IRA and sent them packing, telling them she held them responsible for her husband's imprisonment and that if he didn't return in one piece, she would never forgive them. Matt heard about it, and Harp wished Mrs Galvin could see how much it tore at him to witness this mindless violence. Matt Quinn never wavered from his belief that there was only one way, but he didn't relish it. Quite the opposite. Every drop of blood spilled was a waste as far as he was concerned, but the enemy understood nothing else.

Harp felt tired and sickened at the sight of Seanie Murphy's poor mother, losing her only child, and for what? For Ireland? How did the death of a sixteen-year-old boy further the cause of Irish freedom? She didn't know. She needed to be alone for a while.

Harp let herself out the gate at the top of the property. It was one they rarely used, and the gate was all covered in ivy and creepers, but it led to a lane that came out at the crescent where Matt lived, a magnificent curved terrace high up over the town, commanding a beautiful view of the entire harbour and the Cliff House.

She shoved the gate hard, and it scraped against the moss-covered stone beneath. As she walked up the hill towards the top road that would eventually take her to the old Protestant graveyard, she was deep in thought. Henry's grave had been where she went for comfort since the day he died, and though he would have laughed at her belief in such things, she felt close to him there.

She and Rose had arranged to have a Mass said for Molly and they'd all attended, but Harp didn't get the sense of peace one is expected to from such an occasion. They were all so sad about Molly; she was such a larger-than-life character. JohnJoe in particular was very upset. When he arrived in Boston as a lost and lonely boy, she had made it her business to look out for him, and they were firm friends. Harp thought she might suggest to him that they place a little marked stone in the graveyard, or even a bench, to commemorate her life. She wished he had somewhere he could go to feel close to Molly the way she did with Henry's grave.

Those were the kinds of things one could do in peacetime without thinking, but now everything was different.

She had been right in assuming the men arriving that week were G-men. There was a sense of unease among the officers, according to Maeve, the girl Matt had installed as a barmaid in the hotel. The feeling among them was that they were in some way under scrutiny. Everyone was making sure his part of the operation was in order so as not to be found wanting when the detectives from Dublin Castle arrived. The G-men had been already scheduled to come to Queenstown before the attack on Peary Tower, but they would undoubtedly be focusing on that now as well.

A large shipment of weapons from Pat Rafferty and his supporters had landed last month. They came off a fishing trawler but had in fact been liberated off an American vessel a few miles out, away from prying eyes. Danny and JohnJoe had made sure of it.

The weapons had been stored in coffins until they were needed and then used to ambush three lorries of Black and Tans going from Cork to Bandon. They had wounded ten and killed six Tans, as well as destroyed two lorries. The raid had been successful, but one IRA man was shot and his weapon taken, and when it was analysed, it was found to be an M1903 Springfield bolt-action rifle, standard issue to American troops in the Great War. That was another nugget picked up from a loose-lipped drinker in the Queen's Hotel. The British had correctly suspected all along that the rebels were getting weapons from the United States, and now they had proof. The purpose of the G-men's visit to Queenstown was to find out how the weapons were getting in, so surely it was only a matter of time before they made the connection between Pat and Danny and JohnJoe.

The relationship with the Raffertys had deepened. Kathy missed the boys very much but was heartened to hear how well they were doing. Over the years, Rose and Kathy had become regular correspondents, and Kathy was so grateful to Rose for the care she took of Danny and JohnJoe. Both women were sure they would meet in person one day, and Rose's eyes would light up when Harp described Boston – the restaurants, the shops, the beautiful new buildings that the Americans thought were old.

She passed the crescent and continued to climb until she reached the graveyard. The Cameron Highlanders were stationed at Belmont Barracks just before the little Protestant church, and several of them, in their kilts, were gathered around the gates. She tried not to look either intimidated or defiant.

'Afternoon, miss,' called a cheeky-looking one, who was smoking a cigarette.

'Good afternoon,' she replied, keeping her eyes on the road ahead.

He stood before her, grinning. 'Nice day for a stroll, isn't it?' His Scottish accent burred.

'Yes.' She tried to walk past, but he stood in her way.

'Ah now, no need to be so hasty. What's your name?'

'My name is Miss Harp Devereaux of the Cliff House.' While Harp would never countenance an English accent – that was for people attempting to seem more elevated in society than they were – she still spoke imperiously. 'And I am going to visit my father's grave in that cemetery.' She pointed at the churchyard. 'And I would be grateful if you would allow me to pass please.' Her palms were sweaty now and her heart was racing.

'Private Gordon, report to my office now.' A booming voice from the gate caused both Harp and her would-be waylayer to turn.

The voice belonged to a burly man with the bushiest eyebrows Harp had ever seen; his eyes were barely visible beneath them. He had iron-grey hair cut so short, he looked almost completely bald, and his accent was even more Scottish than the private's.

'Yes, sir.' Gordon saluted and quickly withdrew inside the gates.

'Good day to you, miss.' The man nodded and ushered the remainder of his men inside.

Harp carried on and pushed the gate open, picking her way across the higgledy-piggledy churchyard to the instantly recognisable Devereaux tomb that dominated all of the others. The stone angel with one outstretched wing, the other folded in as she drew a limestone finger to her mouth, always seemed to Harp to be a trifle overly dramatic for a family so notoriously dour.

Henry wasn't dour, and admittedly he was the only one she knew apart from the repugnant Ralph, and the dreadful Matilda, Henry's mother who'd died when Harp was eleven, but the people of Queenstown had long memories, and the Devereauxes were not well liked.

Henry was nothing like his parents or grandparents, though. People might have thought he was. He wasn't sociable and disliked interactions with almost everyone except her and Rose, but he was warm and loving in his own quiet way. Even now, eight years after his death, she missed him so much it hurt, and she felt close to him here.

She sat on the kerbstone of the grave and rested her head against the stone plinth bearing the names of all the Devereauxes that lay there. She tried to imagine how the bones buried beneath her were her family's bones. She was a Devereaux, and the daughter of the maid. Most of the people in Queenstown thought Henry was her father – he had claimed her in his will and bequeathed the house to her as his heir – but her biological father was in fact Ralph. She shuddered at the thought; how she hated him. Henry Devereaux was a father to her in every single way that mattered and as different from his brother as it was possible for two human beings to be.

She sighed. A bee buzzed, and the breeze rustled the branches of the willow tree that overhung the graveyard. There were bluish-green cedars too and several old oaks, lending the place an air of solitude and peace.

'It might seem so up here, but it's anything but peaceful in Queenstown, Mr Devereaux.' She sighed. 'It would break your heart to see what's happening now. That Beckett is a monster, nothing short of it, and his wife and I have become friends. She's nice, but I'm just using her for information. It doesn't sit well with me, but we have to win this war. We have to get rid of them for once and for all.'

She thought of her next Cumann na mBan mission. There was a grenade-making factory in a valley in North Cork. The land up there was wild and uninhabited, so it was an ideal location. The factory was buried deep underground and supplied the entire movement. It was a good place to hide men who had become too visible and risked being picked up.

A consignment of triggering pins from America was to go there, and she was selected to deliver it. The pins were small but vital to production. She was to take the train to Cork, ostensibly to the library in the university to study, and then to Mallow, where she would be met and escorted to a place where the handover could be made safely. The box of pins was light and could fit in the bottom of a carpet bag, which JohnJoe had bought for her the previous Christmas.

How she longed that she and JohnJoe could live happily and peacefully instead of on high alert all the time. Some people enjoyed the adrenaline rush of danger, but she didn't. And neither did he; he wanted this to be over too. Danny, on the other hand, she thought, enjoyed the excitement of it.

She looked down and saw JohnJoe then, at the gate. He looked so different to the skinny boy with the red-blond sticking-up hair and freckles who'd arrived to the Cliff House in 1912, terrified at the prospect of being taken to Boston. Now he was a handsome, filled-out man, and she adored him. Not just because he was attractive but because it was as if their souls or spirits were conjoined when they were children and had never uncoupled. He knew her better than anyone except possibly her mother, and he confided in her in ways she knew he didn't with others. She had never envisaged herself in a relationship, but it was how it happened, and now she could not imagine life without him.

She smiled and waved as he walked over.

'I thought I'd find you here.' He smiled. The mixture of Boston and Ireland in his accent was so endearing. He sat down beside her and kissed her gently.

'I was just thinking about you.' She snuggled up to him. 'It's almost time for me to go back to university, and while I love it there, I miss you.'

'I miss you too, but…' – he yawned – 'Uncle Pat keeps us busy…'

Harp knew he was telling the truth. Dark circles had formed under his eyes; his pale skin looked almost translucent there.

'A boat came in last night but three hours later than we thought. I had to walk up and down the beach to stop myself falling asleep. And all I could think about was you, in your cosy bed, your beautiful hair all over the pillow…' He nuzzled her neck and she giggled. 'And then I got to thinkin' about creepin' in there beside you, holding you in my arms and…'

'Snoring your head off for a fortnight,' she finished for him with a laugh.

He chuckled. 'You could be right, Harp. I don't think even having your gorgeous self beside me would keep me awake right now, but when I woke up…now, that's a different story.' He winked.

They had never been more intimate than kissing, and she looked forward to the day they would fully give themselves to each other every bit as much as he did. She was only sixteen and he eighteen when JohnJoe first confessed that he loved her, and he'd respected her youth so much that he never once pressed the point. But she was twenty now, and something had changed. The deaths of the IRA lads all over the country, the risks she was taking every day carrying messages and weapons, JohnJoe's management of American weapons and money – any one of them could be caught any day, and she didn't want to die not knowing what it was like to be with the man she loved.

He frequently flirted like this, telling her how beautiful she was and how he burned for her, and she'd always gently rebuffed him. He took it in good humour.

'I want that too,' she said slowly. 'Very much.'

He sighed and leaned back against the plinth, pulling her head onto his chest. 'Well, someday we'll get married, and then, well, then, Harp, we'll check into a hotel and nobody will see us for a week.'

'I don't want to wait until then,' she said, surprising herself with how decisive she sounded.

'What?' He moved from her slightly to gaze quizzically down at her, his mouth a curve of confusion.

'You heard me.' She coloured.

'Are you saying that...' – he paused and furrowed his brow – 'you want to sleep with me now?'

'Well, I should hope we don't just sleep, and not right here – that would be somewhat macabre, don't you think?' She grinned. 'But yes, that's what I want.'

The fact that she was making this audacious suggestion, or that the priest might hear her offering to commit a mortal sin, didn't bother her in the slightest. She thought of Henry, lying in rest beneath, and how he loved Rose all his life but never said a word. He would understand. He wasn't prudish. He'd told her that there was a copy of *Fanny Hill* in the library as well as some other worthy literary books deemed obscene by the Church because of their sexual content, but not by him. And while he didn't forbid her from reading them, he suggested waiting until she was older. She'd followed his suggestion, but at sixteen was curious and had read voraciously on the subject.

What had taken her by surprise was the desire. As a young girl reading about such acts as took place between men and women, and in the case of the Greeks and the Romans and Oscar Wilde at least, between men and men as well, she had not been horrified, merely interested. But she could never have imagined wanting to do such a thing with anyone. The idea that throughout history men and women had died in the pursuit of their ultimate bedfellow was something she found mystifying, but not now. Now she understood that primal sensation, that need to be close, to own and be owned, to share that intimacy.

'Well, Miss Devereaux, that's sure a racy suggestion.' JohnJoe smiled and stood up, offering her his hand as he pulled her to her feet.

'Don't you want to?' she asked, her grey eyes locking on his.

JohnJoe smiled. 'Do I want to?' he repeated slowly. He buried his face in her hair and groaned, then whispered in her ear, 'I think of nothing else. Danny says if we don't do it soon, he's going to take me down to the Holy Ground to one of the girls below, just so I don't explode.'

Harp laughed. 'You'd better not!' She punched him playfully. It was well known about the prostitutes who roamed the docklands in the poorer part of town.

'Don't worry, I won't.' He winked at her. 'I'm too tired.'

'That had better not be the only reason,' she warned darkly, then turned to lay her fingers on the stone. 'See you soon, Mr Devereaux,' she whispered. In her mind now he was always Henry, but when she spoke t him directly she reverted to the way she always used to address him.

'We'd best be getting back,' she said to JohnJoe. 'I have to call to the Devlins this evening and get home to help with dinner.' She took his hand as they walked across the churchyard. 'But, JohnJoe, I've been thinking – if anything were to happen to me, I'd like to be buried here, with Henry. I know I'm not Protestant or anything, but can you try to make that happen if I'm gone and you're not?'

He stopped and looked down at her. 'I promise I will. And I want to be buried here in Ireland – don't take me back to Boston. I love Aunt Kathy and Uncle Pat, but this is my home.'

She nodded. How sad that two young people had to have such a conversation, but they did, and now they each knew what the other wanted.

'"I pray for no more youth to perish before its prime, that revenge and iron-heated war may fade with all that has gone before into the night of time,"' Harp quoted quietly.

'Easy. Aeschylus.' JohnJoe smiled.

She laughed affectionately. The boy who had arrived to her house couldn't read, and now he devoured books and could recognise Greek playwrights.

He stood behind her, his chin resting on her head, his arms around her waist. 'Look.' He pointed to the harbour.

'What?' She scanned the scene that had been the seascape of her entire life.

'Nothing really, just that from up here…it all looks so peaceful, like nothing bad is happening.'

Harp sighed sadly. 'I know, but it is, and it will continue if we don't do something to make it stop.'

JohnJoe nodded and took her hand, helping her over some rough ground. 'So were you serious?' he asked, all joking gone.

'About us having sex?'

JohnJoe hooted with laugher. 'Harp Devereaux, yes, about us *having sex* as you so scientifically put it. You really are a quare hawk, you know that?'

She'd told him how the boys at school used to call her and Henry quare hawks, a colloquialism for an odd person, and it used to hurt, but JohnJoe used it now as a term of endearment and it had lost all its power to injure her. He loved using Irish slang, and when he said words only Irish people used with his American accent, it caused no end of hilarity.

She shrugged. 'I suppose I am.' They walked on. 'And yes, I was serious.'

'When?' JohnJoe asked. 'Danny is going to collect timber in Carrigtwohill tomorrow.'

'And what are you supposed to be doing?' Harp asked, smiling.

'I'm supposed to be in the workshop, but Matt has to go to Cork and our place will be empty. Say around two o'clock?'

Danny and JohnJoe shared a two-bedroom flat over Matt's undertaking business. Danny often entertained ladies there, and JohnJoe frequently complained that he was turfed out while his cousin was romancing. But his displeasure was always short-lived. The cousins were devoted to each other. Besides, it was impossible to stay cross at

Danny for long. He was terminally cheerful, according to the dour Liz Devlin, but nobody ever doubted his dedication to the cause.

Danny had been born and raised in Boston, and initially there may have been a little distrust as to his motivation to be involved with the movement. Not that he wouldn't be true to them, but that it might be just a bit of a lark for him and that at the first sign of real trouble, he'd be back to the much safer city of Boston. But Danny Coveney had more than proved he was worthy of the task. He was a happy-go-lucky man by nature and had a terrible weakness for a pretty girl; his romancing had got him into far more scrapes than his rebel activity ever had. He was good-looking by any standard, charming and funny, and his American accent and fine clothes made him seem so much more exotic than the local lads. Rose and the Devlins were forever despairing of the entanglements he got himself into.

While Kathy accepted Harp and JohnJoe, she lived in terror of some Irish girl catching Danny's eye in a serious way and him deciding to stay in Ireland as well. She was bereft without them, having had no child of her own; JJ and Danny were more precious than diamonds. Pat, on the other hand, was so proud of them both and supported them in every way imaginable. He was a prominent member of Clan na Gael, the Irish association in America dedicated to Irish independence, so having the two boys he thought of as his sons back on the home soil, fighting for the liberation of his country, was a source of deep pride.

Danny and JohnJoe had only come to Ireland for a visit in 1916, and to accompany Harp home with a fur coat full of cash for the cause, but the U-boat activity in the Atlantic and the possibility of conscription of the boys in America led to them staying.

'See you then.' She kissed his cheek as they approached the junction where he would turn left and she right to return home.

CHAPTER 10

*A*s Harp lifted the latch and opened the Devlins' back kitchen door, she found Matt, Liz and Cissy all gathered. Matt had summoned her there, but for what purpose she had no idea. The delivery of the grenade pins was arranged for the next week, but perhaps there had been a change of plan. Whatever it was, she would only be told what she needed to know and at the last minute.

The command structure of the IRA was sacrosanct even among friends. The Queenstown Company, of which Matt was the captain, was made up of around a hundred men. Each town around the region had its own company, and together they made up a battalion. The flying column, the group of men who were wanted by Crown forces and had to live on the run, worked closely with the Queenstown Company as well.

Normal day-to-day activity for their company involved receiving weapons and money from the Irish abroad, surveillance of the activities and stealing from the Crown forces stationed in every corner of the town and secreting on boats to America the IRA men who were in extreme danger of being picked up or who knew so much that if they cracked under interrogation, they would reveal the entire operation. Matt explained to each new recruit in the IRA, and Liz and

Cissy the same with Cumann na mBan, that a person should not feel that they were not being trusted with information but that they would only be told the absolute minimum. It was for their own safety.

There were horror stories coming out of West Cork, the town of Bandon in particular, where the activities of the Third West Cork Brigade of the IRA were hugely successful but at a terrible cost – fingernails wrenched out, near drownings, savage beatings. And then the bodies of Volunteers who were arrested were found dumped, either dead or almost dead, in the streets.

A deck of playing cards was spread on the table – forty-five, their favourite – and they made sure that even the cards made sense for the game should anyone come in. They sat around the Devlins' dining table, tea in cups, cards in hand. In the event of a raid, they were just friends meeting up for an innocent game of cards.

Cissy produced a plate of queen cakes.

'Thanks for coming at such short notice, Harp.' Matt spoke quietly. 'Something has come up. As you all know, Mr Bridges has been very helpful, and we know the G-men are coming this week to stay at the hotel. The whole place is up in heap over it, and I was wondering why they were all getting so het up over a couple of G-men. According to Maeve O'Connell, the bar has been very quiet all the week. They're all at their desks, making sure everything is shipshape, hardly an officer in there since last weekend.'

'That's strange. If the G-men are coming to investigate anyone, surely it's us, after the raid on Peary Tower, not the Crown forces. So why are they all so worried?' Harp asked.

'They're not here to find out who was behind the attack on Beckett, though I'm sure they'll be interested in that as well. No, there's something much bigger happening.'

Harp saw a gleam of enthusiasm in Matt's eyes, something she'd not seen before. Normally he was understated and stoic, but this, whatever it was, had him excited.

'They're keeping it very quiet, but Lord Winters is coming, we've seen some intelligence to suggest the visit will be several months from now. The G-men are here as scouts ahead of the visit, just to make sure the place is safe for him.' Matt allowed the news to sink in.

'Winters,' Cissy said softly. 'If we could get him…'

'We'll need further instructions from Dublin, but provisionally we have the go-ahead to come up with a plan at least. It will have to be presented to Collins, and he'll have final say, of course, but to get the Lord Lieutenant, well, it could be the thing we need to bring this to a head.'

'When you say "get him", you mean kidnap or…' Harp asked.

'No possibility of kidnap, I would think – we'd never get near enough. We don't know yet what kind of guard he'll have, but we can assume it will be substantial given that he's the supreme commander of the Crown forces in Ireland,' Matt answered. 'As I say, we'll need a detailed plan, and then it will have to be brought to Dublin in person. Too risky to post it. I was hoping you'd do it, Harp. You can memorise it all so easily, so we don't need to risk writing anything down.' Matt turned to her.

'Of course. There's a symposium on Romance languages in Trinity next week. I could attend that as my reason for travelling up,' Harp replied instantly.

'Good, that's ideal. Are you all right to go alone? You'd have to stay overnight, possibly two nights – it will depend on how quickly Collins responds to the plan.'

Harp thought for a split second; a night in a hotel with JohnJoe would be heaven. 'It might be best if JohnJoe came with me, for safety?'

Matt didn't react and agreed absentmindedly. 'Right, yes. Things are very tense everywhere now, so it would be better, I suppose, to have him with you. No weapons, though – we can't risk a search. And go to the meeting with Collins on your own.'

Matt had spent the entire winter training the ragtag group of Volunteers and Cumann na mBan recruits in combat techniques, with and without weapons. He'd allowed no rest until he was sure each person could handle themselves.

Rose had explained when Harp expressed astonishment that Matt had such skills. 'Matt never knew his parents. He was placed in an orphanage when he was a baby, and there he had to learn how to defend himself. Then when he was thirteen, he was apprenticed to a shipbuilder, Lacey's. They're gone now, but they had a big boatyard. There was a man there – he was French. I never knew him as he died before I moved here, but Matt told me about him. Jean-Claude Bellac. He served with the French Foreign Legion in the Mandingo Wars in Africa, and he took Matt under his wing and taught him all he knew. In the evenings all the other apprentices went home, but Matt lived in quarters in the yard provided for him and so did this Frenchman. They had nothing better to do. Matt said Bellac didn't want to teach him at first, but Matt wore him down.'

'Right so,' Matt said as the three women listened. 'Winters is coming in, presumably to the main quay. I can't see them trying to land him anywhere else. And from there he'll most likely be taken to the Admiralty, where he'll have dinner or lunch with Beckett, Hodges from the naval base, the new RIC man, whoever he'll be.' He shot a sideways glance at Liz, who shrugged innocently.

The most recent commander of the RIC and the Black and Tans, Anthony Edgar, had only lasted three months. Like Beckett from India, Edgar had been taken from Cairo, where he'd been successful in dealing with insurgents there. He'd been very vocal on how he would easily rout out a few Irish rebels and deal with them. He was married with one young child. Ten days ago Liz had shot at him from the upstairs of a derelict house adjacent to the one Edgar was renting. She calmly let herself out the back door and walked past the scene of him prostrate on the street, bleeding, and not one eyebrow of suspicion was raised. She deliberately only inflicted a flesh wound – to do otherwise would invite sharp reprisals – but it was enough that he was taken to the military hospital on Spike Island to recover. Even from his sickbed, he continued with his rhetoric that he would crush the IRA. Clearly a message wasn't enough.

While her husband was still in hospital, a stranger crept up behind Mrs Edgar as she watched her daughter play in the garden. The ominous click of the removal of a safety catch of a pistol, combined with the cold of the muzzle on her neck and the instruction to not look around, chilled her to the bone.

'Take your husband and child and get out of here. Don't come back. Ever. He chose to ignore the last warning. There won't be another.'

Edgar resigned his post the following week.

'We'll assume they'll come up from the quay, turn right at the Porthole Bar and continue up the hill to the Admiralty. We can position people all along the route. Some lads in Quinlan's stables – they can hide in there. I'll put three upstairs in Moll Lyden's – her top floor overlooks the route – and another two in Burke's on the other side of the street. We'll have several lookouts all the way up from the port.'

Cissy and Liz seemed to share an unspoken conversation.

Matt went on. 'I think our best chance of success is a grenade or two into the car. It will hopefully be open, but if not we can lob them into the support vehicle and create a diversion. Snipers then at the junction of Admiralty Road and Burma Lane. I'll be in the window of Linehans's – I think that's the best vantage point as he goes around the bend there, and Dan Cotter across the road in Kelly's in case I miss or am obstructed. Between the grenade and the two of us, we have the best chance.' Matt Quinn was a crack shot, and if anyone could get Winters, he could.

They chatted on for a few minutes, working out the various roles. Liz and Cissy would coordinate access and message deliveries by the women of Cumann na mBan; they were less likely to be stopped and searched. Grenades under babies in prams, bullets in brassieres, notes and coding ciphers in hairdos – they were incredibly resourceful. Liz had removed all of her books about socialism and feminism from her bookshelves, carefully storing them in the cellar to be replaced when the possibility of a British soldier or a Black and Tan barging into her home was gone.

'So a few more bits and pieces,' Matt said to finish up the meeting. 'Rose has two young couples pretending to be on honeymoon this week in the Cliff House, and the lads need to be got out. The girls are Cumann na mBan posing as their new brides. The men were Mac

Curtain's personal bodyguards and Terence MacSwiney has ordered that they be sent to the States. Pat Rafferty will take care of them, and they can tell everyone there firsthand what's going on. Our supporters over there like to get word anyway, and it's not safe for them to stay. We'll get them out on the evening tide on Thursday, so if you can let Ernie know, Liz?'

Liz nodded.

'What about the G-men?' Harp asked.

'We'll keep a watch on them. I've people on that, and it's absolutely critical that we give them no cause for suspicion whatsoever. But we need to keep our attention on the big one, Winters. If we can eliminate him, then the British will have to come to the table. If we get him, they've lost.'

CHAPTER 11

*H*arp was just about to turn up the Smuggler's Stairs when she heard Marianne calling her. Her classes had been suspended as the city was in such turmoil, and she was completing her assignments and returning them by post to her professors. She missed attending the university, but it was good to spend more time with JohnJoe, and the Winters visit was making a lot of work for everyone.

Harp turned and waved and then waited for her. Marianne was dressed in a pale-pink summer dress with gold shells embroidered round the hem and a short dove-grey velvet jacket. She seemed to have a new hat every time Harp saw her. This one was a grey cloche under which her blond hair was pinned into curls. She wore lipstick and powder, and though she was a year younger than Harp, she looked older and certainly more sophisticated.

'Harp, at last.' She smiled. 'I called twice this week but you were out.'

'Hello, Marianne,' Harp said with a smile. 'Sorry. I was probably running errands for my mother.'

'No matter. I just wanted to tell you what happened. Shall we go up to your house for tea and I can tell you all my news?' Marianne was fizzing with excitement, whatever it was. Harp wondered if she was pregnant.

'Of course, more than welcome.' Harp allowed Marianne to link her arm as they climbed the steps together.

'You won't believe what's happened. I got a little upset a few nights ago, and Oliver asked what was wrong. He can be, well, if not nice, at least not a grumpy ogre all of the time, and I saw my chance. I just said I was so lonely for my old life, for my home and my mother, and how the attack had frightened me and how I had no friends my own age and I was truly desperately unhappy.'

'And what did he say?'

'Well, astoundingly he asked what would make me happy.' Marianne issued this statement as if it were the most astonishing piece of information. Harp thought surely it was the role of a spouse to at least try to make their husband or wife happy, but perhaps not.

'And you said?' Harp asked.

'I couldn't tell him the truth, which is that I long to get out of this wretched place and return home, because I said that once and he was furious, telling me it was incredibly disloyal of me as his wife to express displeasure in where his career took us. I mean, honestly, disloyal to him? I never even agreed to the marriage! It was arranged and I was told about it.'

Harp knew Marianne didn't love Beckett, but surely she wasn't forced into the marriage? 'You truly had no choice?'

'Not really. My mother told me it was for the best, and that it was a good match. She wanted me to go through with it, and I thought it might get better, that over time I would grow, if not to love him, then at least to like him somewhat. But no, we are utterly different creatures with not one thing in common.'

Thinking that Marianne reminded her so much of her namesake in *Sense and Sensibility*, Harp quoted, '"It is not time or opportunity that is to determine intimacy; – it is disposition alone. Seven years would be insufficient to make some people acquainted with each other, and seven days are more than enough for others."'

The other girl sighed wistfully. 'Marianne Dashwood, my heroine.

I loved her, and while I could see that Elinor was a good sort, she was rather dreary, wasn't she?'

Harp was surprised. Marianne didn't strike her as the literary type, and Harp was used to people looking at her oddly when she quoted. She used to do it a lot more often as a child – it was almost instinctive that she would think of a quotation pertinent to the conversation – but had learned over the years to curb that habit for fear of looking and sounding like an oddball. Sometimes, though, it just slipped out.

'Do you like Jane Austen?' Harp asked.

'Oh yes, but I prefer Arthur Conan Doyle – I love Sherlock Holmes – and Wilkie Collins of course. You know *The Moonstone* is about an Indian diamond? Marvellous story. I like detective stories the best, though. Sure did love *Northanger Abbey*. The spookier, the better for me, though little did I realise I'd be living in my very own haunted house in awful Dreary Towers. Anyway, listen to me blathering on and I've not told you the best news.'

Harp stopped at the bend in the steep steps for a breather, turning around as she always did to admire the view of the harbour.

'Oliver has agreed to move in to the Cliff House!' Marianne said with a delighted grin. 'I told him the hotel was so dreary, and anyway he doesn't like it either, being in the centre of town, so when I told him about this place, he agreed. Isn't it marvellous?'

Harp had no time to answer before Matt came around the corner. 'Oh, er…Mr Quinn, hello.' Harp knew she sounded rattled and tried to compose herself. The idea that she would in a moment be introducing Marianne to the man who tried to kill her husband and burned her house down had shaken her.

'Hello, Harp.' Matt smiled gently, giving no indication that they were anything more than passing acquaintances. 'Lovely day, isn't it?'

'Beautiful,' she agreed. She turned to Marianne. 'This is Matt Quinn, the local undertaker. Mr Quinn, this is Marianne Beckett. Her husband has been stationed here since last month.'

To Harp's impressed amazement, no glimmer of recognition crossed Matt's face. 'Nice to meet you, Mrs Beckett.' He smiled and extended his hand.

'And you, Mr Quinn.' Marianne gave him a flirty smile.

Matt was good-looking, Harp supposed, if older men were your thing, but she never saw him like that; if anything, Matt was a kind of father figure.

'I think I passed you doing some work at the hotel?' Marianne asked.

'That would be me all right,' Matt joked. 'Mr Bridges had a bit of a woodworm problem.'

'How marvellous to be able to turn your hand to such things. I always admire men who are good with their hands.'

Was Harp imagining it? Or was Marianne being very suggestive?

'Jack of all trades, master of none, that's me,' Matt replied warmly.

'Oh, I doubt that.' Marianne eyed him coquettishly. 'I think you'd be a very useful man to have around.'

'Well, my clients rarely complain.'

Marianne giggled. 'Oh, you *are* naughty, Mr Quinn.'

'Well, we'd best let you get back to it,' Harp said desperately, wanting to put an end to whatever this was.

'Righto. See you later, Harp, Mrs Beckett.' Matt nodded respectfully and was gone.

They climbed the last few steps and turned into the garden.

'My goodness, he's very attractive, isn't he?' Marianne whispered.

'Em...I...I never thought about it. I've known Matt Quinn all of my life, so I don't really...' Harp answered awkwardly. 'Now, you were saying you wanted to come to stay here?'

It was a great idea. If Marianne and Beckett stayed under their roof, they would be in a good position to monitor his comings and goings.

'Yes!' Marianne was triumphant. 'It will be perfect. We can be friends, and I could help in the garden – I would really love that. You could have the most spectacular little rose garden in that sunny corner.' She pointed across the lawn. 'And Oliver is out all of the time anyway, so we'd never see him.'

'Wonderful,' Harp replied. 'I'm sure we can accommodate you.'

They would have to be extremely careful, especially with an IRA man on the run, but it would be worth it.

The men they put up before they sailed were always sent with a girl, a Cumann na mBan volunteer usually, to pose as his wife, and they had got away with it easily so far. On a few occasions, the men were injured and that was a more difficult task, but they managed to bring them in the back stairs and put them in the attic room out of everyone's way. She supposed they would have to be even more careful in that event.

Visiting British officers stayed all the time if the Queen's Hotel was full; some just preferred the Cliff House. The barracks accommodation at the naval base on Haulbowline Island and the army base on Spike were less than salubrious, and the officers enjoyed their comfort.

It would be fine. It had to be.

Harp smiled. 'Come on inside and we'll talk to my mother about which room we'll put you in.'

'"Lead on, Macduff,"' Marianne said in a deep voice.

'You know that's a common misquote.' Harp grinned. Despite who Marianne was, she really liked her.

'Aha, a Shakespearean scholar too! You really are a swotty boots, aren't you? Yes, I *did* know actually. Macbeth says, "Lay on, Macduff. Though Birnam wood be come to Dunsinane, and thou opposed, being of no woman born, yet I will try the last. Before my body I throw my warlike shield. Lay on, MacDuff and damn'd be him that first cries, 'Hold, enough!'"'

Harp laughed. 'I have never met anyone who can remember things like that the way I can. My boyfriend thinks I'm very peculiar indeed – in fact, most people do.'

'Well, yes, I can see how they would,' Marianne said bluntly, but with no malice. 'My mother was always telling me not to be too clever, that chaps don't like it. It intimidates them. They prefer ladies to be silly. I was very clever at school, got top marks easily, and I never really revised. I wish I'd had a mother like yours who allowed you to go to university – I would have loved that. But no, it was Chateau

Mont Choisi in Lausanne for me. Poor Papa nearly collapsed when he saw the fees, but Mama pointed out that I needed to find a rich husband on my own merits. He had lost his fortune, so deportment and etiquette were the way to achieve that, at least according to my mama.' Marianne shrugged theatrically. 'You had a narrow escape, Harp, you lucky thing.'

Harp replied, 'I would be useless at any of that, and besides, we're not the class of people who would go somewhere like that. My mother was the housekeeper here and my father owned the house, so though I have the Devereaux name, we've been destitute. Only that my mother worked so hard at this business and saved up enough for the fees and my books, I would never have got to university.'

'She's a remarkable lady, your mama, by the sounds of it. I like her a lot. You're lucky.'

'Do you get along with your mother?' Harp asked. Marianne was so much more than one initially thought.

The other girl shrugged. 'Yes, but I don't really know her that well, not compared to you and yours anyway. It was my papa I really loved. He came to England on business a lot and would come to take me out of school, and we would go for cream teas. He was lovely. I was sent to school in England when I was five. I remember it still, being taken away from our house in Shimla – my governess took me. I sobbed and sobbed. I loved our life in India. It was perfect. We had staff, and we loved them and they loved us. We had a kitchen *wallah* called Arun who used to take me out in the monsoon, when it was torrential rain, to play in the huge puddles that would form in the grounds. I had a pet monkey, Fred, and he slept in my room. Mama and Papa would insist on British food being served, but I loved eating in the kitchen, *pappadams* with lime chutney and *saag aloo* and all of the Indian spices. The food here is so bland in comparison.'

Harp felt a pang of pity for this girl. She could not imagine being taken from all she knew and loved at five years of age.

They entered the house and sat in the drawing room – Mammy would not want Marianne in the kitchen – and waited for Rose to arrive. She was upstairs, Harp knew, and would be down shortly. 'And you only went home once a year?' she asked.

'Not even then, really. One time it was three years between visits. The passage was so expensive and took so long, so I stayed with my Aunt Emily in the holidays, my mother's unmarried sister. She was kind to me, though my father thought her a boring blue stocking. She had a wonderful personal library and was a librarian herself by profession. I only saw my mother a handful of times between the age of five and seventeen.'

Harp hid her shock at such dereliction of parental duty. Perhaps in their world it was normal. She poured them each a glass of homemade elderflower cordial from the jug on the sideboard. It was these little touches that endeared the Cliff House to the guests. 'And are you close with your aunt now?'

'Yes, she's wonderful. She tried her best to talk me out of marrying Oliver. She cared so much, she even came out to Shimla to see me, but my mother told her to mind her own business, and Papa had promised my hand to Oliver by then. My mother feels bad now, of course, but she did think it was a good match for me at the time. And I think she didn't like the idea of me hanging around her, getting in the way.' She leaned over conspiratorially. 'She more or less told me that there was no need to be faithful to Oliver so long as I was discreet. That women of our class married strategically, but if you were clever, you could have love affairs as well.'

Marianne laughed at Harp's shocked expression. 'I know it must seem awful, but everyone in Shimla is carrying on with other people. I suspect my mother is too, though I've never actually met him.'

'And there were no other options?' Harp asked, making no effort to hide her shock.

'No. Aunt Em lived in a draughty old house in Bristol with her friend Janet, and they were as poor as church mice.' Marianne smiled ruefully. 'It was shallow of me, I suppose, but I was raised to be a lady, and Mama thought Oliver could provide that lifestyle for me. Grandpa was shrewd and made a packet, but Papa was a gambler so that was that. I couldn't imagine a life other than one as a lady of my class. Oliver offered that, and it seemed the best option at the time.'

'And now?' Harp asked tentatively. They were steering into dangerous waters, but any information about Beckett would be useful.

Marianne looked around, though they were alone, reached across the sofa and took Harp's hand. 'I can't bear him,' she whispered. 'Truly, he's awful, Harp. He's cold and unfeeling. And I know those people came and burned our house, and I don't pretend to understand why, but I'm shocked at how callous he is. When we were in Shimla, Papa brought Oliver home for dinner one evening. I knew something was wrong. Papa looked wretched and Mama was tight-lipped, but Oliver stayed and spoke to me, in this condescending way he has, like I was a child, but then he looked at me as if he wanted to eat me alive. It was horrid and made my flesh creep.' She visibly shuddered. 'After dinner I shooed him out and came back into the lounge and remarked to my parents, "Thank goodness that's over. He's dreadful." And then poured myself a sherry. I saw it then, the look between them. Pleading in my papa's eyes, loathing in Mama's. I knew something was wrong, and then they told me.'

'What?' Harp was intrigued.

'That Papa was losing in a game of cards. He'd staked all his remaining money and lost it all to Oliver, who was about to clean Papa out when he said there was a way of winning back the money. Papa jumped at it. He heard Oliver's wager and...' – Marianne fought tears, but Harp could see she refused to let them flow – 'agreed. My hand in marriage was the bet.' She swallowed. 'If Papa won the last hand, he got his money back and I was not available, but he didn't win and so...'

'Oh, Marianne, that's terrible. I'm so sorry.'

Marianne shrugged. 'As Aunt Em said, I could have said no, but by then it was all arranged.'

'Didn't you tell your parents that night that you didn't want to marry him?'

'I did. We had a terrible argument. I said some unforgivable things to my papa, that I would never forgive him, that he was such a disappointment, that he was a weak fool who wasn't a fit husband or father...'

Marianne took a sip of cordial and steadied herself. Her voice sounded strangled. 'He never fought back, never argued, just sat there and took it all, my rage, my mother's stony silence. I went to bed. The garden *wallah* found him the next morning, in the pergola. He'd shot himself in the head.'

Words seemed so inadequate. Harp just squeezed her hand.

'The following day, some creditors came. They wanted to have first call on any available money, I suppose. He owed money everywhere. Mama has private means, from her own family, but she didn't want to waste it on Papa's debts.'

'So what's happened?' Harp asked.

Marianne shrugged. 'I don't know really. Mama is still living in the house, but she must have settled enough of his debts to allow that or something. We don't really speak about it.'

'That's awful. You poor thing.' Harp found herself meaning it.

'Well, it's the situation so I've no choices. My mama and her new chap are coming to London soon, and Oliver and I are going to meet up with them. I was surprised that he suggested it, actually, but I told him she was coming and asked if I could go to meet her and he said we'd both go. He's an odd man, Harp. He doesn't like talking to me – he seems to find me tiresome, if I'm honest – but he wants to control every aspect of my life. He tells me how to dress, what to eat, how to speak, and he insists on his conjugal rights every night. But it's so lonely.'

'I'm sorry life is so difficult for you, Marianne,' Harp said, surprised at the compassion in her own voice.

'Well, having a friend makes it much easier, I can assure you.' Marianne smiled. 'You won't tell anyone any of this, will you, Harp?'

'No, of course I won't,' Harp said, meaning it.

CHAPTER 12

*H*arp and JohnJoe located the first empty compartment they could find on the Cork-to-Dublin train. He sat beside her, though the seat opposite was vacant.

'I just want to be near you,' he murmured in her ear as the whistle blew and the train began to chug out of the station.

It felt good to be getting out of Queenstown, even if it was on a dangerous mission. She was word-perfect on the plan to assassinate Winters. Timings, personnel, the route were etched in her brain to regurgitate to General Michael Collins himself. She was schooled on the plan, over and over, and cross-examined by Matt, pre-empting any questions Collins might have. She was to make contact with a representative of his in the post office on Bachelors Walk and would be given instructions as to when and where she would meet Collins to deliver the news.

JohnJoe was not to go to the meeting; it was an unnecessary risk, and a girl alone would raise fewer eyebrows. Michael Collins was the most wanted man in the British Empire, and he did not remain at large easily. He was notoriously audacious but had so far evaded capture mainly because the British had no idea what he looked like or who he really was.

JohnJoe had written to Kitty and was going to meet her and Jane in St Stephen's Green for a walk while Harp met Collins, and they would go for tea afterwards at the Gresham Hotel. He was excited to see them again.

'How's Beckett and his wife getting along?' he asked.

JohnJoe didn't approve of them staying at the Cliff House, fearing it put Harp and Rose in unnecessary danger, but Matt had overruled his objections.

'All right. He keeps to himself, but at least we know a little more of his comings and goings. He really is the worst they've ever sent. He does nothing to control the excesses of the Tans – he encourages them if anything. He actually told the Devlins that they should invest in a cash register, knowing full well what had happened. He's vindictive and cruel.'

'Matt should just put a bullet in him in his bed,' JohnJoe said.

'The IRA might just do that. God knows he deserves it, but we'll need to bide our time. All energy has to go into the plan at hand now. Beckett wanted to flex his muscles after the attack on Peary Tower, and he has done – people are terrified. But he'll settle down now probably. They are all caught up in the Winters visit, every uniform in the place, from RIC to Tans to the Cameron Highlanders. All the gang at the naval base and on Spike, every last man jack is focused on Winters coming.'

'I hate the thought of him sleeping in your house, I really do. Her too, with her fake friendship with you while all the time her husband is terrorising the whole place,' JohnJoe said.

Harp felt so conflicted. She should see Marianne as the enemy, and in some ways she did, but in other ways she just couldn't. Beckett was the devil incarnate of course – she had no mixed feelings about him – but the fact that Marianne couldn't stand him endeared her even more. She wanted JohnJoe to understand something. 'JohnJoe, I know she's his wife and all of that, but she's really nice, and she...' – Harp would not betray Marianne's confidence, even with JohnJoe – 'and she hasn't had it easy, you know?'

'I know you're such a good person and you try to see the best in everyone, but that Beckett... He's such a monster, and she married him, so...'

Harp bit her lip. 'It wasn't her choice.'

'Well, probably not – he's about thirty years older than her. But she *is* his wife and nobody is holding her there at gunpoint.' JohnJoe was adamant. 'Look, Harp, I know you like her, but honestly it's not a good idea to let her get too close. Use her to find out what Matt needs, but other than that, keep your distance. If she's gonna be loyal to anyone, it's gonna be him.'

Harp knew he was probably right, but it all seemed so unfair. This Irish struggle was as much to do with equality of the sexes for her as it was national liberation. The two were inextricably linked in her mind, and she found herself drawn to the movement precisely because there was an equality to it. Cumann na mBan was a critical part of the operation, with women using the sexist society to their advantage. Women were less likely to be searched, and less likely, if found with contraband, to be executed. Brutal as the British were, they still baulked at beating up women.

She and the Devlins and the many other women she met in the course of the struggle all were united in the belief that with Irish liberation would come the liberation of women. The opening lines of the Proclamation of Independence read on the steps of the General Post Office on Easter Monday, 1916, opened with the line 'Irishmen *and* Irishwomen'. It spoke of cherishing all the children of the nation equally. And Harp believed that no matter how hard the sacrifice, it would be worth it to realise those aspirations of a socialist Ireland, in the true sense of the word, where the downtrodden, the poor, women, children, the uneducated, all would be elevated to stand shoulder to shoulder with men of power and influence. To truly effect change, that was her dream.

Marianne was every bit a victim of that rotten system as the Irish were. Subjugated and oppressed, made to bend to the will of others, denied the right to follow one's own destiny, Marianne Beckett was forced into a life she never chose.

'You're probably right.' She sighed, knowing that without telling him the truth of what Marianne had revealed to her, there would be no way to convince him. Besides, Marianne was entrenched in that system. Her family was, at least in the past, a wealthy if not aristocratic one, and she was steeped in the glorious British Empire. She loved India but had never once uttered a word about how wrong the occupation of that country was or the appalling treatment of the Indians at the hands of the British.

'So what time are you meeting Kitty?' she asked, changing the subject.

'I said I'd go to her house. She and Seamus are renting a place off Dorset Street, and Jane is going to school nearby and likes it, according to Kitty's last letter. I can't wait to see them. She can't write much, as she's afraid of being intercepted, but I think Seamus is really in the thick of it up there, and she's kept very busy as well.'

Harp knew how proud JohnJoe was of both of his sisters, but the copper-haired Kitty with her infectious smile and curvaceous figure was a huge asset to Cumann na mBan; she could flirt with the British soldiers in a way no other Irishwoman could. She and Jane had been taken to England by their aunt and raised there after the death of their mother, and so both O'Dwyer girls spoke with cultured British accents, which hid in Kitty's case a burning Irish heart, intent on rebellion. Harp could well imagine Kitty being used to get messages and information all over the city.

'You'll come there once you've met him?' JohnJoe asked.

He was anxious for her, she knew. Michael Collins was the commander in chief of the IRA, and nothing happened without his say-so. He was a Corkman and allegedly very charismatic and handsome. According to Matt, close shaves were a regular occurrence as the British did everything they could to catch him. He had spies everywhere; it was how the whole thing worked. Not just men, but girls and even children too. British officers were careful not to discuss matters of importance around Irishmen, no matter how innocuous their position as waiter or barman, but they ignored girls. So Collins's army was made up of waitresses and chambermaids every bit as much as men with guns. He realised information was the key to success.

Knowing what the British planned to do before they did it and thwarting them every step of the way was his modus operandi.

'I will. I've memorised the address – 31 Richmond Street.'

'And you'll be very careful? Dublin isn't like Queenstown, you know.'

Harp sighed exasperatedly. 'No, JohnJoe, I'll shout from the rooftops why I'm there.'

He smiled and raised his hands in defence. 'I know, sorry. You're perfectly capable, but you're my girl and I worry about you.'

She smiled. She was his girl and she loved him.

The train was searched twice, and on both occasions Harp and JohnJoe showed the soldiers the details of the symposium in Trinity and Harp showed her university library card proving she was a student. JohnJoe had his newly minted American passport, which so far had exempted him from any questioning. He hammed up his American accent too when approached and was instantly dismissed each time. The idea that an American would involve himself in Irish politics seemed unlikely to the British.

'It would have been nice to have had time to meet Brian,' Harp said with regret. 'I wrote, but he's working a long shift at the hospital today and another tomorrow, so he wouldn't have time. He was cross I didn't give him more notice because he could have taken a day off if he'd known, but I wrote and said I only knew myself a few days ago. But it would have been nice to meet him up in Dublin.'

'Hmm.' JohnJoe was noncommittal. Though the men had met several times since JohnJoe came to Queenstown permanently in 1916, there was a wariness there. JohnJoe claimed that he knew that Brian held a candle for Harp, no matter how much she denied it.

'Well, he'll be home in the summer anyway, so I'll see him then.' Harp was defiant. As much as she loved JohnJoe, he would not dictate who her friends were. 'He's got a new girlfriend,' she added, to soften the blow, seeing the sting in his eyes.

This news perked him up. 'Really? That's great. What's she like?'

'Lovely apparently. He's mad about her. She's a nurse, from up north someplace. Anyway, he was all talk about her in his last letter.'

'So I can relax?' He gave her a sheepish grin.

'You could always relax.' Harp rolled her eyes. 'I've told you a thousand times, Brian and I are just friends. That's all we've ever been. And we will always be friends, so you'd better get used to it.'

'I know, I know.' He held his hands up again. 'But you don't see how he looks at you. When you sang and played the harp for Matt's birthday back in February, he looked at you like his heart was breaking. I know, because I felt the same before I finally got up the guts to tell you how I felt.'

'Except he did tell me, and I told him the truth, that I loved him like a brother. And now we're friends,' Harp said, not unkindly but firmly. The idea that she had any man interested in her at all, let alone two, was astounding to her.

Arriving finally into Kingsbridge station in Dublin, Harp took her bag containing just a notepad and some pens and set off directly to the rendezvous. She didn't bid JohnJoe goodbye and left the train ahead of him. Matt had warned them that everyone was being watched in Dublin these days. Every day there were killings of Crown forces, many of them high ranking, and Collins's Squad, as the band of specially chosen assassins were called, were feared at the highest echelons of the British administration in Ireland. Even within the fortified walls of Dublin Castle, the bastion of Crown forces in Ireland, they didn't feel safe. And with good reason. Collins's army was everywhere, impossible to see and buried deep in every strata of Irish society, from top to bottom.

Harp followed the instructions she had been given by Matt and stood in line at the post office on Capel Street. She had a letter in her pocket, addressed to a Mrs Kathleen O'Brien in Bruree, County Limerick, to be posted in case she was stopped. This was also her calling card. The clerk would know who she was and what she was there for based on that letter.

Thankfully, a young man entering the post office seemed to occupy the attention of the three Dublin Metropolitan Police officers who were outside, observing everyone and everything. They looked far more like heavily armed soldiers than policemen. They took no notice of her. She tried not to watch as they questioned the young man aggressively, a commonplace sight all over the country nowadays. Matt was right; everyone was on edge.

Either the man couldn't or didn't want to answer their questions, and within seconds he was dragged away. Harp didn't dare catch his eye.

'What is the reason for you being here, miss?' An officer in the uniform of the army was at her elbow. He and his comrade had appeared as the policemen left.

'I'm posting a letter to my aunt before going to a lecture in Trinity College,' she replied calmly and in as neutral a voice as she could muster.

'Let me see it,' he said.

She handed over the letter and he examined it. For a second she thought he might rip it open, and she was relieved she'd thought to write a few short lines to the fictitious aunt.

'What time is the lecture?' he asked. He wore the insignia of a major. Harp thought he was young to be of such a high rank, but then the Great War had made officers of boys, as their superiors were mown down before their eyes in the trenches. He was clean-shaven with sandy hair and a ruddy complexion.

Harp glanced up at the clock. The symposium was on all day. 'It's resuming at 2 p.m. I just popped out to post this letter.'

He glanced at her askew. 'You came all the way up here to post a letter? Could you not have posted it down at Stephen's Green?' he asked, and his hazel eyes bored into hers.

'I could have, but after sitting down all morning, I wanted to stretch my legs,' she lied, feeling herself blush.

'Well, if you want to get back for two, you'd want to get going, miss.' He handed her back her letter.

The clerk eyed her cautiously as she left the officer and approached the hatch.

'A penny stamp, please,' she said, sliding the letter under the grille.

The clerk took the letter and passed it back, this time with a stamp on it. She was a middle-aged woman, a portly person with a severe hairstyle that dragged her thick hair back from her deeply lined forehead.

Harp didn't know what to do. The officer and his comrade were still in the post office, seemingly just standing there.

'The postbox is outside on the left,' the woman said mechanically as Harp took the letter and the stamp.

'Thank you.' She licked the stamp and walked outside to place it in the box. Letter posted, she wondered what she should do. For fear she was being watched, she strode off in the direction of Trinity College. She had never been to Dublin before but had studied the map and knew where it was. She kept the River Liffey on her right as she walked down the quays, passing first the ornate pedestrian Ha'penny Bridge, then crossing over the huge O'Connell Bridge, named for 'The Liberator' Daniel O'Connell, the father of Catholic emancipation. Harp glanced to the left and felt a surge of pride. The enormous bronze statue of O'Connell on the bottom of Sackville Street was pockmarked with bullet holes from Easter Week in 1916, when a motley crew of poets and schoolteachers read aloud the Proclamation of Irish Independence on the General Post Office steps not a hundred yards away. She would have loved to go up there and just stand where they stood, to soak that historic place up, but she didn't dare. To do so would attract attention, and that was a dangerous business in Dublin these days.

As she crossed the River Liffey, she felt someone beside her. It wasn't a jostle as such, and there were crowds trying to cross the bridge, but she felt something. A note was placed in her hand. On the other side of the bridge, the traffic came to a stop and everyone crossed onto Westmoreland Street, and Harp allowed herself to be carried along. Opening the note as inconspicuously as she could, she read the contents. *South Anne Street, 14, second floor.*

She tried to conjure up in her mind's eye the map of the city she had memorised.

South Anne Street was off Grafton Street. She'd have to bypass the gates of Trinity. If she was being followed, now she would have to come up with a reason why. She remembered a shoe shop, Hillier's, that her mother said she used to go to for shoes when she was a child. It was on Stephen's Green, so if questioned she'd say she was going there. She just prayed it was still there.

Everywhere she looked were Crown forces, and though the business of the city seemed to be going on unimpeded, there was a tension in the air. The destruction caused by the Rising four years earlier could still be seen everywhere, and the eyes of the city's inhabitants were darting and wary. She tried to stroll as nonchalantly as she could, remembering each detail of the plan over and over in her head.

She turned left onto South Anne Street and noticed the buildings were odd numbers on one side and even on the other. She crossed from a door bearing the number 11 and spotted number 12 almost opposite. Beside 12 was a doorway, slightly ajar. Unlike the other premises on the street, it seemed not to be a business of any kind.

Glancing left and right to ensure nobody was watching her, she pushed the door open. The hallway was dank and smelly, the brown wallpaper was peeling, and the dark-green linoleum was ripped and had holes in patches. She walked in and climbed the stairs. The one lightbulb hanging from a single electrical cord wasn't working. There were two doors on the second floor, one directly in front of her, the other to her left. She stopped, trying to hear if there were any indications of inhabitants, but she heard nothing. She pushed the door in front of her, but it was closed. Did she dare turn the handle? Or should she knock?

The decision was taken out of her hands when a large man in an elegant three-piece suit opened the door. She was in no doubt as to who it was, and she tried to quell her nerves. As good-looking as he was reported to be, she was surprised at the sheer size of the man. He was well over six feet and broadly built. He had dark hair that fell in a quiff over his forehead and a beaming smile.

'Miss Devereaux?' he enquired.

'Y-Yes, Mr Collins...' She found herself tongue-tied.

'Come on in. I'm sorry, this is no place to be entertaining anyone, but beggars and choosers and all of that.' He shot a bolt on the door, one that looked shiny, so she assumed it was a recent addition.

The room had an old bed, on which was a jumble of bedclothes of dubious cleanliness, a large oval mahogany dining table that looked out of place in its ornate beauty and three mismatched office chairs. In a corner was a dangerous-looking gas ring and a small table with a few chipped cups and plates and half a loaf of bread. He pulled out one tubular steel chair with a tattered seat and offered it to her; he took another and sat on it himself.

'Not exactly luxury, but we need it from time to time. Now so, Matt Quinn sent you to me.' He crossed one thick muscular leg over the other and leaned back as if they were taking tea in the Shelbourne, not having a covert meeting in a smelly semiderelict house.

'Yes, Mr Collins,' she began.

'Call me Mick, everyone does. And what's your first name?' He smiled and his eyes crinkled.

'Harp, Harp Devereaux.'

'Well, if you risked your neck to meet me, and I'm running the British gauntlet by coming into town to meet you, we might as well be on first-name terms.' He chuckled and she found herself relaxing. 'Now then, Harp, tell me this first – are you the lady behind our most successful cipher?'

Harp coloured. 'Well, I...I did suggest a simple polyalphabetic cipher that can be used, but I don't know if –'

'Oh, 'tis your idea, all right. The lads were trying to explain it to me, but to be honest with you, Harp, they hadn't a bull's notion what it was about either, except that it works. But I'll tell you this – it's saving lives, so it is, every day of the week. People can deliver messages much better with your system. Writing anything down is a disaster. So could you explain, using small words now, to this big thick Corkman how it works?'

'All right.' Harp tried to find a way to explain. 'A polyalphabetic cipher is any cipher based on substitution, using multiple substitution alphabets. So a monoalphabetic cipher can be broken because the same plain letters are encoded to the same cipher letters – the underlying letter frequencies remain unchanged. So for example, if F always encrypts to V, then all the interceptor needs to do is find the twenty-six corresponding letters and they can break your code. But with a polyalphabetic cipher, there is more than one possibility, so it makes it much harder to break. I didn't invent it – it's a system in use for centuries. I just adapted it for our use.'

'Right so. You use lines of poetry or famous quotations or words from songs, and the letters can correspond to a number of other letters, is that it?'

'Yes, exactly.'

'And how does the person receiving the message know how to decode it?' he asked, fascinated.

'Well, either they know the encryption or they can use a disc, which will show when you line up the inner disc what letter it potentially corresponds to.'

'And the quotations, where did you get them from?'

Harp smiled. 'I just know thousands of quotations, poems, songs. I can remember them easily.'

Collins chuckled. 'Will I tell you something, Miss Harp Devereaux?'

She nodded. There were lots of rumours about this man, that he was fearless, that he was audacious, that men admired him and women loved him, and while she knew these were common myths of freedom fighters everywhere, in the case of Michael Collins, she believed it to be true. There was something compelling about him, and she could imagine people, men and women, doing anything for him. He had a kind of gentle charisma, and he inspired confidence and trust.

'I'm damned glad you're with me and not against me. I doubt too many of us would stand a chance against your wits. But I thank you. All joking aside, it's amazing what you've done. Your system saves lives, never doubt it. Now, what's Matt's idea?'

Harp recited the plan to assassinate Lord Winters en route from his pickup at the dock to his lunch at the Admiralty.

'And how do we know what the timings will be?' Collins asked.

'One of our people works in the Admiralty as a cook, and Winters is allergic to onions apparently, so he was instructed that there were to be no onions in the lunch or dinner but that it was all right to have them in the kedgeree for breakfast, so we knew he was expected for lunch. He'd have to come in on the morning tide, and high tide is due at 11 a.m., so we thought he would be landed at eleven, transfer directly to the Admiralty in time for lunch. They serve lunch there at one usually.'

'That's marvellous. And what about security? What do we know about his entourage?' Collins was hanging on her every word.

'Every branch of Crown forces is on alert. The navy will be in charge of his vessel and his transfer to the port. The Cameron Highlanders are stationed in town, so we are fairly sure a detachment of those will be his main protection. But the Tans and the RIC will be stationed all over town looking out for unusual activity.'

'Right, they'll be peppering all right. But go on anyway – how will we get him?'

'There are three houses we can use along the route. We'll have snipers with grenades in each one. The idea is to lob the grenade, ideally hitting his vehicle if it's open top, but if not, creating a diversion by means of an explosion, and our sniper will shoot him once the support personnel are distracted. We have a backup sniper in the event of anything going wrong.'

'I'm assuming Matt himself is the sniper?' Collins was thinking aloud.

'He is,' Harp replied.

'Yes, Seamus O'Grady says he's the best shot in Cork, and that's saying something. We sent a group down to Matt for training a while ago. I've loads of fellas up here, mad for mayhem, but they couldn't hit a cow's arse with a banjo.' He winked at her and grinned. 'Seamus is connected to you, isn't he?'

'Yes, he's married to my boyfriend's sister,' Harp answered proudly.

'Seamus is a great lad. I'd be lost only for him, saved my skin more than once. And his Kitty is a lovely girl too. Ah sure, I know who I have now.' The recognition was evident on his face. 'Your fella's American, isn't he? Him and his cousin, they're Pat Rafferty's boys.'

'That's it.' She smiled.

'Well, it sounds like it's a very well-thought-out plan, and if anyone can pull it off, 'tis Matt. I was thinking maybe we should send down a few of my lads from here… But you have it well in order already, and as I say, I'm hearing great things about your setup down there.'

Matt didn't want anyone from Dublin, Harp knew. If they were sent, there was nothing they could do, but he'd told her that if it was offered, she should decline. 'Matt is very confident he has the right people,' she said, not daring to call him Mick.

Collins shrugged. 'If he says so.' He thought for a moment. 'Right, tell him I said to go ahead. You've really proved yourselves, relieving the enemy of their weapons at every hand's turn. They tell me the Queenstown Company are supplying most of Cork with weapons. Well done. Please pass on my congratulations to everyone down there. God knows you've a lot to put up with down there with every class of English eejit in a uniform to contend with.'

'It is hard,' Harp conceded. 'And as a town, we have suffered, but it does make people there more determined. It's more immediate, I think. Out in the country, people see less of them and perhaps don't fully appreciate the full impact of complete British occupation.'

'That's a good point. It's the same up here. Crown forces are everywhere and it has an effect on everyone, but you have the right attitude down there – tear into it and get it done.' He leaned back in the chair, his bulk entirely dwarfing the spindly piece of furniture.

'Well, I think it's the effective leadership and having a clear strategy that everyone adheres to that's at the root of our success.'

He looked at Harp as if seeing her properly for the first time. He cocked his head to one side and nodded, as if contemplating her statement. '"Soldiers generally win battles. Generals get credit for them,"' he said slowly, as if to himself.

'Napoléon Bonaparte,' Harp answered instinctively. 'But he also said if you want a thing done well, do it yourself.'

He looked at her quizzically. 'How do you mean?'

'I just mean that *you* do it yourself, as well as us. You risk your own neck every day. Not like the British field marshals and admirals of the last war, issuing instructions from well behind the lines. You're in the thick of it alongside us and as likely to get a bullet or be picked up as the rest of us, more so really, and that's what gives us courage.'

He nodded. 'I'm just an ordinary man, Harp, who wants to put an end to this bloody mayhem for once and for all. I am the son of decent people, but I'm not from a big house or a fancy background. My family were working people, and they want what we all want, to live in peace and quiet.' He sighed, and she heard the enormous toll this war was taking on him. 'And you're right, we *are* all in this together. Because, Harp, let me tell you this. We might look like we're winning – and we are rattling them, no doubt about it – but this is the mighty British Empire we're taking on, and it will take the sheer determination of every man, woman and child on this island to achieve what we want, nothing less.' The passion burned in his grey eyes, and Harp understood on a much deeper level now the degree of devotion and loyalty 'The Big Fella' commanded among those who knew him. There was something about him, not just his famous charm or his handsome face or strong athletic body, but something else; he was lovable.

'We're ready,' she said solemnly.

He smiled and they both stood up. He placed his hands on her shoulders, and for a moment she thought he might kiss her, but he didn't.

'It was lovely to meet you, Harp Devereaux. With a name like that, I won't forget it. You're a remarkable young woman, and I pray God keeps you safe and that you get to marry and have children who'll grow up in their own country, with no foreign forces tormenting them. And please God, when that day comes, we'll both be alive to see it.'

'And if we're not, it will be worth it to achieve what we need to,' Harp replied with conviction.

'Indeed it will. Now, do me a favour, will you?'

Harp nodded; she would do anything for this man.

'When you go home, tell Matt Quinn I said Cobh is a much better name for your place than Queenstown. We'll go back to the days before that auld misery Victoria landed herself on top of us, t'was Cobh then and Cobh it will be again. I'll hopefully get home to Cork myself one of these fine days – I miss it – but for now I've to stay here, ducking and diving.' He went to the window and, standing to one side of it, peered out. 'Cork lost out badly in 1916. Nobody down there's fault, of course, but it was a mess. Since MacCurtain was shot, MacSwiney is in the City Hall now as mayor. And the icing on the cake is that Harp Devereaux is on the team. So I've no doubt the south will rise victorious.'

'I'll tell him.' Harp smiled as Collins opened the window, revealing a small flat roof four or five feet below that joined to another building.

'Take care, Harp, and thanks very much.' He climbed out the window, winked and was gone.

CHAPTER 13

*H*arp loved being reunited with Kitty and Jane. They sat around Kitty's little kitchen table, filling each other in on the news and happenings in each other's lives. Kitty had got a job as head receptionist at Doyle's Hotel on Westland Row, based on the glowing reference she'd received from Rose, and loved it.

JANE SAT beside JohnJoe the entire time. She was thirteen now and growing up. Though still very quiet, she did speak occasionally, and seemed a much happier child these days. The long years with their very conservative aunt and her vicar husband had killed any of the natural *joie de vivre* that Jane might have possessed, but now at least she smiled and spoke a little.

'I was just telling Janie she should come down to Queenstown in the school holidays, Harp,' JohnJoe said.

'You all should. Mammy would love to see you all,' Harp agreed.

'We'd love to, but Seamus wouldn't be able to get away.' Kitty glanced at the clock. 'In fact he should be home now.'

Harp could tell Kitty was agitated. Seamus and his two brothers had been born and raised in Liverpool but had come over to be involved with the Rising in 1916. He was imprisoned in Wales for his involvement with an armed insurrection, but once he was released, he and Kitty married. His brothers went back to Liverpool, but Seamus stayed in Ireland, and because of connections he'd made in prison, he was now in the top ranks of the IRA. Harp was sure he knew Michael Collins well.

They ate and chatted amiably, but Kitty couldn't keep her eyes off the clock.

Harp and JohnJoe had mentioned to Kitty that they would catch the last train home, but they'd told everyone at home they would stay overnight with JohnJoe's sisters. Harp hated lying, so JohnJoe said that he'd have a quiet word with Kitty and tell her the truth, that they were booked into a hotel, but swear her to secrecy. They knew she'd understand. Harp's cheeks burned at the idea of that conversation, but she so wanted a whole night with him, alone and uninterrupted. She wondered if he'd said anything yet.

There was a knock on the front door of the little terraced house. Kitty left to answer and Jane went upstairs, so Harp used the opportunity to speak to JohnJoe. 'Did you say about us staying at the hotel?' she whispered.

'I did, she was –' JohnJoe began, but a wail from the hallway sent them both out. Kitty was leaning against the now-closed front door, slowly sinking to the ground, in clear distress.

'What? What is it, Kit?' JohnJoe ran to her.

'They've got Seamus...' was all she managed to get out before collapsing into her brother's arms.

They led Kitty inside, and Harp made her a cup of tea. When she'd recovered enough to speak, she told them all she knew.

'A young lad came to tell me. Seamus and two others – you wouldn't know them – were on a job. They were caught. Maybe a routine checkpoint, but more likely someone informed on them, and they were caught in arms. They've been taken to the Castle.'

'So now what?' Harp asked. 'Is there someone we can call?'

Kitty shook her head sadly. 'No, there's nothing to be done. His superiors know he's been taken, and all I can hope now is that he can withstand the beating they'll give him, not give anything away, before they shoot him.' The last words came out in a sob.

'Is there any chance they'll come here? Search the house or question you as well?' Harp asked. Matt had instilled in them the need to lay low if one of their own was picked up.

'Good thinking, Harp. Come on, we need to get you and Jane out of here.' JohnJoe stood, went into the hallway and called, 'Janie, pack a bag for you and Kitty, as much as you can carry.'

'Where are we going?' Kitty asked, tears running down her face, clearly stricken and in shock.

'We have that hotel room,' Harp said, all thoughts of romance gone. 'We'll go there first and decide from there.'

Janie appeared moments later with two carpet bags. 'What happened?' she asked, her eyes wide and terrified.

JohnJoe was consoling Kitty, who was barely functioning.

'Seamus has been picked up by the police.' Harp decided honesty was best. 'We need to get you and Kitty away from here in case they come looking for you. JohnJoe and I booked a hotel room, so we're going to go there first and see what happens and then we'll decide. Can you do that, Janie, just be brave and trust me?'

Jane gazed into Harp's eyes and nodded.

As they left, Kitty took an oval brass photo frame from the mantle. It was of her and Seamus on their wedding day in Queenstown. Rose had arranged the photographer and bought the frame as a wedding gift.

'Here, let me take it.' Harp placed it in her bag along with her notebook and pen. 'It will be dusk soon. I know the curfew isn't until midnight, but it's still best to be off the streets as soon as we can.'

They walked briskly across the city to the Excelsior, where Harp had written to book a room. Instructing Kitty and Jane to wait outside, she and JohnJoe went to check in as Mr and Mrs Delaney. The room was just for two, one small double bed, and they didn't need any questions. Harp had a small brass ring she'd saved from a barmbrack years ago, pressed into commission as a wedding ring. Marianne had wormed it out of her that they were going to a hotel and she was the one who said it would be best to wear a wedding ring, it had never occurred to Harp.

Marianne had not known of the tradition of the currant cake served at Halloween, when a pea, a stick, a coin and a ring were all added to the mix and whoever got each one it was a portent for the year to come. Whoever got the ring would be married by next Halloween but Harp had scoffed at that when she bit down on the piece of brass.

The young man checking them in was clearly preoccupied and took no notice of them as he handed them a key. As they left to climb the stairs, Harp overheard him say, 'Alice was supposed to relieve me and she's not after turning up, and I've to go home. This is the third time this month...'

They paused on the stairs, around the corner from the lobby, and listened. An older male voice said, 'Sure, let you go on, Frankie. I can manage. They were the last booked in anyway, and sure won't Mrs McAleese be in in the morning to do the breakfasts, so there's nothing for me to do except keep an eye to the place. I've to polish the brasses, but sure if anyone wants me, I'll be in the kitchen. They'll just ring.'

JohnJoe nodded and led Harp by the hand upstairs. They found the room and watched the front door below until the young man emerged and walked up the street.

'I'll go down for the girls,' Harp said. 'The other fellow is in the kitchen, so we'll just slip in undetected.'

Before she left, JohnJoe grabbed her hand and pulled her towards him, kissing her gently. She reluctantly pulled herself away from his embrace and went down to get the girls.

Hour after long weary hour they waited. The city fell silent apart from an odd gunshot. Kitty sat on the bed, her arms around her knees, staring into space. Harp was not much good at small talk or platitudes, and anyway there was no point. Kitty knew as well as anyone what was probably happening to her darling Seamus. Jane sat beside her sister, holding her hand. The little girl's silent presence seemed to give Kitty comfort.

117

Once the dawn streaked the city sky, JohnJoe stood up. 'The curfew is over at five. I'll go, see if I can find anything out.'

Harp intervened. 'JohnJoe, you can't. It's not like home – you don't know anyone. And if you go asking about Seamus, it will immediately raise suspicions. It's not safe, and there's no point in you getting picked up too.'

'Well, I can't just sit here...' he objected.

'She's right, JohnJoe,' Kitty said quietly, her voice sounding like it was coming from far away. 'We just have to wait.'

'But surely some people Seamus knows, could we not contact them?' JohnJoe was agitated now.

Kitty shook her head. 'Too risky. When Seamus was picked up, he wasn't alone. They'll all be gone to ground now, and rightly so.'

'So what should we do?' he asked.

'I could go back to the post office when it opens, try making contact again,' Harp suggested. 'Not with Collins, obviously, but maybe someone else can tell us. It's the only way I can think of.'

JohnJoe looked at Kitty, so pale and wan, still in her clothes, having not slept a wink. 'All right, we'll try that.'

They sat, falling into silence again until 9 a.m., when the post office opened.

'Will I come with you?' JohnJoe asked as Harp washed her face in the sink and repinned her hair; they'd splashed out on a room with a bathroom. He leaned against the doorframe. She was dressed in the only other outfit she had, a pale-blue dress and black jacket, and she set her black hat on her strawberry-blond hair. She drew him into the bathroom out of earshot. 'No, you'd better stay with Kitty. She's in shock and Jane is worried. I'll be as quick as I can.'

'Be careful. What will you say if you're stopped?'

Harp sighed. 'Just that I came up for the symposium, that I stayed at a hotel last night and am planning on going home this morning but need to post a letter first. Stick as close to the truth as possible.'

'I hate to think it, but he's probably dead, so I was thinking, shouldn't we take Kitty and Jane back with us? Take care of them for a while?'

Harp shook her head. Queenstown was not safe. Even if they didn't kill Seamus outright – though it would be a charity if they did because the alternative was torture – either way it wasn't going to end well. Being caught in arms was a capital offence. 'Let me see what I can find out and we'll take it from there. She might want to stay.'

Before she opened the door, he took her in his arms and kissed her. 'I love you, Harp Devereaux. You know that, don't you?' he whispered.

'And I love you,' she replied, clinging to him for a moment before going back into the bedroom.

She took some hotel stationery, wrote a note similar to the prior day's and put it in an envelope, writing the same name and address on it as before.

Harp crossed the city once more, the streets wakening now, with factory workers, deliveries and shopkeepers all going about their business. Harp went into a store to buy a newspaper. The front line told her all she needed to know. Crown forces had raided several properties last night known to be in the hands of rebels, and a large number of arrests had been made.

Paid spies and informers were the downfall of every attempt made at Irish freedom, and Collins's harsh and summary dealing with them was certainly reducing the numbers of people willing to take such a risk but had not eradicated them completely. She found it hard to equate the idea that the genial, charming man she'd met yesterday was on the other hand a ruthless general who had no qualms whatsoever about ordering executions of anyone who got in the way of the cause. It had to be done, of course, and she supported him, but it didn't sit easily with his personality, she thought.

She walked on, her head not lowered but not held high either. Her years of being tormented by Emmet Kelly and his gang in school had taught her the art of being inconspicuous.

The post office was deserted this time, and to her relief it was the same stern-looking woman behind the counter. This morning she was alone. Harp approached and slid the envelope under the grille, just as she'd done the day before.

The woman looked up and asked, 'What?'

'I need to find out about my brother-in-law – he was picked up last night,' she murmured. She was taking a bit of licence here as Seamus was JohnJoe's brother-in-law, but a family member might be more successful in finding out information.

The woman eyed her disapprovingly, as if to say her use of official channels for private business was not acceptable. 'Who is he?' she asked.

'Seamus O'Grady.'

The woman's face softened ever so slightly. She got up and opened the side door, beckoning Harp into the inner office. 'Look, I'm sorry to have to tell you, but he and two others were picked up and their bodies were dumped in Dame Street in the early hours. We've had them taken to the morgue.'

Harp tried to remain stoic. The Cumann na mBan women, wives and sweethearts of the leaders of the revolution, set the standard in 1916 as they were brought in to say goodbye to their men before they were executed. Show no emotion; do not give the enemy the satisfaction of knowing how much they hurt you. Harp nodded, not trusting herself to speak.

'We'll see they get a proper burial,' the woman went on. 'Best you get back where you came from as soon as you can.' She ushered Harp out the back door into a smelly alleyway.

'We're staying at the Excelsior if anyone needs to contact us. We thought it safer than their house,' Harp managed.

'Very wise. They've picked up the brother and sister of one of the other lads already.' The woman nodded. 'But get out of Dublin, and take his wife if you can. It's too dangerous for her here now.'

Harp barely registered the streets as she walked back to the hotel in a haze of grief. There was no doubt in her mind that the woman was telling her the truth. Seamus was dead. She tried to block the image of his beaten body, forcing herself instead to remember him as he was, tall and gangly, with chestnut-brown hair and warm brown eyes. He had a crooked front tooth and the most infectious laugh; he and Kitty seemed to always be laughing together. They had fought so hard to be together. Poor Kitty. Harp knew this would break her. She'd defied her adopted parents to see Seamus, someone so far beneath her status in society, and she'd left England and worked at the Cliff House while waiting for him to be released from prison. Their wedding was one of the happiest days Harp could ever remember.

She'd been a maid of honour, and Kitty looked amazingly beautiful in a cream lace dress the Devlins were able to borrow from a niece of theirs. They'd married in the cathedral in Queenstown, and they'd had a wonderful wedding breakfast afterwards in the gardens of the Cliff House. The weather that September day had been unseasonably warm, and the day turned into a night of singing songs and happy conversation. Harp and JohnJoe had sat together, holding hands and singing songs. She'd even taken her harp out, and they performed together. Everyone stayed after the bride and groom were long gone. Rose had treated the newlyweds to a night in the Queen's Hotel. There was no time for a honeymoon as Seamus was needed in Dublin, so they left for the capital the next day.

But Seamus was dead. The sentence kept stomping around in her brain, obliterating all other thoughts.

How could this be true? Poor Kitty and Jane. It was so unfair. How could the British sleep at night, knowing that they were illegally occupying this country and beating to death anyone who dared object? Rage and hurt and loss and grief pounded through her veins as she walked. Some people she knew felt that the actions of the IRA were only riling the British up, making things worse, and possibly they were right, that the IRA *were* making things worse. But to live under a cruel regime, to have no autonomy, all for the veneer of peace, would never do. Freedom was not free; it had to be paid for. And the price was heavy, but there was no alternative.

She summoned the words of Thomas Jefferson. 'Timid men prefer the calm of despotism to the tempestuous sea of liberty.' They were in the eye of the storm now, being tossed about on the tempestuous sea of liberty. It was within their grasp; they could almost touch it. She had to keep reminding herself. It was closer now than at any time since 1169, when the first Anglo-Normans came to conquer Ireland.

The darkest hour was always just before the dawn. They had to press on, regardless of the personal cost.

She entered the hotel. The clerk was someone new now and took no notice of her as she climbed the stairs. She knocked on the door and waited for JohnJoe, but it was Jane who answered. Kitty stood behind her. There was no need for words; Harp's face told her all she needed to know.

Kitty sank to the ground and howled, and Harp knew the sound the other woman made was one she would never forget. Jane tried to comfort her, but for once Kitty couldn't bear to have anyone near her.

'Just leave me be, please,' she begged.

JohnJoe emerged from the bathroom, freshly shaved and cleaned up. He took in the scene and put one arm around Jane and another around Harp.

Harp understood Kitty's need to be alone. She needed time to process, to accept this awful reality. Harp valued her own time alone so much that she knew what Kitty needed now. There would be time for support, time for friends and family, but now she needed to be on her own. 'Let's go downstairs, have some breakfast.'

JohnJoe caught her eye, understanding what she was doing. 'Come on, Janie, let's get something to eat.'

Jane followed her brother, her dark eyes glittering with pain. 'Is Seamus dead?' she asked as they descended the stairs.

JohnJoe stopped and drew her into the alcove on the turn. 'He is, darling. I wish so much that he wasn't, but he is.'

Harp put her hand on Jane's thin shoulder. 'We all need to look after Kitty now, and make sure you and she are all right. You're not on your own – we'll look after you.'

Jane nodded slowly, one fat tear sliding down her cheek.

JohnJoe took his handkerchief and gave it to her. 'But starving ourselves is not how we help her, so let's eat something and have a cup of tea, and we'll decide what to do then.'

They operated as if underwater. The whole thing was surreal, but they sat and ordered breakfast. Harp knew she must have eaten it because the plate was empty when the waiter came to clear the table, but she had no recollection of it. Jane just played with a piece of toast and didn't touch her scrambled eggs.

Suddenly an idea occurred to Harp. She told JohnJoe and he agreed wholeheartedly, but convincing Kitty would be another story.

Upon returning to the room, they found Kitty dressed, her hair done and her bag packed. JohnJoe hugged her, and she stood in the circle of his arms for a long time.

'Right, we have to get on,' she said, her voice sounding not like her at all. 'We'd best get home, Jane, and make arrangements.'

JohnJoe caught Harp's eye, and she gave the slightest shake of her head.

'Kitty,' Harp began, 'I think it isn't safe for you and Jane to go back to the house. The movement will take care of the funeral, but it would be too risky to stay. I know you won't really want to, but would you consider going to Boston?'

'What?' Kitty looked confused. 'Boston in America? Of course I can't. I'm needed here...'

'Kit, just for a while, till things settle here. They'll know how close Seamus was to Collins, and you're at risk just because of who you are, you and Jane. You could come to Cork with us, but the place is swarming with British down there, and Uncle Pat and Aunt Kathy would take such good care of you, give you the time and space you need to grieve. Harp's right – staying here is too dangerous, Kit.'

'And you won't be able to do anything now anyway,' Harp said. 'Even if they don't pick you up, they'll be watching you both like hawks to see who you contact, where you go. You'd be of no use to the movement, so it would be safest and best for you not to be here, just for a while.'

'Where is Seamus now?' Kitty asked.

JohnJoe and Harp exchanged a look. They'd discussed it over breakfast, and the truth was the only way.

'His body is in the city morgue, and arrangements will be made to have it taken to an undertaker. That's what the contact I spoke to said.'

'Can I see him?' she asked.

'It would be best not to, Kitty. They roughed him up. I think you should try to remember him as he was. If you saw him now, that image would stay with you forever and it wouldn't help. Seamus is gone. He's not in any more pain. It's over for him, and he died for the one thing he loved as much as you, his country.'

Kitty nodded sadly, unable to speak. Harp didn't reveal that the relatives of the man arrested with Seamus had been taken into custody, but if Kitty refused to go, she would have to tell her.

Before they had time to say anything else, there was a gentle knock on the door. JohnJoe shot them a look and gestured they should get behind him. Going to the door but not opening it, he said, 'Who is it?'

"Tis not our British friends, if that's worrying you.'

Harp recognised the voice instantly and opened the door.

'Ah, Miss Devereaux, we meet again.' He smiled. 'Is Kitty inside?'

'She is,' was all Harp could manage. 'Come in.'

They moved aside and allowed him to enter. Kitty stood as he approached her. He took her in his arms and hugged her. Kitty descended into sobs in his arms.

'I'm so sorry, Kit.' He rubbed her hair with one hand, the other arm firmly around her. 'I wish I could have got him out. I tried, but they knew they had a big fish when they caught Seamus. They got Ned and Con too. I suppose you heard?'

Kitty stood back and nodded. 'I did.'

'Seamus O'Grady was a fine Irishman despite his accent.' Collins smiled and Kitty returned it; it was small and pale, but it was a smile nonetheless.

It was a source of constant teasing, Seamus's Liverpudlian accent, but it had proven useful on more than one occasion when he needed to pass himself off as an off-duty soldier at a checkpoint.

'He was.' Apparently suddenly realising that no introduction had been made, she turned to JohnJoe. 'Mick, this is my brother, JohnJoe O'Dwyer.'

Collins stuck out his hand. 'I've heard all about you and your cousin below in Queenstown, though Harp and I decided we're changing the name, didn't we?' He turned to her and she nodded.

'We're changing the name back to Cobh. It used to be called Cove years ago, before the arrival of Victoria, when it was changed to honour her.'

'Honour that auld bat, my arse.' Collins snorted. 'And she painting pictures in the middle of the harbour and filling her belly with tea and cakes while starving people left their homes and families to get on boats to other countries in rags and in chains.'

'It's an honour to meet you, Mick.' JohnJoe shook the proffered hand.

'Thanks for coming, Mick,' Kitty said sadly. 'But you'd better go.'

'What'll you do now?' he asked kindly.

'I don't know. Harp and JohnJoe think I should go to Boston...'

'I think that's a good idea. Pat Rafferty will look after you both. Dublin Castle got nothing out of Seamus – I know that from my contacts inside. He never told them a thing, but they know who he was and who he was connected to, so it would be safer for you and Jane. And if you need a few bob or anything...' He smiled and placed his big hands on Kitty's shoulders. 'Will you go? 'Twould take a weight off my mind if I knew you were safe. You won't be able to do a bit up here for now – they'll be watching you like a hawk.'

'I'll go,' Kitty said resignedly. 'And thanks, but we're grand for money.'

'Good.' He kissed her forehead. 'He was a great man, your husband, and he died for his country. I wish to God nobody had to die, them or us. If they'd just leave us be... But they won't, so it has to go on. If there was any other way, I'd take it, I swear I would. I know this is a dark day for you, for us all, but we're close. I can feel it.' He shot a glance at Harp. 'And if things go to plan in Cork, well, we'll be even closer. So go on, let you, and please God this will end and we can all live in peace.'

'Mind yourself, Mick,' Kitty said sadly. 'Seamus might have been a good catch, but you're who they're after.'

'Yerra, they're blue in the face looking for me. They're after a fierce good-lookin' fella altogether, so they're barking up the wrong tree entirely.' He chuckled. 'I've kept away from them so far, and sure, God is good, so hopefully he'll keep me out of their clutches for another bit anyway.' He made for the door. 'Good luck to you all, and I pray I'll see you all again. God bless.' Within seconds he was gone.

'So you'll go to Boston?' Harp asked gently.

The other girl swallowed, her eyes bright with unshed tears. 'I suppose I will.'

CHAPTER 14

*B*y the time they arrived back to Queenstown, Matt was anxious to get moving. Harp had telegrammed him as arranged with the code that indicated Collins had agreed: *Auntie Mary doing much better.*

The night they arrived, Harp, Matt and the Devlins gathered in the Devlins' kitchen once more, the usual tea and cards arranged on the table.

Harp repeated verbatim Collins's reaction and his approval for the assassination attempt. She also reported on Marianne and Beckett's plans for London. If all went as scheduled, Beckett would be absent from Queenstown – or Cobh as they now called it – for Winters' visit.

'Not a coincidence, you may be sure,' Liz said darkly. 'If there's an incident, Beckett wants nothing to do with it. This is essentially a navy task, so he will let them do it, and if they mess it up, he'll be nowhere near it.'

'It's good news for us, though, one less thing to worry about,' Matt said. 'He's getting information from somewhere, though. He knows things. He's made some strange remarks to me and others about Pennington's disappearance and things like that, so someone is talking to him but I can't figure out who.'

The four of them went through the plan meticulously. The cemetery was full with weapons that would be exhumed the day before. Matt had arranged two fictitious funerals for the morning of the arrival, complete with mourners, so that the activity in the graveyard could be explained.

'We'll have to try to get rid of them again immediately afterwards, so we can use the usual methods. You can set that up?' He looked at the Devlins.

'We can,' Cissy confirmed.

The process was smooth by now, as they'd done it so often. A woman would be walking by the gunman with a baby in a pram or a basket of groceries, and the weapon would be secreted away within seconds of being fired. That way if any man was picked up, he was not caught in arms and therefore could claim ignorance and not be executed.

The Winters visit was still on track as far as they could ascertain, but his route and schedule were top secret. Though he wasn't officially involved, Matt knew Beckett was privy to all the arrangements. Beckett was systematically working his way through every male aged between sixteen and sixty, randomly bringing people in for questioning, and he'd really pulled the Black and Tans into shape. Under the previous brigadier general, Potts, they'd become unruly and were frequently drunk on the job, but under Beckett that all changed. Their behaviour was every bit as savage – he did nothing to curb that – but they were a much more efficient and ruthless force under Beckett.

Despite having an IRA watch on him constantly, Beckett was slippery. He knew what he was doing when it came to guerrilla warfare, and he kept all important information on his person at all times.

'We need more information on Beckett,' Liz said. 'What he knows, who he has working for him. He's wily, nothing like Potts – he hadn't a clue. If there is the slightest crack in this operation, we're in trouble.'

'Does he drink in the bar?' Harp asked.

'He goes in there occasionally,' Matt answered, 'but he doesn't drink anything but water. He doesn't say much.'

'What about the wife – did he tell her anything about Winters coming?' Cissy wondered.

Harp immediately felt herself bristle.

Matt seemed oblivious to her discomfort. 'We don't know, but we're trying to find out. But he's not our priority now that we know he won't be here for the visit, thanks to Harp.'

They finalised the plan, Matt outlining what would be required of Cumann na mBan in terms of relaying messages and acting as lookouts before moving on to the next topic. 'I've made contact with the Raffertys, and they are more than happy to take Jane and Kitty. There's a boat coming into Cork tonight, in the city. It's sailing under a Canadian flag, but it has consignments for us under lumber, so I've arranged for them to be on it for its return. They'll have to get from Montreal to Boston, but Pat assures me he'll send someone to fetch them. They'll be fine.'

Harp was relieved. They'd taken Kitty and Jane to Queenstown with them and had hidden them in JohnJoe and Danny's flat over the undertaker's, keeping them out of sight, but the sooner they were gone, the better for everyone.

'I'll call to them now and let them know,' Harp said. 'Can we have a car take them to Cork? The train is too public.'

Matt nodded. 'JohnJoe and you could take them in my car, if that is all right?'

Harp nodded. 'Of course.'

JohnJoe had learned to drive in Boston and had proved useful as a taxi in extreme circumstances. Matt tried when possible to keep him and Danny out of IRA business. They were too conspicuous for a start, with their American accents, but also they were so valuable as points of contact for Pat Rafferty, it was best for them to stick to that. But on occasion JohnJoe was called upon to drive the car.

Harp left the meeting and went straight over to the workshop, where she explained the plan to JohnJoe. Kitty and Jane were there and had not unpacked, knowing their departure could well be immediate. JohnJoe left to collect the car at Matt's.

'You're to go tonight,' Harp said as she hugged them. 'JohnJoe and I will take you to Cork now, and the ship docks in two hours.'

'Right. Let's go, Janie. It's a new adventure.' Kitty tried to look cheerful, though her heart was clearly broken.

'You'll be fine.' Harp reassured her. 'Kathy and Pat are lovely people, and we'll see you soon, I hope. Try to enjoy it, Kit. Boston is a wonderful city, and Seamus wouldn't want you to grieve forever.'

'I know, but I'll grieve him for now.' She smiled sadly. 'Look after my brother, won't you? And yourself? And that big eejit Danny too.' She chuckled. She and Danny enjoyed a teasing friendship.

'I will.'

'Thanks, Harp, for everything. If you hadn't found me that time, I would never have been reunited with my brother, or met any of you, and I just can't imagine my life without you and your mother and everyone.'

Harp looked outside and watched as JohnJoe pulled the car up at the back of the workshop. She took the blanket off the bed. 'Just to cover you two until we're out of town.'

They went down, and Kitty and Jane got in the back, their small bags beside them. Harp covered them with a blanket, and JohnJoe slid some pieces of timber in over them.

'Let's go, sisters. The bright lights of Boston await.'

Harp squeezed his hand. She knew he was so sad to see them go, but it was for the best.

The ship was waiting, and they kept the goodbyes brief. JohnJoe hugged his sisters tightly, and Harp saw the brightness in his eyes as they walked hand in hand up the gangway. She slid her arm around his waist. 'Come on, let's go home.'

As they approached Cobh, she asked him not to turn up to the Cliff House but instead down to the workshop once more.

'I can drop you home first, save you climbing the hill?' he asked.

She shook her head, and he gave her a sidelong glance. 'Danny is busy tonight,' she said. 'He told me he'll be out until late, and it's only seven.'

'Oh yeah? Is he?' JohnJoe smiled.

He pulled up and wordlessly they climbed the stairs back to where they'd left with the girls only a few hours earlier. He put his arms around her and kissed her. 'I missed you,' he whispered gruffly.

'How could you miss me? We were together all week!' Harp giggled.

'Yes, but not alone,' he murmured, holding her close. 'When you said you were ready, and we were to spend the night together in Dublin, I... Harp, it's all I think about, and now, urgh...' He groaned in frustration.

Taking his hand, she led him to his room. JohnJoe's books rested on the bookshelf under the window, and his clothes were hung on a rail behind the door. She was ready, and if the events of the past few weeks had taught her anything, it was that there were no guarantees. Life was precious and precarious.

She knew her mother wouldn't approve, but Harp didn't mind about that. Rose felt she had let herself down badly by succumbing to Ralph all those years ago, and felt judged by society for it, she didn't want that for her daughter. She loved her mother so much, but Rose saw the world very differently from Harp and worried much more about appearance and what people would say. Harp was more like Henry in that regard; she couldn't care less.

They stood there, looking at each other, for a long moment.

'We don't have to if you don't want to...' JohnJoe began, and she could see he was as nervous as she was. She'd never asked but assumed it would be his first time too.

'I do want to,' she said confidently.

They made love passionately at first, but later, much more slowly, and Harp knew for the first time what all the fuss was about.

Afterwards, she lay on his broad chest, her hand over his heart. She could feel it thumping. She watched him in profile, lying on his back. She loved his copper-blond hair and noticed the beginnings of a flame-red beard appearing on his cheeks and chin. He had that kind of sandy tan that redheads get. She thought him perfect.

'That was... I...I know we shouldn't have, not until we're married, but I'm so glad we didn't wait, Harp. You're so beautiful, but it's more than that...' He paused. 'It's like what we're doing is so important, so necessary. As Collins says, it has to be done. But any one of us could be dead tomorrow, do you know what I mean? Seamus was alive. He was a living, breathing, vibrant man, loving Kitty, with his whole life ahead of him, but it ended. And not just our side – theirs too. I'm sure some lad growing up in Essex or Edinburgh who joins the forces dreams of lying with his girl in his arms, making a living, maybe having children. He doesn't want to end his days as a corpse in Ireland any more than we do, but it could happen. Every day we get out of bed could be our last, and...well...if tomorrow is mine, I'll know that at least once I made love to my girl and she knew how much she meant to me.'

'I know what you mean,' Harp answered. 'I've no regrets either.'

He kissed her head. 'You're remarkable. I know I'm always telling you, but even Michael Collins saw it in you.'

Harp dismissed it. 'I'm sure he's nice to everyone.'

JohnJoe smiled. 'Well, I doubt anyone in a British uniform would agree with you, but yeah, he's nice to our side anyway. But people are intrigued by you, Harp. You don't know how unusual you are. When we were kids and knew each other first, you were such a sad little girl, that oaf Kelly bullying you in school and living alone here with just your mother and Henry – and his loss was so hard for you. I remember seeing the sadness in you that first time we came here. But you've blossomed, and as Henry said you would, you found yourself, found out that you aren't odd or peculiar but so smart and so kind and so talented. That cipher you came up with – I mean, I don't know a single other person who could do that. And you were so confident in Dublin, meeting Collins, helping Kitty. I'm glad you finally get to see yourself the way we've all seen you forever.'

'I feel like a totally different person now,' she mused, contently lying in his arms. 'When I was a child... I don't know, I think I wasn't very good at being a child. I was too odd, too clever or something. I had no idea how to relate to other children. It wasn't their fault, I guess. I feel like I grew into myself. I love books and music, and I feel so passionate about Ireland and about what we're doing. Those are adult feelings, I suppose, and I've always had them. My mother bought me a doll once, when I was about seven. I didn't want to hurt her, but I looked at this thing, wondering what on earth I should do with it. Why would anyone want to pretend it was real?'

JohnJoe laughed. 'I hope our children look like you, have your brains and talent and kindness, but I hope they are like me too. I loved playing. I used to make Kitty dress up and we'd play soldiers, and I was forever building camps and damming rivers and climbing trees just for the fun of it.'

'Well, let's continue to make sure that isn't a possibility for a few more years to come,' Harp replied dryly. All birth control was illegal in the country, but Danny had managed to have some condoms sent from the United States – he had quite the side business selling them among the Volunteers apparently – and JohnJoe had been carrying some around with him since she first mooted the idea of them becoming intimate.

'I'll have to endure Danny's knowing winks now.' JohnJoe chuckled. 'But yes, I'll take care of that side of things, don't worry.'

'Well, better that than the alternative – my poor mother distraught and us being marched up to Father Dunne and married in a side aisle with the whole parish counting the months before the baby arrives.'

'I'd marry you tomorrow, Harp Devereaux, and you know it.' He rolled over and began kissing her again.

She did know it, but Harp had no intention of marrying for years, if ever.

CHAPTER 15

'Something has you grinning, Harp,' Marianne remarked as she and Harp weeded the flower bed outside the front door. Rose had asked Harp to do it and would not have been happy to have a guest down on her hands and knees pulling nettles and briars, but Marianne had insisted.

'Oh, it's just a lovely day, that's all,' Harp answered.

'Hmm. How did it go in Dublin, at the symposium? Did you enjoy it?'

'Oh, fine. It was interesting actually. There was a central focus on Baudelaire and Cervantes, which was good, but I really enjoyed the talk on Pedro Correia Garção, who composed the "Cantata de Dido".'

'And did you enjoy the night away?' Marianne asked, glancing at Harp wickedly.

'I did,' Harp replied simply.

'Well, are you not going to fill me in on all the details? I know you took JohnJoe with you.'

As far as Marianne was concerned, Harp and JohnJoe were childhood sweethearts and he was an American and had come to live in Ireland to be with her. That was as much as Harp had told her.

'What details?' Harp asked, digging to remove a particularly deep-rooted dock leaf.

'Oh, Harp, come on, tell me. I won't say anything. Who would I have to tell anyway?' Marianne knelt back and rested, stretching her back.

'There's nothing to tell,' Harp insisted. Marianne really was the most forward person Harp had ever encountered, and though she found it disconcerting, she liked her.

'You expect me to believe you spent a night in a hotel room, alone, with the young Adonis that is your JohnJoe, and there's nothing to tell? Then if that is truly the case, Harp my dear, we need to have a talk!' She nudged Harp and laughed. Marianne had seen JohnJoe but never spoken to him.

'Nothing I'm going to tell you anyway.'

'Aha! So there was something! Tell you what – you tell me and I'll tell you.' Marianne winked.

The thought of listening to Marianne detail the bedroom activities of Oliver Beckett sent a flush to Harp's cheeks. She didn't know how Marianne brought herself to do it with him; he was so old and so bad-tempered and mean. 'Your and your husband's activities –' she began, knowing she sounded prim but dreading the conversation.

'I don't mean Oliver! Goodness knows it's bad enough to endure his attentions without subjecting you to it as well. No, I have someone much more interesting in my sights. You mustn't breathe a word, though, to anyone, even JohnJoe, if I tell you, all right?' Harp could see Marianne was bursting to tell her.

Harp hoped it was just a silly infatuation and not anything more. Oliver Beckett was a cruel and ruthless man, and Harp had seen him with Marianne. He didn't find her delightful or funny the way everyone else who met her did; he ignored her when she spoke. He rarely arrived to the Cliff House before eight in the evening and was gone before breakfast. Harp felt a pang of deep pity for her friend, to have to be married to such a man.

'Marianne, you should be very careful...' Harp warned, glancing around in case they were being overheard, but they were alone.

'Oh, Harp, I grew up in Shimla. Everyone was having affairs all the time – it was the way of it. Mummy had a dalliance once with a very handsome major in the Hampshire Regiment, and Daddy, well, goodness knows what he got up to. But it was just how it was, as long as one was discreet.'

Cobh was thousands of miles from India, geographically but also morally. Affairs were not commonplace in Ireland, and intense shame and scandal followed anyone who strayed from their marriage. Harp felt Marianne needed to understand that, but the girl was so excited, it felt wrong to be so strait-laced and puritanical.

'Besides, nothing's happened yet, I promise you.'

'And who is it?' Harp asked warily, thinking it was one of the officers staying at the hotel. There was nobody eligible in the Cliff House at the moment. There was a moustachioed old colonel and his ill-looking wife; Rose said she thought she had had the Spanish flu last year and was not yet fully recovered. A few other guests too, but they were in couples.

'Oh, Harp, the most wonderful man! He's so handsome and funny and kind, and when he flirts with me, honestly, I go weak at the knees. He looks like Jack Dempsey, you know, the boxer, all dark and brooding, but his personality is nothing like that. He's so young and full of life and fun. And his accent... He's American like your chap, so he sounds so exotic. Oh, Harp, I think I've fallen in love.'

Surely not. Harp's heart was racing. There was only one person in Queenstown who fit that description. 'And his name?' she managed.

'Danny. I don't know his surname. He is simply divine. I can't stop thinking about him. Do you know of him?'

Harp nodded. 'I do. He's JohnJoe's cousin.'

'Oh really? He never said. My goodness, how marvellous. Now if we are seen together, it won't look so odd. You're my friend and he is your beau's cousin – how perfectly proper.' Marianne clapped her hands in glee.

Harp thought. This was actually a good development. Danny could surely get close enough to her to hear more about Beckett and his plans. She would be more interested in telling a potential lover what her husband was up to, to avoid being caught. Marianne hated talking about him with Harp, so details were scant.

'So when did you meet him?' Harp asked encouragingly.

'Well, the day you two went to Dublin on your amorous pilgrimage.' She grinned. 'He came up here, looking for your mother actually. He wanted to book a room for a visiting friend or something. I was reading in the drawing room, and we just struck up a conversation. We instantly hit it off.'

Danny was a law unto himself when it came to girls, and Harp knew he possessed none of the scruples that other men did. He had lots of girlfriends, often at the same time, but despite his philandering ways, the local girls seemed to find him irresistible. But she would not share that information with Marianne.

'He's a charmer, all right.' Harp laughed.

'Does he have a girlfriend?' Marianne asked.

Harp shrugged. 'Nobody serious as far as I know.'

Marianne gave a tinkly laugh. 'Marvellous! Please don't be shocked, Harp dear. I'm a married woman, I know, but I'm not looking for anything from him except a bit of fun and romantic excitement in my life. I'm stuck with Oliver, rightly or wrongly. I know you think I was mad to allow the marriage, and maybe I was, but it's done now and I have to make the best of it. He's obsessed with catching these rebels or whatever they are, and he cares nothing for my company. His only interest is carnal. So I can endure it, but why shouldn't I have a little fun in the meantime with a handsome chap nearer my own age? He makes me laugh, and he finds me entertaining too, and he won't want to put a ring on my finger or take me home to meet his mama.'

'Well, just be cautious, all right? Your husband doesn't strike me as someone who'd take kindly to his wife with another man.'

'If I can make anything happen, we'll be careful, I promise.' Marianne smiled, and her blue eyes twinkled with mischief. This was all a game to her, but Harp knew there was nothing fun about this; it was deadly dangerous.

CHAPTER 16

*D*anny lit a cigarette and leaned on the workshop wall, his saw resting beside him. The demand for coffins was relentless. It was becoming increasingly difficult to store the weapons they acquired, stole or bought from British soldiers down on their luck as well as ones coming from the USA. The movement was always in need of more, and there was an almost unlimited supply between all the Crown forces in the area and Pat Rafferty, but storing and transporting guns and ammunition was a major issue.

He waited until Harp was finished speaking.

Honesty is the first chapter in the book of wisdom. The words of Thomas Jefferson swirled around her mind. What she was asking him to do wasn't exactly a hardship, but it wasn't right either, she knew that.

He took a long pull of his cigarette and exhaled a thin plume of blueish smoke before he spoke. He ground the cigarette out with his heel, mashing it into the sawdust, and then stuck his hands in the pockets of his moleskin work trousers. He was handsome, she could see that, and Harp knew what girls found attractive about him, though he wasn't her type. He had a strong jaw and a symmetrical face, twinkling eyes and a full mouth that always looked on the brink of a smile. But there was something compelling about Danny, something that exuded honesty despite his romantic antics around the town.

'So if I were a woman being asked to seduce some guy for the cause, would that be OK with you and the Devlins and all the other feminists?'

Harp instantly regretted her request. He was right. How demeaning. If someone approached her and asked her to have physical relations with a man to gather information, she would be appalled. Danny was right. It was a terrible double standard and the kind of thing she normally railed against. 'I'm sorry, Danny.' She felt her face burn with shame. 'I should never have asked. You're right, of course. I...' She looked up and saw he was suppressing a smile. 'Danny!' She punched him, and that sent him into fits of laughter. 'I thought you were insulted.'

'Then you don't know me much at all, brainbox.' He winked and mock rubbed his arm where she'd punched him. 'I was considering having a crack at Mrs Beckett anyway – she's gorgeous – but I thought Matt might have a canary. But if I'm getting the go-ahead...'

'Well, I haven't asked Matt, but I think he'd be all right if it was for intelligence gathering. We can't get a handle on Beckett, and we can't find out where he's getting his information, who is telling him things. But someone sure as anything is, and we need to find out. Everything is at risk, everything, if there's an informer among us and someone is feeding him information about Queenstown and the people. He knows who to look for and where, he's uncovering arms dumps that are completely concealed, and he's finding safe houses that are in the middle of nowhere. Once or twice might be just luck, but it's happening too often to be a coincidence. We need to find them and eliminate them. Marianne never wants to discuss him with me – she changes the subject any time I bring him up – and I thought if she liked you, you might get more out of her.'

Danny nodded. 'I'm on it, if you get the green light from Matt.'

'All right. But Danny...' She paused, not sure how to phrase it. 'I know that you, well, you have a lot of girlfriends, but Marianne's nice and she… Well, just go gently.'

For once Danny looked serious. 'Harp, I know you're fond of her, and of course I'll be nice to her, but I think you're losing sight of what's important here. Beckett is intent on eradicating us from the town, by whatever means necessary. He doesn't care who he hurts or kills in the process – he just wants to go back to London and say he's crushed the IRA in Queenstown –'

'Cobh,' Harp interrupted. 'Cobh is the name now.'

'Right, sure, Cobh. He's a very dangerous, slippery individual, and what has made this war the success it is, is information. Collins says it all the time, and he's right – knowledge is power. But Beckett is using the same counterintelligence against us, and we need to find the leak and plug it or we are all at risk. Simple as that. His wife is closer to him than anyone, and if he doesn't talk to her, fair enough, but she can ask him things, she can give me information, she can let me know who he sees or where he goes or who communicates with him, at least some of the time.'

'She might not tell you anything – that's the other risk. I mean, she's British and –'

'Exactly. She is, and you'd do well to remember that, Harp.' His hand on her shoulder softened the words. 'I'm not a cruel man, Harp, but I know I can play her like a fiddle. She won't willingly inform on him, but I'll get anything there is to be got out of her.'

'And if he finds out, you're a dead man.'

Danny shrugged. 'And the battering to death of Seamus O'Grady? Or the shooting of Eamonn Foley or Richard Greene? Mick Daly died after the kicking he got. I could go on all day listing names, but, Harp, you know what we're dealing with here. Of course it's dangerous. But what's the alternative?' He ran his hand through his hair and lit up another cigarette. 'What else can we do? Lie down and take it? Be slaves forever, living at the mercy of such cruel masters?'

'I know, but…' Harp wanted him to know the risk.

'Look, Harp, I'm an American – that will give me a lot of protection. Lloyd George is trying to court the Americans and won't want to do anything to rile them up, and they get very upset when their citizens fall foul of foreign regimes.'

Harp knew he was right, about that and about everything else. The sheer exhaustion of it all suddenly bore down on her. The scene out before them, the harbour full of navy ships, fishing boats… She could hear the hammering coming over the water from the dockyard on Haulbowline Island, and she recalled the words to the song she sang with Chief O'Neill in Boston four years ago. *The chainless wave and lovely land, freedom, Nationhood demand, be sure the Great God never planned, for slumbering slaves a home so grand.*

The tears shocked her – they were unbidden and unexpected – but she allowed Danny to take her in his arms and hold her. She cried for her country, for Kitty, for Marianne, for herself. Danny stroked her hair and let her sob.

'I know, Harp, I know,' he soothed.

His cotton shirt was soaked from her tears, and he handed her a handkerchief. 'You're so brave, Harp,' he said. 'Always were. It's hard, all of this. Some days I wish I was back in Boston. Life was nice, calm, easy, y'know? But then I think about my folks that came over there from here, and how they'd want me to do this thing, and I see the sacrifices everyone makes and think, why not me? I may not sound Irish, and to everyone here I'm a Yank, I know, but I feel Irish' – he laid his hand on his chest over his heart – 'in here.'

'And we see you as one of us too, Danny, so much. I never had a brother, but you're as close as I'm ever likely to have, and I want you to stay safe.'

'Don't worry about me, brainbox. I'll be fine.' He squeezed her once more companionably.

She turned to go and heard him chuckle.

'I'm glad you put our kid out of his misery too, by the way. But you two better take care. I might be ready to be a big brother, but I'm not lookin' to be an uncle, you hear me?'

She didn't turn, feeling her cheeks burning. She knew exactly what he was referring to.

CHAPTER 17

*R*alph Devereaux ordered a bottle of Veuve Clicquot. It was so pleasant to see all the white faces again, and he found the cool London air so refreshing. Pamela was down at the front desk, checking for post, and he kicked off his shoe and lay on the bed. His leg ached where the prosthesis was strapped to the stump, but he was too vain to remove it in daylight. Pamela had seen his injury and usually spouted some claptrap about king and country, but he saw the revulsion in her eyes. He didn't blame her; it disgusted him too. If he ever thought he was getting over the gnawing need for revenge, all he had to do was look below the knee on his right leg and it came flooding back.

He should really telegram Sarita, but he knew he wouldn't now. Pamela's fortune was safe according to the solicitor they'd seen today; her inheritance was for her alone and could not be touched by Alfie Pascoe's creditors. So all he needed to do was pop the question the correct way and it would be his.

Sarita was in such a strop because he was leaving Shimla that she refused to see him, which was a disaster. She had so much jewellery, gifts from her late adoring Babu, that she wouldn't have noticed if he filched a few things. It had been his plan in the weeks coming up to the trip to pocket some things here and there, but to his astonishment the moment he mooted the idea of his departure for London, she was uncharacteristically aggressive and told him to get out and never contact her again. That part was fine – he'd frankly had enough anyway – but it did deprive him of an opportunity to make his travels a little more comfortable. Pamela knew he wasn't a really wealthy man but thought he was better off than he was, and he'd have liked to keep it that way at least until he married her and her money.

She burst in the door, beaming and brandishing a letter. 'It's from Marianne! I wrote and sent the hotel address, so she's written to me here. I was worried that she might think it improper to come to London with my new beau – I mentioned you in my last letter, and I was afraid she'd think it was too soon after Alfie – but she telegrammed saying she was delighted I was coming, so at least that.'

She clearly saw the shadow cross his face. He didn't know she'd blurted about them to Marianne.

'She had to know about you sometime, darling, and I didn't name names, just said that I'd met someone and he made me very happy.'

He stood, popped the champagne and offered her a glass, smiling. 'Of course, I'm sorry. I just didn't want you to have to face any unpleasantness. But it's wonderful. She is such a thoughtful girl, but then you're a caring mama so no wonder she adores you.' He kissed her cheek. 'Read it to me.'

Pamela ripped the envelope and extracted a cream sheet of writing paper. '"Darling Mama, I hope you survived the voyage to London. I always hated that trip as a child, taking me away from my beloved Shimla, and it always seemed so much shorter and more pleasant going home."'

'"Life here in Queenstown – for some reason people have started to call it Cobh, which drives Oliver scatty so I do it sometimes, just to see his face – plods along. It's something the rebels are doing – it's the old Irish name and they don't want it named after a queen any more, though which one it is named for, I've no idea and couldn't care less. Victoria perhaps? Who knows?"'

'"I'm so excited that you're coming to London, and I can't wait to see you. I am astounded that Oliver offered to join me, but he seems quite animated on the subject. There's some bigwig coming here at the time we'll be away, but he doesn't seem to care about missing it."

"'Now, Mama, don't be shocked, but I have met someone. I know I'm married and all of that, but you did say that women of our class marry strategically and love with our hearts, so I'm doing just that. I know you won't breathe a word, and I have to tell someone."

"'His name is Danny and he's American. Oh, Mama, he's simply dreamy, all tall, dark and handsome. He's so funny and young and sees the humorous side of everything. He thinks I'm hilarious. We just laugh all the time; it makes such a nice change. His cousin is my friend Harp's chap, so we make quite an innocent foursome. You remember I told you about JohnJoe, the golden-haired Adonis from Boston? I confess I long to leave Oliver and run off with Danny, but he says we must wait. And please don't worry that I'm considering it on a whim and will end up a penniless old maid like Aunt Em. Danny's uncle is a millionaire as far as I can see – a chap called Pat Rafferty in America – and this uncle sends him oodles of dollars. I saw an entire suitcase of notes under his bed one day when I was waiting for him. And besides, he and JohnJoe have a very good business going, making coffins, would you believe? They work with the local undertaker, and the demand for coffins is huge. It's truly amazing the number of people who die here every day. It must be the war, I suppose. Anyway, it's a thriving business so there is nothing to worry about. There's a funeral every day, several some days, but Danny isn't a bit morbid about it."

"'Anyway, that's it for now. I'll fill you in more when I see you. I need to make the post, and Harp is going down to post something for her mother, Rose, so if I'm quick, I'll catch her."

"'Love, Marianne."

"'PS. Living at this Cliff House is so much nicer than that awful first place. You should come over here. It really is very pretty, despite everything.'"

Pamela folded the letter and turned her attention to Ralph. 'What is it?' she asked. 'You look miles away.'

Ralph had had a realisation. The two men on the train that day he was shot and left for dead in the cold waters of Cork Harbour, a dark-haired one and a redhead, they'd been American. One of them now was hooked up with his treacherous niece, and it wasn't a leap to say the other was now mauling Marianne. He seethed inside and looked down once more at his leg, the ire fuelling his need for revenge. 'Oh, it's nothing... I...' He fought for words to come out, to sound authentic.

'Please, Ralphie darling, talk to me.'

'Talk to you?' Ralph made himself blush. It was a skill that had served him well all his life; women were like putty in his hands when he came across all vulnerable and insecure. 'Well, yes, I would, but...'

'But what?' she asked gently.

'Nothing, I'm just being stupid.'

'No, sweetheart, please tell me.'

'Well, I was listening to you reading about handsome men, and I was thinking how I've never felt about anyone like I do about you, Pam. And since my injury, well, I never imagined anyone would want to...' He allowed his voice to fade away.

'Oh, my love, you got that injury fighting for your country! How could anyone see it as anything but a badge of honour and pride? Besides, it hasn't affected your abilities in any way.' She winked in what she thought was a seductive manner, but it made her look so foolish, he fought a sneer. 'I love you so much, I want to shout it from the rooftops that Ralph Devereaux is my man.'

He sighed. 'I wish that too. How proud I would be.' He eyed the sandwiches – he was starving – but now was not the time. He needed to reel her in like a particularly stupid but tenacious pike. 'But apart from anything else, I couldn't keep you in the manner you deserve. With Alfie you had everything, but I've had a lot of expenses. My only brother died a few years ago.' He allowed his voice to crack, and like clockwork she took his hand, her eyes soft with love. 'His child is completely dependent on me – the girl's mother is incompetent – so I have to support her and it takes all I can do financially. My brother never worked. He was not quite... Well, he was wonderful, but... And so the care of my niece and her mother and our home estate has fallen to me.'

She fell for it as he knew she would. 'Oh, Ralph, is that why you never married?' She was tender and gentle in her questioning.

He nodded sadly. 'I had responsibilities, and no girl with any intelligence is going to marry a poor cripple, even if her father would allow it, which none in their right minds would.'

'But you have a job. Surely that would be enough...'

Ralph had let her and everyone think he did something nonspecific for the British government. 'If it were just me, then of course. I have quite a fine salary.' He needed her to feel sorry for him but not pity him, or worse, deem him beneath her. 'But my brother rather callously seduced one of the maids, my niece is the result, and they live now for nothing in my house, which is extremely expensive to maintain. You know how it is, these old piles. They look so impressive but the bills are eye-watering. I'd let it go, but my niece, well, she's not really right in the head, you know... I've never told anyone this, Pam...'

'Oh, Ralphie,' she crooned. 'You're such a good man, so modest about your heroics on the battlefield, and now this. I love you even more for telling me. Thank you, darling, for opening up to me, and I promise to do all I can to help you.'

'No...definitely not. I didn't tell you to come with the begging bowl, just so you'd understand my situation. I would dearly love to marry you, be with you every day. But I simply can't.'

'But I don't care about such things, Ralph, honestly I don't!' Pamela pleaded.

He shook his head sadly. 'I know you don't, my love, but where would we even live? All of my salary, especially so now that my niece's mother has been diagnosed with a wasting disease...' Wishful thinking on his part; how he longed to hurt and punish Rose and Harp.

'No. I'm giving you some money, Ralph. I won't hear another word about it. What I have is yours, and this way, it will ease some of your burden. Please, I know you don't want to take it, but for me? Please? I can't bear to imagine you struggling.'

'No, my sweet, I can't. The only way I could take it is if you knew for definite how I feel about you.' *In for the kill*, he thought.

He'd managed to pilfer a ring of Sarita's before the bust up, so at least that. He went to his suitcase and extracted it. He'd bought a velvet box and had an unscrupulous forger he knew in Shimla write 'Hancocks' on the silk lining. He couldn't kneel, but he stood before her, showing her his best vulnerable face. 'Pamela, my darling, will you do me the tremendous honour of becoming my wife?'

He was tired, and a life of comfort on her father's money was just the thing. If his association with her brought him closer to destroying Harp and her gaggle of degenerates, then so much the better.

'Oh, Ralph!' She threw her arms around him.

He held her tight and even managed to squeeze out a tear.

'Oh, my darling, please don't be sad. This is such a happy day! Of course I will. I would love to marry you.'

He kissed her passionately – she liked it a bit rough, he'd found – and threw her on the bed.

Later, as she dozed, he got up and stood gazing out on the London street. He would meet Beckett and tip him off about the American money. Surely if they were getting cash from America, they were getting weapons too, and what better place to hide them than in coffins? Several funerals a day? Not a chance.

He could use Beckett to catch his prey. Beckett was in Queenstown, so if he knew where to look, it should be easy. Matt Quinn employed the two who shot him in the leg, so he was in on it too, of that Ralph was certain. Rose was besotted with him, so he would be the first to go, and one by one he would, through Beckett, pick off every single person around Harp and Rose until they were alone and caught in his web like helpless little flies. Then slowly and painfully, they would pay for what they'd done to him. And the best of it all was that Beckett would pay him to do it.

CHAPTER 18

Marianne had never laughed so hard in all her life as when Danny told her the hilarious story of how he and JohnJoe had encountered two English soldiers trying to change a tyre. They were being assisted by some locals, who made the entire situation worse with their deliberate meddling but did it with such willingness that the polite young Englishmen couldn't refuse their help. Danny's Irish accents were wickedly flawless and his impression of the young soldiers was so funny, she could picture them perfectly.

She was lying in his bed over the workshop, her lithe young body wrapped around his. The room smelled of linseed and wood, the pleasant aromas wafting up from the timber yard below. It was sparsely decorated, just a double bed, always made with fresh white linen – she suspected the hand of Harp's mother in that since Danny had no access to laundry facilities – and a basin to wash at. The floor was untreated pitch pine, and there was a rail for his clothes. There were a few books on a shelf over his bed and a suitcase under the bed, which she'd sneaked a peek in once. It was stuffed with American money, so she snapped it shut again and said nothing but inwardly relaxed; he could afford to keep her in the manner she enjoyed if he had to. There was a dressing table with his cologne, a comb and his shaving things, under which was a single stool. She liked it; it was bright and sunny on rare nice days and warm and cosy when the rivulets of the seemingly incessant Irish rain ran down the window-pane. She wished she could stay forever.

'Mmm...' she moaned appreciatively, running her hand over his bare chest and breathing in the scent of him. 'You are absolutely deli-cious, Mr Coveney, do you know that?'

He chuckled and she loved the gurgling sound. 'You're not too shabby yourself, Mrs Beckett,' he replied.

'Don't call me that,' she said, suddenly serious. 'I hate him, Danny, truly. I want nothing of his, not his name or his...attentions. He revolts me.'

She'd told Danny the story of her father and the debt, and he'd been like Harp, appalled. He'd said it was like modern-day slavery. But since then, she'd underplayed it. Oliver was a peculiar man, deeply possessive of her and sexually aggressive. He frequently hurt her, but she kept the bright side out. She bitterly regretted marrying him, but in the whole turmoil of the aftermath of her father's death, he'd been kind, if not attractive, and it felt like the least awful of her options. How wrong she'd been. He wasn't kind; that was an act. He was cruel.

If Danny knew how horrible he was to her, he might either abandon her, not wanting to risk antagonising such a man, or – and she found comfort in this version of the fantasy – he might confront Oliver. Neither scenario would end well, so it was best to say nothing, pretend he was simply a tiresome old husband and Danny was a bit of fun. But that wasn't true. Oliver was a monster, and she loved Danny Coveney with all of her heart, but she could never tell him.

Danny had a reputation as a ladies' man, and she knew very well why. He was very attractive, and his American accent made him even more exotic. But it was more than that. Danny had a way of making the girl he was talking to feel like she was the brightest star in the sky. That changed and was easily transferrable to the next girl, but while one was in the warm glow of his spotlight, it was heavenly. She'd managed to hold him enthralled for a while now and was fairly sure she was the only one.

'All right, Maid Marianne, I'll never call you that again.' He kissed her head and patted her bottom with his other hand. 'Now, you need to get out of here, and I need to get to work.'

'When will I see you again?' she asked, trying to sound casual.

He was standing now, naked and glorious. He reminded her of those statues of Greeks and Romans in the British Museum. Except he wasn't cold alabaster and marble; he was warm flesh and blood.

Oliver was hairy and thin. With his muscles standing threateningly out from his biceps, he reminded her of a muscular frog. He insisted on his conjugal rights and cared nothing for her experience of it. She was an object to be used.

When she was with Danny, he loved her, caressing and admiring, kissing and tickling to make her laugh. They were both men, but there the similarity ended. They were as different as night and day.

How she longed to never leave Danny Coveney's side, to leave this wretched place with all its violence and mistrust and go somewhere with him, America maybe, where they could dance, hold hands in the street, eat lunch together in public and lay in bed wrapped around each other each night. It was a fantasy, she knew, but it kept her from throwing herself into the cold, wild Atlantic.

'I'm not sure. I've some stuff to do in the next few days, but I'll be thinking about you all the time.' He dressed as he watched her drag herself from his bed.

'I'm sure you will.' She raised a sceptical eyebrow.

'You doubt me?' he asked, smiling.

'I do, my darling Danny boy, because in my limited experience, the past is almost always the best indication of the future, and so I feel sure you say that to all the girls you bed.'

His face suddenly changed as he gazed at her. The dust motes danced in the shaft of sunlight that came through the dormer window in the roof. 'Not this time,' he replied, and something in her knew he meant it.

He couldn't or wouldn't say more, but it was enough. He cared for her, maybe not as she loved him, but she wasn't just another notch on his bedpost, she was certain, and that would have to be enough. She was in no position to push it anyway. He was free as a bird and could do as he pleased; she was the one tethered to a great weight, with little prospect of ever escaping.

When she heard another British officer was killed – it happened daily in this treacherous place – she longed for the news that it was her husband, that she was free, but he had not survived the Great War and the Indian insurgence by being stupid enough to allow himself to get shot. He was like a cockroach – she shuddered at the memory of the huge black insects that scuttled from dark corners of their house in Shimla – he could not be killed.

She dressed in silence as Danny paused. The sound of gunshots rent the air outside. He put a finger to his lips for her to stay quiet and looked out the small window. 'Just Tans flexing their muscles. I think it's nothing, but be careful not to be seen leaving. Here, let me fix your hair.'

He sat her at the dressing table, his eyes on hers in the oval age-spotted mirror. He opened a drawer to find a brush, and there she saw a small teddy bear.

'Ooh…how sweet. Is it yours?' She took it out as he tried to snatch it from her.

'Put it back. No…it's not…'

'Danny Coveney, are you blushing?' she teased.

'No…I… Give it back, Marianne.'

She handed him the little brown bear. The velvet that had once covered its chubby little body had become threadbare, and the stuffing was poking through a part of its leg where the seam had burst. Its brown glass eyes were warm and round, and it wore a little green waistcoat.

'What's his name?' she asked softly, handing it back.

Danny sighed and went to put it in the drawer but thought better of it and placed the bear on his pillow. 'Tuffy hates it in there, scared of the dark.' He smiled.

'So Tuffy sleeps in your bed?'

'Every night. My mom gave him to me for my birthday when I was three. She said I was her little tough guy.' He shrugged apologetically. 'Not exactly tough guy material to sleep with a teddy bear, I guess.'

'I think he's lovely.'

'You know the idea of a teddy bear came from the American President Teddy Roosevelt?'

'I did not know that.'

'Well, Tuffy is from before that time, but when I was a kid, Teddy Roosevelt went on a bear hunt but wouldn't shoot the bear, so one of the newspapers did a cartoon of Teddy and the bear. Then a store in New York asked him if they could start making teddy bears. So he agreed and then every kid had a teddy bear, but I had Tuffy long before that.'

'And one day you'll pass him on to your own children?'

'No way.' He grinned. 'If I ever have kids, and it's a big if, they can get their own. Tuffy stays with me, keepin' me safe. He might look little but he's tough. He can fight off all the bad guys.' He chuckled.

Using his brush, he gently teased her blond curls up and pinned them expertly with the clips he'd removed earlier.

'How did you learn to do that?' she asked. Another man doing a lady's hair would have seemed effeminate or awkward, but not Danny.

He gave a sad smile. 'My mom had too many kids, not enough money, house too small, typical Irish Catholic family in Boston, so when I was seven, they sent me to Aunt Kathy, my mom's sister. I loved her and Uncle Pat. They're my parents in every way that matters. But before I left, I used to do my mom's hair – it was curly like yours. She would sit in front of the mirror and let me brush it. It was the only time I remember ever having her to myself.'

Marianne could hear the pain of loss and rejection in his voice, no matter how much he rationalised it. 'I'm sure she loved you very much, and it would have broken her heart to let you go.'

He shrugged. 'Maybe, I dunno. She's dead now, my old man too.' He ran a finger down the contour of her cheek. 'I ain't never told anyone that.'

'I'm glad you told me. Thank you,' she whispered, her eyes locked with his. 'What was her name?'

'Marion,' he said, and she smiled slowly. 'The less fancy version of your name.'

'What was she like?'

He thought for a moment. 'Nice. She always smelled good. Even though they had no money, she was careful that everyone was clean. And she loved my old man, though he drank. He wasn't a mean drunk. He would come up the street singin', and everyone would laugh and say, "There goes Sonny Coveney, sauced again."'

'I bet they were good-looking.' She smiled as she stepped into her dress.

Danny did up the buttons and kissed the back of her neck. 'They were.' He went to one of his books, rifled through the pages, pulled out a small sepia photograph with scalloped edges and handed it to her. The couple were handsome. Her hair was as curly as Marianne's and he was just like Danny, if a little fuller in the face.

'Oh, you look so much like your father, and your mother really was a beauty.'

He took it back and replaced it in the book. 'It hurt that I was the one they chose to give away. I get it that Pat wanted a son, and I have become his son, me and JJ too, and my mom and Aunt Kathy were close. But...I guess I should have asked my mom before she died. My old man had nothing to do with it.' He shrugged again.

'Maybe they gave you because they loved you the most and knew you'd have a wonderful life.'

'Maybe.' He beamed. 'I never thought of it that way.'

She allowed him to hold her teal and silver coat with the silver fur collar. She put her arms in.

'See you soon, Maid Marianne.' He kissed her once more.

'Will you be my Robin Hood?' she asked.

'I will, but for now you gotta get back to the Sheriff of Nottingham, and I gotta go to work.'

She hugged him, her heart saying all her tongue couldn't.

The street was full of Crown forces. A raid or a house-to-house search was going on; it was a daily occurrence these days. There were a group right outside Danny's yard, but she decided they would not notice her slipping out onto the street; rebels were all they were interested in. Her head held high, she walked past them, feeling their admiring glances.

CHAPTER 19

*H*arp knocked gently on Marianne's door. She'd not appeared for breakfast, and it wasn't like her to sleep late. Harp had seen Beckett stride off after his kippers and toast, so she knew the girl was alone. There was no answer so she knocked again, harder this time.

Eventually she turned the doorknob, fearing that she shouldn't but a greater part of her having an intuition that all was not well. Beckett had arrived early yesterday afternoon, and Marianne was out; Harp could guess where. When Marianne returned, the couple adjourned to their room and Marianne had not been seen since.

She could not see Beckett as a cuckold – he would not take kindly to that at all – and Marianne was too indiscreet to keep such a secret for long. She and Danny had been seeing each other in secret for weeks now, and the flush on her cheeks and the way her eyes danced when she mentioned him was surely as plain as the nose on Beckett's face.

The imminent arrival of Lord Winters was preoccupying every member of the Crown forces, and Marianne had taken full advantage of her husband's obsession with making sure every single detail of the trip went without a hitch. Danny had gleaned a lot more information, presumably from Marianne as pillow talk, about the preparations, and it turned out she was privy to more than Harp had thought. Not that Beckett confided in her as such, but he talked in his sleep, and between those mutterings, the things let slip in conversations and what she observed, Marianne was a font of information. If she suspected Danny's interest was anything more than wanting to stay out of the way of a possibly livid husband, she gave no indication of it.

The longer it went on, the more the affair sat badly with Harp, despite it being her idea. Marianne was falling for Danny, and it was going to break her heart to know she was being used. This struggle was, to Harp's mind, as much about equality of gender as it was about national freedom, and the exploitation of a young woman who was in love seemed wrong. She was a flirt, it was true, but there was a kind of vulnerable innocence to her for all of that. She reminded Harp of Molly Bloom in *Ulysses*, where Molly, for all her sexual expression and admirers, loved Leopold. She was painted as a femme fatale, but she was a romantic at heart, believing in true love, enduring, everlasting, no matter what the world did to disavow her of that notion.

She'd discussed her disquiet with her mother, who surprisingly disagreed.

'Marianne Beckett knows what she's doing, Harp. She's playing with fire and must expect to get burned. Her husband is a cruel and callous man – we've seen it almost every day since he got here, the lengths he's willing to go to – and she's not blind. Danny didn't put a gun to her head. She went willingly.'

'But apart from the morals of it, it's so dangerous, not just for Marianne, but for Danny too. If Beckett ever found out...'

'And what if he found out you carried a pistol under your coat? That you went to Dublin to meet Michael Collins himself to get the green light for the plan? What if he finds out about the Devlins passing information, storing money and weapons, Matt out all hours drilling, attacking, rescuing? Do you not think that's as dangerous?'

Harp was surprised at her mother's stern tone; it wasn't like her. 'Well, yes, of course, but we are choosing it. We know the risks and we're doing it anyway because we want to be free,' she reasoned.

'And she's choosing to have another man in her bed because she dislikes her husband or wants a bit of excitement or whatever her motivation. She's choosing it too, Harp. Never forget that.'

Rose was wringing out pillowcases in the scullery's big old mangle as they discussed it. 'It was she who started flirting with Danny, not the other way around. God knows he's a bit indiscriminate with his affections, but he never went after married women. Danny has respect in that regard.'

Harp grew suspicious. Rose was normally so much more understanding than this. And then something struck her. 'Well, Danny is more her own age and Beckett is much too old for her...' She wondered if her mother would confirm her hunch.

'Hmm.' Rose dragged another pillowcase with more force than was necessary. They were beautiful embroidered ones, yet another gift from the Raffertys. Guests often commented on the bed linens, how luxurious they were, and Rose always explained that friends in Boston sent them. 'She's not that fussy. She was flirting outrageously with Matt too, who's old enough to be her father, and shameless about it too, she was.'

Harp hid a smile. Her mother and Matt might not be publicly demonstrative – indeed, very few people knew there was anything other than cordial neighbourliness between them – but Rose was jealous. Harp knew it was hard on both her mother and Matt, keeping their feelings hidden, and Rose especially longed for them to marry. In fact, she'd once confided to Harp that the only person she ever told was Kathy Rafferty. She felt she could tell her, being a woman of her own generation, and it felt like they were dear friends, though they'd never actually met.

Marianne leading Matt on was what had Rose so vexed. Harp was sure what straight-talking Kathy would have offered if Rose had confided her concerns about a beautiful young Englishwoman toying with Rose's man: that she had nothing to worry about, that Matt adored her and her alone, and that it was kind of a compliment that other women flirted with your man so long as he came home with you.

Rose was right; Marianne was a terrible tease. She drove the soldiers half daft with the way she batted her eyelashes and held their hands as she pretended she needed help up into the carriage or off a step.

But despite her silliness, things were becoming more serious by the day. The three G-men whose arrival Mr Bridges had alerted them to had appeared, ostensibly on a fishing trip. The trip had come to a tragic end when the boat they hired, presumably as a ruse, had got into difficulty in the harbour and had sunk before anyone could get to it, with the loss of all three men aboard. An accident surely – there was not a shred of evidence to suggest otherwise. And besides, they were, as far as everyone was concerned, just English fishermen on a little holiday.

Harp opened the Becketts' bedroom door and saw the form of someone in the bed. She crossed the room, finding her friend curled under the blankets despite it being almost eleven. 'Marianne, is everything all right?' she asked gently.

The girl pulled the blankets down to reveal a face puffy from crying, her pretty peaches-and-cream complexion blotchy, and most alarmingly, there were the beginnings of a bruise on her cheek. Her normally perfectly coiffed blond curls were in disarray, and her face was devoid of make-up. She looked like a different woman.

'What happened?' Harp gasped in shock.

Marianne struggled to sit up, her lilac chiffon nightie revealing her bare arms. 'Oliver got very angry. He heard some rumours or something – nothing specific, I don't think. He doesn't know about Danny, just the soldiers' banter to the effect that I was otherwise engaged when he was at work. He came up here and was furious.' She winced, and Harp saw that there were bruises on her upper arms as well as on her wrists. 'Said I was not to be friends with you, I wasn't allowed to mix with anyone without his approval, and that he would tell me who I could see and when. He told me he would choose my clothes from now on, that I dressed like a harlot, and that I was giving the soldiers ideas. It's like he wants to control every single thing about me, Harp.'

'You're sure he doesn't know about Danny?' Harp's immediate reaction was to protect him and JohnJoe.

She shook her head. 'I denied everything. I said I was friendly with you and that your boyfriend came around sometimes and we chatted, but that there was nobody else.'

'And did he believe you?'

She nodded. 'I think so. But he said I was embarrassing him by being so flirtatious, even if it was innocent. That I should behave in a more ladylike manner, more befitting to my rank and station. And he made that point quite forcefully actually.' She gingerly touched her swollen cheek with her fingers, wincing as she connected with damaged tissue.

'And he beat you up?'

Marianne shrugged. 'He's not a nice man.'

'Clearly,' Harp said incredulously. She didn't know why she was so shocked. She'd seen what he was capable of, but still.

'We're due to leave for London today, I'm not sure how long for exactly but I got the impression from Oliver it could be a long trip, though what my mother will say when she sees my face...' Marianne was struggling, and Harp could see the inner conflict. 'Can I tell you something? It's a bit of a shock, but I...I don't know what to do.'

'Of course.' Harp sat on the end of the bed.

'I'm pregnant. And I think the child is Danny's.' The words were delivered with none of her usual animation.

Harp swallowed. This was a dilemma. She did a quick inventory in her head of all the women in literature who found themselves thus and wondered if there was a universal right answer. Finding there wasn't, she racked her own resources. 'And does your husband know?'

'Not yet. I've been very sick in the mornings, though, and he's astute, so maybe he's guessed.' The wooden delivery startled Harp.

'But why do you think it's Danny's? The child could be Oliver's?'

Marianne shook her head. 'Possibly, I suppose, but I'm his third wife and he's never had a child. So I wonder if he's capable of fathering one. I'll have to tell him, I suppose, but I'm terrified.'

'But I thought you and Danny were careful?'

'We were, mostly,' Marianne conceded wretchedly.

'And does Danny know?'

'No.' Her blue eyes filled, a tear hovering on the edge of one lid. 'I can't tell him, and for his sake, I can't ever see him again. If Oliver ever knew...'

'And you're sure he doesn't?'

'Danny is still alive, so that's a sign that he doesn't know.' Marianne was clearly sad and resigned. She threw back the covers and sat on the edge of the bed. 'I'd best get on. You won't say anything to anyone, will you, Harp?'

'No, I won't,' she promised, but immediately wondered if she could keep that. This was information that could be critical to the movement. She didn't know how yet, but it could be.

CHAPTER 20

$\mathcal{T}$he waiter at the Criterion Restaurant at Piccadilly Circus took their order, and the foursome sat in awkward silence. Marianne could not believe her mother's new beau was this man, Ralph Devereaux. She recognised him from Shimla, though she never knew him, and she had no idea what her mother saw in him. There was something deeply unsettling about him, despite the friendliness. The way he looked at her, the way he spoke to her mother... While one couldn't fault him on anything, there was something about the way his smile never reached his eyes that made her mistrust him instinctively. He had been good-looking in his youth – there was a trace of it still there – but he was becoming jowly and the crow's feet around his cold grey eyes were deep. He did his best with what he had, though, and she suspected he was vain, but there was something compelling about him, a kind of burning energy that either attracted or repelled. In her case, she was repelled. There was a cruelty to him, she thought, though he had been nothing but charming. The Indian sun was hard on British skin, but his skin was burnished, as if he had Mediterranean blood.

He filled her water glass and smiled.

She couldn't put her finger on it, but something about him gave her the shivers. Her mother, on the other hand, seemed obsessed with him, constantly seeking his approval and touching him as much as she could. Marianne felt a pang of sadness. *Mama was never like that with Papa.* Marianne knew she should feel resentment or bitterness towards her father, but she didn't. She missed him and loved him still.

Her mother had come to the hotel alone to see her that afternoon; Ralph had some business in the city. She'd instantly suspected Marianne was pregnant. Marianne tried to deny it – she wasn't sure what she was going to do yet, and the fewer people who knew, the better – but there was no point. Her mother knew and was thrilled. Of course she assumed it was Oliver's and made no reference to the affair with Danny.

Since leaving Queenstown, Oliver had been curt and cold. She had felt nauseous most of the time and was utterly wretched. She missed Danny with an actual physical ache. She'd written to him, not of her pregnancy but just a friendly letter, nothing incriminating should it be intercepted, but had not had a reply. But that was probably just as well. Oliver monitored her post as well as her movements. She'd thought of asking Harp to contact Danny on her behalf but decided against it. What was the point? She and Danny clearly had no future. If Danny wanted to get in touch, he would have, and she couldn't bear the humiliation of running after him. She'd seen too many girls do that since she got there.

As her mother chose from the leather-bound menu, asking Ralph's opinion on this and that, Marianne was deep in thought. Could she manage alone if it came to it and Oliver threw her out? She had been presented at court by her mother's maternal aunt, who was married to an earl, and her parents were so anxious that she make a good match that they cultivated friendships with the best families through that connection, so despite living in India, Marianne knew a lot of people. Would someone help her? She could go to Aunt Em possibly. She suspected she and her friend Janet were actually a couple. But they hadn't a bean and she didn't want to be a burden. Her mother had independent means; perhaps she would fund a small flat? But what then? How could she care for a baby alone? As she pondered her situation, Oliver spoke to a waiter. She had no appetite anyway and didn't care what he ordered.

She caught Ralph Devereaux's eye. She wondered about the name, Devereaux. It was Harp's name too, but perhaps there were lots of Devereaux families. Pamela mentioned when they met that his family had a house in Ireland, but she didn't know where. Marianne considered making conversation by bringing up Harp but decided against it. Oliver frowned on her fraternising with the locals, and she had no desire to antagonise him further.

She forced herself to tune into the banal conversation, something about some General being promoted in Malaya.

'You remember the Huntington-Booth girl don't you darling?' Pamela tried to include her. 'What was she called now, Amelia? Agatha? She was presented the same time as you. Anyway it doesn't matter, but she married General Worth's son, and I hear good things about him too, making a name for himself in international trade circles.'

Marianne smiled and nodded. She had no idea who her mother was talking about but it was easier to agree.

A waiter arrived, bearing a plate of liver and onion that Beckett had ordered for her, and as the smell assailed her nostrils, she felt the nausea rise up. 'Excuse me...' She stood up abruptly, fearful she would throw up all over the table, and dashed to the ladies' room, her mother hot on her heels.

'Perhaps something a little more bland would have been a wiser choice?' Ralph suggested, cutting into his asparagus tips wrapped in Parma ham.

Beckett just smirked.

'While I have you alone, I was wondering if we could have a word, in private,' Ralph murmured.

'What about?' Beckett was blunt.

'I have some information that might be of use to you, but it would be imperative that it is kept between us.'

'Go on.' Beckett's face was unreadable.

'Well, as you know, Marianne is in regular correspondence with her mother, and, well, I fear that there are things going on under your nose that you should be aware of. I wasn't going to say – not my business and all of that – but us chaps need to stick together.'

'What sort of things?' Becket's words fell like stones.

'Well, for one thing, your wife is sleeping with an American called Danny Coveney, and for another, the same individual is, I suspect, receiving money and possibly weapons from an American Irishman called Pat Rafferty in Boston. From Marianne's letters, this Danny Coveney, along with his cousin and Matt Quinn, are making coffins at a rate that would not seem warranted for Queenstown. And so I would wager that if an officer of His Majesty went investigating the local graveyard, he might find something interesting.'

Beckett's eyes glittered with fury and a vein throbbed in his temple, but he said nothing for a long moment. 'You mentioned before about the disappearance of a captain in the Norfolk?'

'Yes, Pennington. Nothing was ever done about it, but it was all very suspicious at the time. I had a feeling Rose Delaney, Matt Quinn and Harp Devereaux knew about his death, may have murdered him actually, but Brigadier Potts was ineffectual. They sent a chap over to investigate, but as I said, it was the middle of the war and they had bigger problems.'

'But you think they were behind it?'

'I do.'

'Why? The women are not involved in anything, as far as I can tell, and Quinn's son is a decorated member of the Royal Medical Corps, served valiantly on the Western Front. I've never heard a whisper about him, and he's never come to my attention in any way.'

Ralph shrugged. 'He's very republican, I know that. If I were you, I'd search the graveyard. And though they don't want people to know, Rose Delaney's been having it off with Matt Quinn for years.' Ralph allowed the waiter to top up his glass of Sancerre.

Beckett didn't react. Then he spoke again. 'And they are connected somehow to the Americans?'

'Well, they work for Quinn, and Coveney has money, American dollars in a suitcase under his bed – that's where Marianne saw it.'

Beckett never flinched at the idea that his wife was privy to the contents of a younger, more attractive man's bed.

'And his cousin, I think it's safe to assume, is connected too, given they share this Pat Rafferty as an uncle. The whole thing is a nest of rebellion and criminality. I thought you should know.' Ralph hid his glee expertly. This couldn't be better. He wanted more than anything to make them all pay for what they'd done to him. Beckett would spot a personal vendetta a mile away and would not play ball with him unless it somehow benefitted him either personally or professionally. This did both.

Beckett sat back, pushed his plate away and lit a cigarette. 'She's pregnant.'

Better again. Beckett didn't love Marianne, of that Ralph was certain, but he did seek to possess her, and he would see his cuckolding in those terms.

Ralph took another sip of wine. He was enjoying this. Wanting to play devil's advocate so as not to alert the shrewd officer, he tried to smooth things over. 'But, Oliver, is there not the chance that the child is yours? Could you be cutting your nose off to spite your face as it were? She'll hardly be straying now anyway with a baby in tow, and she is a beauty and quite charming. Maybe it would be best to let it go? Think of what's in it for you, a child and heir, a young beautiful wife who might have blotted her copybook early on in the piece but...'

'Marianne is friendly with your niece.' Beckett changed the subject.

Ralph shrugged. 'We have no contact, so I wouldn't know what she does.'

'She's odd, isn't she?'

'Deeply peculiar,' Ralph agreed. 'My brother, Henry, well, he wasn't quite right in the head. My parents kept him out of sight. But the maid saw the house and his estate going to waste, so like a lot of her gender, she exerted the power they have over us and he fell for it. She took advantage of a simpleton really and got the whole lot, the house, everything.'

'That must have been a bitter pill to swallow?'

Ralph laughed. 'Not at all, I can assure you. My interest in Queenstown ended the day I escaped Rose Delaney's clutches and went back to Shimla. I have no interest whatsoever in either her or her peculiar child. I consider myself well out of it.'

Beckett nodded. 'At least in India, the natives knew their place, and most were willing to serve their betters and not make a fuss about it. But over there, it is populated by ignorant illiterate brutes, their mates and spawn, all ham-fistedly trying to eject us. Of course they won't succeed, but it is damnably tiresome dealing with them.' He took a sip of his water.

'What will you do about the, em, domestic situation?' Ralph asked.

Beckett shrugged. 'Maybe you're right. There's something to be said for an heir, and she is easy on the eye. I'll make her pay, of course, every day, but I'll keep her for now at least. I need to stay in London for a while, people to see and all of that, so I can keep her under close observation.'

CHAPTER 21

*H*arp sat at her harp playing some of the old O'Carolan tunes she'd learned as a child. She used to play for Henry and he loved to hear her; playing now made him feel closer somehow.

Rose was at Matt's house for a rare evening together. It was the night before Winters' visit, and they wanted to be together, just in case anything went wrong. Every day or night in this life could be the last, of course, but Rose just wanted to spend the night with Matt tonight and Harp understood.

She was in the middle of 'Eleanor Plunkett' when the loud knock on the front door startled her. She glanced outside, always fearful of a raid, but to her astonishment, it was Beckett and Marianne. They had been gone for weeks and had telegrammed to say they would keep their room but didn't expect to return for a prolonged period. It had perplexed Rose, why pay for a room you're not using, but Harp thought he wasn't paying for it anyway, it was probably the army so what did he care?

Marianne looked positively green as she stood there, her dress loose now to accommodate her expanding abdomen. Marianne normally wore her dresses cinched to show off her tiny waist.

'Brigadier Beckett and Marianne, welcome back.' Harp smiled. 'We weren't expecting you, but no matter – your room is vacant.'

She ushered them in and noted that Marianne looked miserable. It was a windy and rainy night, and the young woman was shivering. 'There's a fire in the drawing room – I was just in there. Can I get you a cup of tea or some sandwiches?'

'Yes, please do,' Beckett replied, and stalked into the room, leaving Marianne to carry her own suitcase.

She went to lift it, and Harp turned and whispered, 'I'll bring it up, it's all right.'

Marianne nodded and followed her husband into the drawing room, while Harp prepared the snack in the kitchen.

There were a few other guests, but they had eaten earlier. Military people only – the tourist season was well over. It was bitterly cold, and the frost crystallised on the windowpanes.

The moon's rays shone in through the French doors leading to the garden, and Harp noticed it was almost ten o'clock. She tried to hide her loathing of the man as she laid the sandwiches and tea.

'Play something.' The words came from behind the newspaper he was reading, and at first she didn't know who they were aimed at. She caught Marianne's eye.

Then he lowered the paper. 'I hear you play the harp. Play something for me.' His piercing, cold blue eyes were lifeless, and his face gave nothing away. No wonder he was good at poker, she thought.

'Do you know "The Last Rose of Summer"?' he asked.

'I...er...I...' Harp was nonplussed.

'I'm sure you do. A lovely English folk song – it celebrates the English rose, just like my wife, a rare and delicate flower. It goes like this.' He began to sing in a commanding baritone.

"Tis the last rose of Summer,
Left blooming alone;
All her lovely companions
Are faded and gone;
No flower of her kindred,
No rose-bud is nigh,

To reflect back her blushes
Or give sigh for sigh.'

Harp knew by his satisfied smirk that he was trying to rile Marianne, to upset her. Did he know about Danny, she wondered?

'I'm afraid I don't know it well enough to play it,' she managed.

'Pity.' He smirked. 'Play something you do know then. My wife would love to hear it, I'm sure.' He went back to his newspaper, and Harp caught the terror in Marianne's eyes again.

Not wishing to antagonise him, she did as he asked, but a surge of defiance flooded through her. How dare he? How dare any of them come there to take what was not theirs and rain such torment down on the heads of Irishmen and women? They accused the Irish of savagery, but the Irish were defending their home. They could not surely be savages if they never invaded anyone, never denied another people their rights. All that she and her compatriots wanted was to be left in peace, to live, to love, to be free. Why was that so much to ask?

She sat at the harp and heard Henry's voice, as she had done since she was a little girl. He would be proud of her stance against oppression, she knew. *Just feel the music, Harp, heart to fingers, bypass the head.*

She ran her fingers over the strings, adjusting the tuning slightly. Beckett kept on reading, but as she began to pluck the opening strings of the piece she'd selected, he lowered his paper and watched her.

'I'll play "The Harp That Once Through Tara's Halls". It is, like "The Last Rose of Summer", one of Thomas Moore's compositions, the *Irish* poet.' She allowed herself the small emphasis on 'Irish'. They had claimed everything else as their own, but the typically English song he had chosen was composed by an Irishman and she could not let it go.

Before he had time to respond, she began, the haunting melody on the harp strings accompanying her voice.

'The harp that once through Tara's halls
the soul of music shed
now hangs as mute on Tara's walls
as if the soul were fled
So sleeps the pride of former days so glory's thrill is over

and hearts that once beat high for praise
now feels that pulse no more
No more to chiefs and ladies bright
the harp of Tara swells
the chord alone that breaks at night
its tale of ruin tells
Thus freedom now so seldom wakes
the only throb she gives
is when some heart indignant breaks
to show that still she lives.'

He clapped very slowly, the sound echoing around the room when she plucked the last string. 'Very nice. The harp is the symbol of Ireland, is it not, as the rose is of England?'

'Yes, it is.'

'How prophetic that here this evening, both of our countries should be so beautifully represented. Entwined together forever, the harp and the rose.' He stood. 'Now, ladies, I have work to do, so I'll bid you both goodnight.'

Marianne and Harp sat quietly until they were sure he was gone up to his room. *If she and her fellow rebels had their way, and she prayed they did, the Harp would be firmly wrenched from the Rose for all eternity. What could he be doing at this time of night?* Harp wondered. 'So how was London?' she asked.

'Awful,' Marianne replied dully. 'I met my mother's new man, and he's dreadful. A chap called Ralph Devereaux. He's got some association here, but neither he nor my mother went into it. Is he some relation of yours?'

For a moment, Harp couldn't speak. The pounding in her ears drowned out Marianne's voice. 'Yes, a distant...' Her voice trailed off.

Mercifully, Marianne went on. 'Oh really? I never made the connection. I thought there were probably lots of Devereaux families here, like Murphys or O'Sullivans. I knew of Ralph back in Shimla – he's one of those characters everyone knows – but I had never spoken to him.' Marianne was lost in thought. 'He was very successful with the ladies, despite having lost a leg in 1916, on the Somme, I think he said. Mama is mad for him, and he seems to feel the same about her. I'm sorry, though, if he is a relative, but there's something about him I don't like.'

Harp tried to still her racing mind. Should she come clean, tell Marianne who Ralph really was? No, of course she shouldn't. But Beckett knew, of that she was sure. Ralph was trying to hurt them, and he was using the brigadier general to do it. And a more willing weapon he would not find, she was sure of that. Ralph was warned not to return, that the entire IRA would make sure he regretted it if he did, but feeding information to Beckett from the remove of London was the perfect cover. Marianne's mother was being used; Harp was sure of that too. Ralph did nothing that wasn't self-serving and calculating, so he would have become close to her, knowing who Beckett was married to and what his role was.

She needed to think and then to talk to her mother and Matt about this; they might have an idea about what to do.

'You don't know him, do you?' Marianne's question cut through her thoughts.

'Oh no, as I say, some distant relative, I think...' Harp was vague.

'Well, he and Oliver had a very serious conversation. Mama and I were in the ladies' room, and as we returned to the table, they were very definitely in cahoots about something. I don't know what it was.'

Harp had a horrible feeling in the pit of her stomach. If Ralph Devereaux was involved, it could only spell trouble for them. She would need to warn Matt and her mother, but she would wait until the morning; surely nothing could happen between now and then. She wasn't confident that Beckett wasn't watching her, and to leave the house at this late stage of the night would alert him.

'He hates me Harp, truly. He uses every opportunity to be cruel but he does want the baby, I know that. He's spoken about his son, he's convinced it's a boy, and what school he'll go to and things like that. He's made it clear I won't have a say.'

'Do you think he knows about Danny? Is that why he's being so awful to you?' Harp felt so sorry for her friend.

Marianne shrugged. 'He was never exactly nice to me, but these days he's positively loathsome, he's never said, but maybe, I don't know. Either way, I'm doomed. I think he'll wait until the baby is born and then discard me, and keep my child,' tears flowed freely down her pretty face now, 'mine and Danny's baby, being raised by that monster, I can't bear it Harp, I just can't. You don't know what he's capable of, he might even maltreat the child to hurt me, I don't know, I lie awake at night, imagine all sorts of horrible scenarios...'

She collapsed sobbing in Harp's arms.

CHAPTER 22

*T*he day dawned misty and cool. Winters would arrive sometime between ten and eleven and be taken from the yacht by tender to the quayside, where he would travel in convoy to the Admiralty. There he would meet with the top brass of the army, navy and RIC, presumably to be apprised of the situation in Cork generally and in Queenstown in particular.

Matt and Rose lay in bed in Matt's house, the bedroom door locked. Her dark hair was fanned out on the white linen pillow.

'I feel sick,' she said.

He held her, his arm round her shoulder and her head on his chest. They rarely took the chance of spending a whole night together. Matt was very careful that nobody knew of their attachment because of the danger it posed for anyone close to him if he was picked up. He would try his best to withstand torture if the moment came, but of everyone in the battalion, he knew the most. In general, he kept his opinions to himself but appeared jovial and friendly, and it had been remarked upon before how a person could spend an evening in his company, chat easily all night, and the other party would have revealed all while they knew no more about Matt than they did at the start of the night. It was a knack he'd cultivated years ago, and it stood him in very good stead now. But could he withstand some of the brutal methods of information extraction employed by the British now? He was only human, and while he prayed he wouldn't speak, he couldn't guarantee it. So far, though, he was fairly sure he was above suspicion.

When men under his command attacked and burned the RIC barracks in Rushbrooke one night, and Glanmire, Whitegate and Aghada over the next week, he had taken pains to have been overheard to mutter in the Devlins' shop that the perpetrators were foolish hotheads getting everyone in trouble. A British officer was close enough by to have overhead. He didn't proclaim his apparent dissention from the rooftops – it was well known that such public condemnation of the IRA led to consequences for anyone foolhardy enough to do it – but the fact that he muttered it, more than once, in the earshot of Crown forces, marked their cards.

'It's as well-thought-out as I can,' he assured her. 'I'll be the most likely to hit the target where I'm positioned, but if I fail, we have plan B and plan C as well. I'll be in the workshop as he lands, so I've a perfect view of the dock. Once I give the command, everyone will be on alert. It will only take me a few minutes to get into position.

'If we pull this off, Rose, it will change everything, absolutely everything. Winters is their man in Ireland, the Lord Lieutenant, the next best thing to the king himself. If we get him, then it will shake Westminster to its foundations, and the repercussions will be enormous. No more will they dismiss us – this time they'll have to negotiate. If we manage to execute Winters, the boost it will give to the movement will be phenomenal. The reason lots of people don't join us is fear, or thinking that we can't do it, that it's a folly to even try, but this will prove we are a force to be reckoned with.' He blushed a little. He wasn't usually so openly passionate about the cause. His conviction was deep in his heart, but with Rose he could be himself.

'I know all of that, but I'm worried, Matt.'

'Me too.' He grinned and kissed her head.

She smiled, and he thought his heart might break. How he longed to marry this woman, to have her officially by his side, to sleep each night in a free country with her in his arms.

He threw back the blankets, but she pulled him back. 'Not yet,' she whispered.

They made love quickly but tenderly, and though he would have loved nothing more than to stay in this safe bed, away from everyone, he knew he couldn't. Everything would have to be as normal. He would get up, get his bag of valuable tools for the coffin-making business. Most of his things he left in the workshop, but it was handy to have an excuse to carry a tool bag, and because he did it every day, on the day he needed it to transport something else, it didn't raise any eyebrows.

He would call to Liz and Cissy; they were holding the weapons for the men he had stationed around the town. They would each in turn come into the shop to collect and order, and the Luger or grenade would be wrapped carefully under the eggs or rashers. The bravery and defiance of the elderly sisters never failed to impress him.

Once Winters was on the quay, he'd make his way quickly via a set of steps to the sniper position, on the second floor of a loyal house. There was a tunnel under the house, dug out by Volunteers over the last few months. It was invaluable for getting people to and from the port unseen. He just had to lift the flagstone inside the front door, and it would lead him into the tunnel that would bring him out into the yard of the pub beside the workshop. Danny and JohnJoe would swear blind he never left the workshop all morning.

The cars procured to transfer Lord Winters were open top, which was ideal, and they had that information on the authority of the chief army mechanic, who was a Queenstown man and a loyal Volunteer. As far as Matt could see, it was a flawless plan. A Volunteer would lob a grenade from another upstairs window, causing confusion, and he would shoot, aiming exclusively for Winters. He'd arranged other men to shoot from other buildings at the same time, to cause confusion about the source of the assassin.

He groaned as he pulled away from her this time. 'I have to go.'

She watched as he dressed.

'I've written to Brian. The Devlins have the letter, in case...'

Rose nodded. 'I wish you'd tell him, Matt. He'll be so hurt if anything happens and he never even knew. He'll think you don't trust him.'

'No. If he knows, then he's a risk. It puts him in danger. I can protect you by making sure nobody knows about us, or how much I love you...' He rarely spoke so candidly, but it was important to say everything today just in case. 'But Brian is my son, and if he knows nothing, they'll realise that soon enough and let him go. He's a doctor, a respectable person with no links to us in any way, so even if I'm arrested, he'll be able to distance himself from me. He's got his career now, and I'm so proud of him. I explained everything in the letter. It's not that I don't trust him – it's that I'm trying to protect him.'

Rose nodded. She knew as well as he that if he was arrested, there most likely would be no trial. He would die in custody, after being tortured to reveal anything he knew. It was their modus operandi, and everyone knew it. Every day he left her could be the last, but today especially. Despite the meticulous planning and every safeguard implemented, there was always a risk.

'I wish we could marry, Rose, more than anything. You know that, don't you?'

'I wish it too, but I know you're just trying to keep me and Harp safe.'

'Someday, the day we see them take down their flags and take their armoured vehicles and ship out for good, that very day, I will get down on one knee in front of the whole town and beg you to be my wife.' He reached into his pocket. He took out the little ring box and opened it. Kneeling by the bed, he showed her the ruby ring. 'You can't wear this on your wedding finger, and I deliberately didn't get a diamond. Though you should have the biggest one in the shop, there are too many eyes in this town that would spot a new diamond ring. I thought you could say it was a family heirloom or something, just in case, and wear it maybe on the other hand. But with this ring I promise that if you'll have me, Rose, I am yours, body and soul.'

'And I am yours, Matt, forever.' Rose slipped on the gold ring, the band embedded with tiny seed diamonds around an oval-cut ruby in a crown setting. 'It is beautiful.'

'I'm glad you like it.' He kissed her, and then they heard it, the shouting first, then the boots up the stairs.

They looked at each other, stricken, there was nowhere to hide. Someone tried the door, but the bolt stopped them momentarily. Before they had time to react, the door was kicked in and several soldiers appeared, their weapons drawn and trained on Matt and Rose.

Matt raised his hands. 'I don't know what's going on, but you've the wrong house.' He tried to sound calm. He didn't recognise any of the soldiers, but the man behind them was instantly recognisable.

'Matthew Quinn, you will come with us now for questioning, and you too, *Mrs* Rose Delaney.' Beckett emphasised the 'Mrs' and glanced at the double bed. 'We wish to discuss several matters, including the disappearance of Captain Robert Pennington and the recent discovery, just this morning, of a cemetery full of weapons and American dollars, all buried in coffins made by you and your employees.'

'What? I've no idea what you're going on about. You have no business arresting anyone, but Rose is –'

Matt's protests were answered by a rifle butt blow to the temple, sending him reeling. Before he had time to react, he found himself shoved down the stairs and out into the waiting vehicle.

CHAPTER 23

*H*arp sat beside the range in the Devlins' kitchen, shivering. The sisters were managing customers between them, as to close the shop would be to attract unnecessary attention. Besides, they heard what was happening out around the town better in the shop. She'd told them about Ralph's involvement and how he and Beckett were somehow in cahoots.

Cissy was on her hunkers in front of Harp. 'We'll know more in a while. We have people on the inside. Try not to worry...'

Harp knew Cissy was trying to comfort her, but her words were hollow reassurances.

Liz arrived moments later and closed the door between the shop and the living room, something rarely done. 'I've young Eily Keane minding the shop.' She pulled up a chair and sat opposite Harp. 'They've taken Matt, JohnJoe and Danny to Spike, and your mother is here in the RIC barracks.'

'Who else was lifted?' Harp croaked.

The sisters exchanged a glance. 'Nobody else, it seems.'

Ralph. Harp just knew it. He had a grudge against the five of them, and he would exact his revenge.

Liz shrugged. 'Danny might be released. They'll be slow to risk it what with him being American, so he'll tell us more then.'

'But JohnJoe isn't, nor Matt nor my mother,' Harp whispered.

'I know, lovey, I know.' Cissy drew her into a hug.

'We need to get you away, Harp. If Ralph Devereaux is behind this, and you seem sure he is, he won't stop at them – he'll want to get you too.'

'But where would I go?' Harp asked.

'Boston?' Liz suggested. 'Just until things settle down?'

'No. No way can I leave my mother or JohnJoe to their fate. I just can't.' She blazed with determination. 'I'll hide. I know it makes sense, but I won't leave the country.'

'Well, no house is safe, unless we send you to the column.'

The flying column were a band of IRA Volunteers who were wanted by Crown forces and had to live on the run. It was a hard life, out in all weather, constantly in fear of being caught, relying on locals for food and shelter. The idea of being in such a situation terrified her.

'But what about the Cliff House? We have guests…' Harp began. 'Won't it look very odd if I just disappear? I mean if they suspected me, they'd have arrested me by now.'

'That's true.' Liz thought for a moment.

Harp swallowed and blinked back tears. 'I don't know how much more of this I can stand, Liz. Beckett and Marianne are staying in our house, for God's sake, the man who might be beating my mother as we speak is sleeping under our roof. And the others, Major Brompton and the two colonels, they're all staying there.' Harp could hear the hysteria in her voice. 'We live beside them and then they have this power over us… She was making their breakfasts and now…'

'Calm yourself, Harp,' Liz said, not unkindly but sharply. 'We cannot afford to lose our heads. We must stay focused and calm. We don't know exactly why they've been picked up, and the best opportunity we ever had to make a significant difference to this fight has just slipped through our fingers.'

Harp couldn't believe her ears. Liz sounded more upset about the

Winters attack being called off than the fact that her entire world was collapsing around her.

'Liz doesn't mean it that way...' Cissy soothed, glaring at her sister. 'But maybe it's not a coincidence this happened the day Winters came. He'll be landing now and heading up to the Admiralty. Matt and the others are probably not being dealt with yet because the top brass are up there with him. So we can assume they are all right for now.'

'So what to do?' Liz thought for a moment.

'We need some leverage. Something that will give us some bargaining power,' Cissy said. 'Matt and Danny and JohnJoe are on Spike Island, so the IRA will most likely be able to break them out. They don't like doing prison breaks as a rule, but in this case they'll do it. Spike is easy for us given we have so many of our lads working there. And considering who they are... Nobody is going to want to tell Pat Rafferty that his boys are in jail, and Collins will want Matt out. I've sent word to the section leader in Youghal, so it will be coordinated from there. Rose is a bigger problem.'

'Marianne Beckett,' Liz said quietly. 'She's still above at your house, Harp?'

Harp nodded.

'Right. We take her hostage, use her to force Beckett to release Rose. The only other option is to blast Rose out of the barracks. The only cell is in the basement, but there's a grille at street level. I might be able to lay a charge, enough to get her out, but it's going to cause a commotion.'

Harp thought for a moment. 'Before we try either of those options, what about the consul? If we informed Mr Jackson about Danny's arrest, surely he can kick up a fuss about him being an American and get him out at least? Maybe JohnJoe too? Matt said the British are anxious not to do or say anything to sour relations with America.'

She, JohnJoe and Danny had attended a Christmas drinks reception at the embassy, and the consul, Alexander Jackson, was a quiet but nice man. She'd had a few words with him after she played the harp at the function, and he was complimentary and kind. He was tall and wide, running to fat on the belly, and from Tennessee, he told her.

His accent had that slow drawl, nothing like JohnJoe and Danny's broad-vowelled, fast-delivered New England accent. He was married to an Irishwoman, and he reminded Harp of nothing so much as a basset hound. He seemed to have extra flesh on his face and looked permanently mournful, but everyone who knew him said he was reasonable. He almost always dressed in a cream suit and boater hat and a velvet bow tie and was a regular feature walking along the quayside with his wife.

'It's worth a try, I suppose, but I doubt it would work,' Liz said.

'Let me go up there now, see how far I get.'

Harp walked up the town, trying not to look panicked, towards the railway station and up the Burma Steps, as they were known locally, to the consulate, a beautiful Italianate mansion with stained-glass windows. Nervously she crossed the gravel driveway and rang the bell on the front door. A maid in a black and white uniform appeared.

'I wonder if I could speak to Mr Jackson please?' she said with as much authority as she could muster. She recognised the girl as one of the Luceys. The mother used to work at the Cliff House doing the laundry, and she was a loud pushy woman, determined to get each of her many children into good positions in the town. One of the daughters, Katie, was married to Harp's childhood tormentor, Emmet Kelly.

'Have you an appointment?' the girl asked insolently.

'No, I do not, but it is a matter of some urgency and delicacy. Please expedite my request for an audience with Mr Jackson with all due haste.' Harp knew she would need to intimidate this little upstart. Who did she think she was?

'He doesn't see no one without an appointment.' Harp could see the mean little mouth and piggy eyes delighting in the soupçon of power she had.

'He will see me.' Harp breezed past her with an imperious confidence she didn't feel. She had been there only once and was ushered directly to a function room, but to her relief there appeared to be an office off the hallway and she knocked on the partially open door.

'Come in,' a slow Tennessee drawl invited her.

'Mr Jackson, I am so sorry to interrupt, and I wouldn't have come if it were not a matter of extreme urgency. You probably don't remember me, but I'm –'

'Miss Devereaux, who played the harp so beautifully for us all at Christmas. Come in, my dear, have a seat. What can I do for you?'

Quickly Harp relayed all she knew.

His basset hound face looked permanently despondent, so it was hard to tell how he felt about what she'd just revealed. He seemed to take an interminable amount of time to react, sitting in his chair, his hand stroking his chin as he mulled it all over. 'And to the best of your knowledge, the authorities have no reason to detain Mr Coveney or Mr O'Dwyer?'

His sleepy, slow delivery belied a sharper mind, Harp thought. Could she lie straight to his face? Would he believe her if she did? 'Not to my knowledge. They were both busy when the soldiers burst into the workshop and took them away,' she said, which did intimate they were innocent without saying outright that they were entirely without blame. Beckett must have something on them; he wouldn't risk arresting an American on a whim.

He nodded. 'Yes, I realise that today they were engaged in their lawful business, but in general?'

She was right; he was no fool. She thought of Euripides. *The good and the wise lead quiet lives.*

Henry too was a quiet man, and he had no ego to get in the way of his life; he just was what he was. She got the same impression of Mr Jackson. He could have lived a much more lavish life, but he wasn't one for that sort of thing. He was restful and cerebral, though he gave the impression of being a little slow.

Harp blushed.

'Miss Devereaux,' Jackson drawled, 'I know very well who Danny Coveney and JohnJoe O'Dwyer are related to. Pat Rafferty is the lynchpin of Clan na Gael and is at the heart of the American support for the Irish cause, so I'll ask you again – is there any reason that you know of why they would have been taken into custody?'

'Can't you help them? As Americans?' Harp deliberately avoided answering the question.

His pale-blue eyes, slightly bloodshot, fixed hers. Again a long pause. 'Danny is an American, and though I cannot interfere with the authorities in any way, if he has committed a crime, then he must face the rigours of the law, regardless of who or what he is. But in his case, I might have some hope. But in the case of JohnJoe, he's Irish born, so my influence is nonexistent. Miss Devereaux, if your friends are involved with anything...' – the silence hung heavily for a moment – 'that would cause them to fall foul of the police, well then...' – he held his hands out, palms upwards – 'there is nothing I can do.'

'Whose law?' she heard herself ask defiantly. 'The law imposed on us by an illegal occupation of our country? In your own country, Americans did everything in their power to repel the British, that it might be a free, self-determining country. Were those who achieved that criminals or patriots in your opinion, Mr Jackson?' She knew he was one of their only hopes, and she had to make him see.

'I understand your position, Miss Devereaux, but I cannot condone lawlessness.'

'Would you sit by and allow someone to brand Benjamin Franklin or John Hancock a criminal? All of those men – George Washington, Horatio Gates, Nathanael Greene, Henry Knox, Benedict Arnold, John Sullivan – were they enemies of the state? At the time they were, because they were in open defiance of the Crown, but an English king had no business ruling in your country, just as he has no business in mine. And somebody has to stand up and say "no more". Those brave Americans did and it worked. I've been to your country, Mr Jackson. It is indeed the land of the free and the home of the brave, and that freedom was hard fought and hard won. But I doubt very much that you could find a single soul on that continent who is not grateful for that fight. And is it not reasonable and just that we should want the same? One man's rebel is another man's freedom fighter, Mr Jackson, so if you are asking me if Danny and JohnJoe are freedom fighters, then yes, they are, but I'm still asking you to bring your influence to bear on this.' Harp swallowed. 'This is personal, not political. Beckett has a gripe, and another person is fuelling that, and we are the victims.'

Jackson said nothing, but she could tell he was digesting every word. 'And why, young lady, would you imagine Brigadier General Beckett has some kind of vendetta against people of your association?'

'I have no idea,' Harp lied. Jackson did not need to know about extramarital relations or money from America. 'But he's proven time and again he is a ruthless monster. He shoots, kills, tortures with impunity. They all do. And we are powerless to stop them, for, as you say, the weight of the law, their law, is behind them. Justice has nothing to do with it.'

'My role is simply to provide such consular assistance as should be necessary to American citizens while they are on Irish soil. My remit does not in any way stretch to intervening in legal matters, Miss Devereaux.'

'As consul, maybe not, but as a man? As another human being? Be under no illusion, Mr Jackson – Beckett will torture them if he doesn't get what he wants. It is happening everywhere. A dear friend of my family was taken into Dublin Castle a while ago and beaten to death, his body dumped on the side of the street. This is going on under your nose, and if you are the decent, freedom-loving American I know you to be, you will not stand by and do nothing. You know that the Crown forces are being warned to avoid any citizens of any other countries, particularly America, for fear of an international backlash, so all I'm asking you to do is rattle Beckett, send a message that America is watching and won't tolerate any unlawful treatment or incarcerations.'

He glanced at the clock. 'Excuse me, Miss Devereaux, I'm due at the Admiralty for lunch today.' He stood, and his demeanour if not his gesture ushered her out.

'Will you at least try, Mr Jackson, please?' she begged.

He sighed and shook his head. 'Good day to you, Miss Devereaux,' he said firmly.

CHAPTER 24

*H*arp was deep in thought as she made her way back to the Devlins'. It was no good; they would have to go with the hostage plan and try to break her mother out of the RIC barracks. The town was eerily quiet. The Winters visit meant people on the streets were told to go home, so the shops were open but nobody was about.

Could she honestly take her friend hostage? A pregnant woman at that?

Matt had a saying: 'If you're not prepared to finish it, then don't start it.' The inherent threat in hostage taking was that if the demands were not met, the hostage would be shot. Could they do that to save her mother?

Marianne was the enemy. She knew nothing of the struggle the Irish faced from her genteel upbringing in England and India, and now that she'd lived in Ireland for a while, she often spoke of how the ordinary British public had not the faintest idea what was being done in their name. Ignorance was not an excuse, but still. It was why things were the way they were.

The Devlin sisters were both in the shop when she arrived. Liz was serving a naval officer some sweets, and Cissy was cutting cooked ham off the bone and weighing it out on the huge scales.

'Good afternoon, Miss Devereaux,' Cissy called cheerfully.

'Hello, Miss Devlin,' Harp replied brightly. 'Is our order ready?'

'It is indeed. 'Tis around the back. That eejit Billy Mitchell was supposed to have all the orders delivered this morning, but he was fooling with his brothers and fell off his bike, so we've no delivery boy for the foreseeable.' Cissy rolled her eyes, and the naval officer laughed.

'Boys will be boys, Miss Devlin,' he said with a grin.

'I suppose they will.' Cissy sighed. 'Girls are a much smarter species. They wouldn't bother with such caffling and tomfoolery and are overall much more productive.'

The naval officer, a pleasant-looking man in his mid-twenties with sandy-blond hair and a nasty scar on one side of his face, presumably from the Great War, turned and smiled at Harp. 'I would never doubt it. More productive, more clever and certainly nicer to look at. I could carry your groceries for you if you'd like? If the delivery lad's out of the picture? We can't have lovely young ladies carrying heavy boxes around.'

Harp caught Cissy's eye.

'Oh, don't worry about that,' Cissy said. 'I've arranged a replacement. He'll be here this evening, so all the deliveries will go out but just a bit later.'

'Thank you, though.' Harp smiled. He wore the rank insignia of a lieutenant, and it was best not to antagonise him.

He left and Liz beckoned her behind. 'Well?'

Harp told them how everything went with Jackson.

'Right, so he won't get involved.' Cissy sighed.

'Winters is still at the Admiralty, due to sail this evening,' Liz said.

Harp could hear the disappointment in Liz's voice. The operation to execute him had all come to nought, months of meticulous planning wasted. The removal of Matt, and the arrest of JohnJoe and Danny, made it too risky to go ahead, and orders to stand down had come from higher up the chain of command.

'What's coming from higher up?' Harp asked.

Cissy's face was inscrutable. 'Not much more than we knew already. The lads are under armed guard on Spike, separate cells, so no communication. They are in good shape, though – they've not been harmed. At least we know that much anyway.'

Matt had long had an insider in the prison on Spike Island, though Harp had no idea who, so it gave her comfort to know that at least.

'The Cameron Highlanders were above in the graveyard at the dawn this morning, pulling up coffins and God alone knows what else. Bob O'Hara, the gravedigger, came down to tell us. He said they were digging up older graves too, ones that predate the war. Your mother is in the RIC barracks, and we don't have anyone there unfortunately.' Liz's voice was hard. 'So we don't know…'

Rape was a weapon of the Black and Tans and was used frequently and with impunity. There was a code of conduct that was observed by the army and the navy and even the RIC, but the Tans were a law unto themselves. Harp felt her stomach lurch at the thought of her mother's fate. If they were excavating the graveyard and Ralph was involved somehow, they wouldn't just find the coffins full of guns and money – they'd also find Pennington's remains. She fought a wave of nausea as a cold sweat prickled her back.

Before she could answer, the back door opened and all three women turned towards it. They had not set up tea things or any kind of decoy purpose for a visit and so instantly looked suspicious. To their astonishment and huge relief, it was Danny. He'd been badly beaten and his right eye was almost closed, the skin around it swollen. His clothes too were bloodstained, and a line of dark blood ran down from his ear onto his collar.

'Holy mother of God!' Cissy ran to him and brought him in, sitting him beside the fire as Liz brought the medical box. They cleaned him up, and Liz expertly dressed his wounds; he tried not to wince and cry out.

Cissy gave him a bottle of whiskey. 'Drink that,' she instructed, and Danny did gratefully. One of his hands was badly bruised, and Harp suspected some bones were broken.

187

'Is JohnJoe with you?' Harp asked.

'Is Matt all right?' Liz asked at the same time.

'I don't know about the others. I didn't see Matt at all, and they split me and JJ up when they arrested us. But hey, I'm OK. Look – handsome as ever.' He grinned through his cut lip and swollen face, and Cissy smiled. She, like all women, had a soft spot for Danny.

'How did you get out?' Liz asked, making him a cup of tea.

'Someone' – he looked at Harp – 'went to the American consul, it seems, and he got me sprung.'

'That was Harp,' Cissy said proudly. 'It was her idea. What with you being American, she thought the British wouldn't like to antagonise the Americans.'

'I guessed it would be.' He grinned, supping from the whiskey bottle gratefully as the sisters did their best with his injuries. 'Smart move, Miss Devereaux, but then you've a brain the size of a planet so we should not be surprised. Now how to get Matt and JohnJoe out as well.' He accepted a bowl of soup gratefully, wolfing it down.

'And my mother,' Harp added.

'What?' Danny stopped eating. 'I didn't know they'd picked Rose up. Where is she?'

'The RIC barracks.' Harp did not need to explain what that meant.

All joking and jubilation was gone, and a dark shadow crossed Danny's face. 'We gotta get her out, and soon. How can we do that?' he asked.

'That's what we've been wondering,' Liz replied. 'Though you're in no fit state to do anything, so whatever it is, you won't be part of it. Matt would want us to focus our attention on her, that's for sure. He and JohnJoe will manage, but we can't let her stay in there. Who can we lean on? Bridges? He might be able to have a word?'

Cissy shook her head. 'I doubt it. Beckett doesn't like him. He doesn't drink in the hotel, and Mr Bridges has failed to become a confidante of his as he has done with others. Though he's never given him cause, Mr Bridges is sure Beckett doesn't trust him, so there's no question of him having any influence.'

'Well, if he can't be coaxed to release Rose, then he must be forced,' Liz said.

'How?' Harp asked.

Liz Devlin was the most hard-line of the people Harp knew in the movement. She felt that the ends always justified the means and that this was war. Cissy too was of the same opinion, but she was softer in her delivery. Though Harp agreed with them on the subject of Irish independence and women's liberation, their attitude frightened her sometimes. Even Matt, who was totally dedicated, could see the enemy as people too. He hated the killing and pain but felt it was necessary. Some of the soldiers, especially those in the army and navy, were nice, well-brought-up young men who would never willingly hurt a woman or behave in an ungentlemanly way, though the same could not be said for the Black and Tans – they were savage brutes, and it was they who had her mother.

Liz looked directly at Danny, anticipating his reluctance to the plan. 'He has someone we care about, so we take someone he cares about.'

'Marianne.' He said dully.

'Yes, but she's pregnant and that poses its own problems.'

Harp watched as Danny processed this news. His face paled and he looked like he might cry. The normally confident, happy-go-lucky Danny was gone. Marianne had not told him about the baby and Harp had kept her promise to keep it a secret, but the Devlins knew everything. The Becketts would have been under surveillance all of the time. He must be wondering if the child is his or Becketts. Her heart went out to her friend.

'We can't do that, it wouldn't be right, Liz,' Danny managed.

'Maybe not, but she's the only leverage we have, and we have to use it,' Liz said with certainty. 'We'll try to get Rose out, but we need her as an insurance policy.'

'He doesn't even love her, so I doubt she will be enough,' Harp said quietly.

'Maybe not, but I would imagine he wants the child, men usually do and Beckett is childless, and to have it, he has to have her.' Cissy shrugged, and Harp wondered if inside she felt differently; surely she must. Neither Liz nor Cissy had a cruel streak, but to hear them speak so indifferently about Marianne made them feel like strangers.

Harp thought about what happened to women in police custody, and the idea of it made the sweat bead at her neck.

Danny was silent.

They were right, Harp understood; it was all they had. Until they knew the charge, they couldn't be certain, but there was no question of Beckett being approached and asked for clemency. Ralph would have fed him enough to make sure the conviction would stand. He'd probably told him about Pennington, which meant her mother could hang. Matt and JohnJoe would at worst be held prisoner, maybe face trial, but most likely would be helped to escape, so Rose was the one in the gravest danger. And every minute Rose was in the barracks, the risk of her being raped, or worse, grew.

Marianne was a vulnerable girl, pregnant. Matt had told them, from the beginning, not to start anything they were not prepared to finish. If they kidnapped Marianne, then the inherent threat was they would kill her if Beckett didn't succumb to their demands. Could they do it?

'Ralph is behind this, Ralph Devereaux,' she said.

By Danny's face she could tell he was deeply shocked. He paled under his bruised and bloody face. 'What? He can't be. Are you sure, Harp?' he asked. 'Because, look, I know you asked us not to, but the truth is JJ shot him that day. He shot him at close range and Ralph fell into the river, and I was sure –'

'I'm positive. He's lost a leg – maybe that was as a result of the shooting – but he's alive and well. He's having an affair with Marianne's mother, Pamela, something that cannot be a mere coincidence. He's the one who's been feeding Beckett information about the arms and money dumps and who's who. I don't know how he knew. Maybe Marianne saw something when she was at your place and let it slip, or maybe he's been watching more closely than we thought – I don't know. But Beckett and Ralph know each other from India. This is Ralph's revenge on us all, on me, by hurting those close to me. Ralph has his reasons to hurt us all, and Beckett has a grudge against you, Danny, so they've combined forces.'

'Does he know? About me and Marianne?' Danny asked, wincing as he moved.

'I'm not sure, but he could. If he did, it would make sense. She told me that he's not let her out of his sight for months. And she's very upset and worried. He's cold and mean to her, and she's sure he just wants the child. She's thinking he'll discard her when it's born, but then she won't want to leave her child. She's trapped. I've thought this through. Beckett isn't going to do Ralph's dirty work for no gain to himself. But if with Matt's capture he's wiping out the IRA commander, and with your arrest and JohnJoe's he's cutting links to the American Irish and their support for the cause, and he also gets to destroy the man who cuckolded him, not to mention solve a murder of a brother officer from four years ago, then that's motivation enough, isn't it? All of this gets Ralph's revenge nicely for him too, so they both win.'

Danny's muttered expletives at this news drew no admonishment from the Devlins as his cursing normally did. He was merely expressing what they all felt.

'All the more reason,' Cissy said. 'If this is personal as well as strategic, then let's make it even more so. Beckett hurts us, then we hurt him. Personally. We need to get Rose out as a priority.'

The ding of the shop bell startled everyone. Liz went out and returned moments later. 'We've had word – they are going to rescue Matt and JohnJoe tonight. There's a boat ready at low tide, and they are down to a skeleton staff as all hands are being deployed to keep Winters safe, so it's their best chance.'

'And did they say anything about my mother?' Harp asked.

Liz fixed her with a sympathetic stare. 'No, we'll have to take care of that ourselves.'

'She's not a priority,' Harp added dully.

'It's not that, Harp,' Cissy rushed to explain. 'Rose is a civilian to all intents and purposes, and so for the IRA to kick up a fuss would cause too much of a furore and muddy the waters of what we are trying to achieve. This is personal, and so we must deal with it as such. But we will get her out, by hook or by crook.'

'Beckett knows about Pennington, and if they found his body – and we can assume they did if they are digging up older graves – my mother could hang.'

'So the top brass of the movement can't get involved,' Liz said. 'That's a criminal matter. I'm not saying your mother wasn't right to do what she did, but if Beckett can prove it, Collins himself couldn't get her off the hook.'

'We have no choice, Harp. It has to be this way.' Cissy took Harp's hand.

'Are we all in agreement?' Liz asked, her eyes fixed on Danny. 'We take Marianne Beckett into our custody. We have a safe house out in the country that they have never found or raided even once. We can take her to it and hold her there till Beckett releases Rose. We'll give him six hours. Once Rose is out, we'll get word to the safe house and she can be released. Cissy and I can't go – our absence would look too conspicuous. And besides, we're not as young as we used to be.'

'I'll take her,' Harp heard herself say. Marianne was a friend no matter the circumstances, and at least she could make sure she was safe.

'There needs to be a man too, for safety,' Liz said. 'I can send for a Volunteer if you'd like.'

Looking much older and wearier than his years, Danny sighed. 'No, I'll take them.'

'You can't go out looking like that…' Cissy began.

'Why not? I've been released, no charges brought, and they won't dare touch me because of being American. I'm the safest bet we've got.'

The sisters exchanged a glance. He had a point.

'Are you sure you'll be able?' Harp asked.

He nodded. 'I just got a hiding, nothing critical. I'll be fine. Beckett had to let me go, he knew that, but he wanted to hurt me for going near Marianne, so…' He shrugged but winced. 'I'll live.'

'And if he refuses to release my mother?' Harp asked. 'Marianne is not at all sure of his affections. He might not think she is worth the trade.'

There was a pause, and Harp observed the unspoken conversation between the two sisters.

'Then we execute her. Agreed?'

Liz's words hung in the air. What she was suggesting was a horrific prospect, even without the added complication of Marianne being pregnant. Surely it would not come to that? The three women, believers in equality of gender, sisters in revolution, each needed to examine her own conscience. Once it was agreed upon, there was no going back.

'Agreed,' Harp and Cissy said together.

'Danny?' Liz asked.

His eyes gave nothing away of the turmoil he must be feeling. He cared for Marianne, much more than he ever intended to, Harp knew. It was impossible not to. She was funny and kind and as much a victim as they were.

He exhaled and gazed down at his hands, his elbows on his knees. Harp's heart went out to him. They were asking the impossible, and she hoped against hope it wouldn't come to it, but if it did, they had to have his assurance it would be done. Not only was what they were asking grotesque because he loved her, but also because very probably the child she was carrying was his.

'I don't know if I can,' he said, never raising his head.

'Please God it won't come to it,' Cissy soothed, her hand on his back. 'We'll try to get Rose out.'

CHAPTER 25

*H*arp knocked on Marianne's bedroom door and turned the knob, letting herself in. Marianne was curled up under the blankets and seemed to be sleeping.

'Marianne.' Harp shook her shoulder gently. 'Danny's here to see you.'

The girl sat up blearily. 'Danny?' She'd been crying again, and her face was puffy.

He stepped into the room and she saw his injuries.

'Danny, my God, what happened to you? Oh, you poor thing...' Marianne rushed to him, not caring how it looked.

He stood back, not allowing her to embrace him, offering her no comfort. Harp could see it was killing him.

'You need to come with us now,' Harp said gently.

'Come where? What's going on, Harp?' Marianne asked.

'You need to get something warm to wear and strong walking shoes.' Harp went to the wardrobe and extracted a woollen coat and some fur-lined boots.

'I don't understand – what's going on? Danny?'

Turning with the boots and coat, Harp saw Marianne was in tears.

'You're being taken hostage, Marianne.' Danny's voice sounded choked. 'Beckett has arrested Matt, JohnJoe and Rose. He had me but had to let me go. The IRA will look after the men but we're going to hold you until he releases Rose.'

'I thought you were coming to save me,' she wailed. 'How stupid I was, Danny! I thought you cared about me, about us.' She placed her hand on her belly. 'This is your child – you know that, don't you?'

'Marianne, please, I wish it wasn't this way, I really do, but –'

'I'll scream! They'll hear me and the soldiers in the house will come running...'

Harp stood behind her, and without Marianne realising what was happening, Harp gagged her with a white handkerchief. She then tied Marianne's hands behind her back. 'Nobody wants to hurt you, Marianne, I swear we don't, but we have no choice. Your husband is holding my mother in the RIC barracks, and I'm so worried about her. We're hoping he'll trade her for you.' Harp tried to reason with Marianne, who was protesting furiously.

'We're taking you someplace safe. Nothing will happen to you, I promise you that.' Danny caught Harp's eye; she didn't contradict his lie.

Marianne's blue eyes filled with tears, and they slid down her face. Danny draped her coat over her shoulders and helped her into her boots; the coat wouldn't close over her bump.

Feeling wretched, Harp led her to the pony and trap outside the back door, hidden from view. They helped Marianne up and told her to lie down on the blankets they had placed on the rough timber floor. There was a pillow too, and Harp saw that Danny had tried to make it as comfortable as possible for her. Then Harp drew another warm blanket over her and sat on the side seat of the trap, Marianne at her feet. Danny then placed some bags of potatoes around her and jumped up to take the reins, and they were off.

There was normally a checkpoint on all approaches to the town, but the Winters visit meant all staff were redeployed. There might still be an odd patrol, and if the soldiers looked in the trap, they were in trouble, but they had decided to stick mostly to back roads and lanes. Once they were out of town, they would be safe enough.

Harp hoped against hope that JohnJoe got out and managed to make his way to the safe house too. If he was an escapee, he would have to go on the run, or realistically go back to America. She and her mother had provided safe accommodation for so many young men who'd had to flee, hours ahead of the authorities. Now her JohnJoe would be one. The thought gave her a physical pain. They'd been separated by the Atlantic Ocean once before, from 1912 to 1916, but they wrote each week and they were just children then. To be apart from him now was an entirely different prospect. They were soul mates, and she hated the thought of a life without him near her. JohnJoe accepted and loved her for who she was, and he never found her odd or was confused by her reactions, as others were. She had learned the ways of the world more slowly than others. Her isolated childhood didn't help, with just Henry and her mother for company, but she would not have chosen another. Nobody else understood her the way JohnJoe did. Nobody made her feel as safe. Except possibly Henry Devereaux.

As she always did in times of difficulty, she thought about Henry. His gentle, calm presence was something she could summon up at any time, and she always felt that he was with her. He would have scoffed at such a fanciful notion, being himself a committed atheist, but she knew he was wrong. It probably didn't have much to do with religion, she thought, but she was sure there was something else after death, another dimension or something. Henry wasn't gone; he was still around her and her mother.

Much as I need you now, Henry, go to Rose, she urged. Henry Devereaux had loved Rose Delaney for all of his adult life, a fact that only became clear when he died and left a letter declaring his feelings. He was a recluse and found social interactions difficult, but he would have done anything for Rose. Harp thought back to her childhood and realised now that it was obvious even then, if she'd been able to see it. The way he gave Rose his undivided attention when she spoke, how his face lit up when she entered the room, how much he loved Harp, her daughter.

If only Henry really was her biological father and not his malevolent brother, Ralph. She hated the thought that Ralph's blood flowed in her veins. At least Ralph had no idea of their connection, and if she could, she would make sure he never did. Ralph would stop at nothing to hurt her; she knew that. She'd seen the naked hatred in his eyes. He believed that all of the hardship he'd endured – financial, social, and now physical with his leg – was her fault and not his own. He blamed her completely, and Rose too, and he would, like the discontented wife in 'Tam o' Shanter', nurse his 'wrath to keep it warm'. She remembered Henry explaining that image to her as they read Burns together.

Harp tried not to imagine what was happening to Rose. She was so beautiful; it would make her such a target. Men had looked at her mother with lust in their eyes since Harp was old enough to recognise what it was. Not that Rose ever gave them encouragement; it was just that she was such an attractive woman, men noticed her. If Beckett had found Pennington and he could get Ralph to testify, then there was no hope. She racked her brain, trying to think how much Ralph could have revealed. He knew something had happened that night, he knew Pennington had an eye for Harp, and he knew after that night Pennington was never seen again. But did he know that Matt and her mother had buried him under old Mrs Duggan, whose funeral was the next day? How else could they explain him being there? She wished she knew the state of decomposition of a body over that period of time. Matt would know, but she couldn't ask him. Could Pennington be recognised? Could it be proven it was him beyond reasonable doubt? If it could, Matt would hang. She wondered if Beckett knew or suspected who Matt really was.

Danny turned the horse off the main road and up a country boreen, rutted and full of potholes. The bouncing around on the hard timber seat of the trap must have been agony for him because of his injuries. It was a bitterly cold day, and she heard Marianne groan as the wheel of the trap bounced in and out of the dips and depressions on the road.

'Can we let her sit up now?' Harp whispered at Danny.

He shook his head. 'No, there could be a patrol anywhere, and they'd recognise her. Are you alright back there? I'm trying to avoid the worst of the holes, but this darned surface is awful.'

'We're fine, just keep going.' Harp's teeth chattered and her breath was visible in the cold air.

'Should we check on Marianne?' he asked, and Harp could see how much he hated doing this.

'All right.' Harp drew back the blanket and Marianne gazed up, her face tear-stained and her body curled in a ball. 'It won't be long more. Are you alright?'

Marianne nodded and swallowed and shifted position slightly.

'Can't you untie my arms Harp? It hurts so much.'

'Of course, I…I wish it didn't have to be this way Marianne.'

Harp untied her and the other girl stretched her limbs and winced, then settled herself back down. As she did, Harp saw her take something from her coat pocket and crook it in her elbow, cuddled up to her face. Danny flicked the reins and they were off again.

The rain began shortly after, that driving winter rain that stung as it hit your face. She pulled her scarf up and her hat down to try to protect herself. A part of Harp was envious of Marianne; at least she was dry and relatively warm.

Mile after mile they went through farms and fields, the hedgerows dripping the rain that had by now become relentless. Fear of the soldiers and the inclement weather meant people stayed indoors. In recent weeks the temperature of the conflict had risen as steadily as the temperature of the weather had fallen. Every day more and more attacks were mounted by the Volunteers, and the British were rattled. The foiled effort to take out Lord Winters had been a blow, but they would carry on regardless. The Cobh area had more than acquitted itself in the supply of weapons alone. It was used as the conduit to remove Volunteers in danger of execution too, many spirited away to America. It was where money and people of influence came into the country, as well as where the efforts of Crown forces were most concentrated and therefore most hindered.

The entire county of Cork was doing remarkably well. British bastions around Ballincollig and Macroom, and further afield in West and North Cork, were being set ablaze, and the tension in the air was palpable. They were close; the British were on the back foot. They just needed to keep up the pressure. For the Devlins and Matt too, the cause was the most important thing, but for Harp right then, all she could think about was her mother and the possibility of JohnJoe being caught or sent back to Boston.

They turned off yet another rutted track and this time entered a wooded area. The canopy above was thick and dense, and they were almost immediately plunged into darkness. Harp drew back the blanket from over Marianne, which was now sodden. Incredibly she appeared to be asleep. This time Harp had a closer look and saw she was cradling a stuffed bear with a green waistcoat.

'Marianne.' Harp shook her shoulder gently, and the girl's eyes opened as she tried to orientate herself to her surroundings.

'Harp...are we there...' she asked.

'Almost, I think. Would you like to sit up? It must be terribly uncomfortable down there.'

'It was all right,' Marianne said, trying to sit up. 'But yes, I'll sit up.'

Harp managed to get her into a sitting position.

Marianne nodded. 'Harp, I really need the lavatory,' she murmured, clearly in some distress.

'Oh dear, it will have to be over there in the bushes, can you manage that?' Harp asked sympathetically.

Marianne nodded.

She tapped Danny on the back. 'We need a rest stop.'

Danny stopped once more and tactfully gazed ahead, knowing what she meant. Apart from the few words they exchanged back at the house they'd not communicated at all. Harp knew they were both suffering and wished she could do something to alleviate their pain, but this was not the time.

Harp helped Marianne over the uneven forest floor to an area behind a large oak. Marianne did the necessary and walked slowly back to the cart, allowing Danny to help her back up.

'You're soaked through,' he said, brushing a damp curl from her forehead.

'So are you.'

He turned to Harp. 'Can you give us a minute please, alone?'

'Of course.' Harp walked away. She should probably say they needed to press on, get to the safe house, but a few minutes couldn't hurt. She wondered where JohnJoe and her mother were and sent up a silent prayer to Henry to watch over them. She couldn't bear the thought of anything happening to either of them.

She turned briefly to see Danny and Marianne talking, their heads close together, and then he kissed her. Moments later they were all back in the trap and heading deeper into the woods.

CHAPTER 26

*R*ose had never been so cold in her entire life, she was sure of it. When she'd been arrested, she'd not been given time to get dressed and so was still in just her nightgown and bare feet. There was nothing in the cell except a wooden cot without blankets or a pillow, and no candle was provided either. It was a cell in the basement, and facing the gate through which she'd been pushed unceremoniously was a blank wall. Apart from the scratching and scurrying of rodents, she'd not seen or heard anyone since she arrived. A night had passed, she was sure of that, but more than one? She had no idea. High in the corner of the room was a grille, through which water poured. She thought it was most likely a grate on the side of the street above and that the flow of water through the night was caused by the heavy rain. The grate itself was clogged with leaves and debris and allowed in no light, so she spent all the time she was there in darkness.

She'd not been given anything to eat or drink. There was no lavatory either, so she'd had to make do with the bucket in the corner of the dank cell. She'd sat most of the time against the wall, on the wooden cot, her knees pulled up to her chest, trying not to panic. The ubiquitous sounds of gunshots that had become part of their daily lives caused her so much distress now. Was that shot meeting a target in Matt? In Harp? She had no idea who had been picked up besides her and Matt, and she wondered if he was here too somewhere. She tried calling out, but her voice went unanswered. She was alone. She assumed they knew about Pennington and the coffins.

She recalled the words of a poem Harp had learned off by heart at only seven years old for no reason other than she liked the images in it. To Rose it sounded terrifying, but Harp loved it. 'L'Allegro'? Or was it *Paradise Lost*? She wasn't sure. If Harp were there, she'd know. John Milton, was it? Rose was not the literary scholar her daughter was, but when Harp was younger and she would get anxious, reciting the words of this poem calmed her. Henry had started it, reading it to her at night, while other children heard stories of the three little pigs or princesses in towers. Rose had heard the words so often, she wondered if she could remember them.

Hence, loathed melancholy,
Of Cerberus, and blackest Midnight born,
In Stygian cave forlorn,
'Mongst horrid shapes, and shrieks, and sights unholy;
Find out some uncouth cell,
And the night-raven sings;
There under ebon shades, and low-brow'd rocks,
As ragged as thy locks,
In dark Cimmerian desert ever dwell.
But come thou goddess fair and free,
In heav'n yclep'd Euphrosyne...

'Rose...Rose are you in there?'

Was she dreaming it? Was it someone calling her name? No, it was real.

'Rose, can you hear me?'

She leapt up. The sound was coming from the grille above her head. The cell was underground and this grille was on the street overhead.

'Yes, I can hear you. This is Rose. Who is that?'

The person was removing the leaves and dirt debris from the

grille, and she could make out eyes in the darkness. Whoever it was must have been on their hands and knees on the footpath above to lean down so far.

'It's me, Liz.'

Relief flooded through Rose.

'Can you climb up to this grid? I can blow a hole in it with some explosive, but I need to be quick. Cissy and some others have created a diversion, and there are a few of our lads going to give us coving fire, but I only have a second or two. If I can blow a hole big enough up here, do you think you could get up to climb out?'

Rose gazed around. The grille was about a foot square and was about eight feet up the wall, and there was nothing but the bed. Liz would not need to make the hole much bigger for her to wriggle through, but how to get up that high? She thought quickly. Luckily the iron bedframe wasn't fixed to the wall, so she lifted it up and placed it on its end. She could use it as a kind of ramp possibly. It was worth a try.

'I think so,' she called.

'Right, stand back so,' Liz instructed.

Within seconds there was a loud bang. Dust, bricks and debris flew everywhere, and a hole just about large enough for her to climb out was made. Luckily there was so much noise around the town – there was a lot of unrest – the sound might have gone unnoticed long enough to escape. It was early morning and the dawn was just breaking.

She leaned the bed against the wall, wedging the legs on a flag-stone that stood proud of the one beside it. She clambered up the bed and dragged herself through the hole; Liz pulled her from the other side. Both women took off across the street. Liz threw a dark blanket over Rose, as a white nightdress would be seen, and they immediately entered a lane off the main street. It smelled awful – it was probably used as the latrine for the nearby pub – but Rose didn't care. Liz took a crowbar from where it leaned against a wall, obviously placed in readiness, and lifted a manhole cover. The smell intensified, and Rose covered her nose and mouth with the blanket.

'Is Harp all right? And Matt?' Rose asked.

'Matt was in Spike. They got him and JohnJoe out an hour or two ago. Harp is with Danny – she's fine. Now, down you go,' Liz whispered urgently. 'Turn left and stay straight. I can't give you a light, I'm afraid. Keep walking until you come to where it widens into three tunnels. It should take about fifteen minutes. At the junction, there will be an open manhole there with someone waiting to pull you out. It comes out by the customs house, which should be unwatched at this time hopefully. Good luck, my dear.'

Rose wasted no time. Every second they were there, they were at risk. She sat on the edge of the manhole and dropped down, landing painfully in the wet sludge below. She was immediately plunged into blackness as Liz slid the manhole cover back on, and she forced herself to stay calm.

Breathing was nauseating; the smell of human and animal excrement filled her nostrils and congealed in the back of her throat. Involuntarily she gagged, but did not vomit. She pulled the blanket around herself, as much as for warmth as camouflage – it was so cold.

Her feet squelched in the mud beneath her bare feet, the cold slimy stuff oozing up between her toes. She tried not to think about rats. She remembered how she and Harp had been too afraid to go into the old stables because they feared one was in there, and now here she was in the pitch-dark traversing a sewer, no doubt home to hundreds of the terrifying rodents. The alternative, however, was the end of a rope, of that she was sure.

She was convinced Beckett knew about Pennington, though how, she had no idea. He had an uncanny knack for finding things out. Matt was sure he was getting information from outside of the town, but he could never determine who it was.

Matt. The thought of him drove her on. And Harp. She prayed the girl had kept her head down. She was so impetuous sometimes that Rose was terrified she would fall into the hands of the Black and Tans. Matt had escaped; something had told her he would. He was so resourceful and so brave. She longed to marry him, for everyone to know he was her man, but he was right – it was too dangerous. Clearly the secret was out now, though, with Beckett finding them in bed together, so they might as well get married. The old Rose would have been mortified to have been discovered in a man's bed. Having a child out of wedlock with Henry Devereaux, or so the story went, had caused enough shame without people thinking she was so loose in her morals as to sleep with any man who came along. But she didn't care any more. She knew the truth, that apart from one ill-advised encounter with Ralph Devereaux when she was seventeen, Matt Quinn had been the only other man to touch her. She knew that, Matt did, and so did Harp, and that was all that mattered.

She tried to imagine what would happen now. They were all wanted fugitives, so returning home wasn't an option. Would she ever see her house again? If JohnJoe was arrested too, then he would have to be got out of the country, Danny as well. If they were picked up, and it seemed they were – why else would Liz have said they were rescued from Spike Island prison – then it was the end of everything. The boys would have to be taken back to America. Kathy would be thrilled at least, but poor Harp would be heartbroken. She and JohnJoe were like two peas in a pod. Rose hated the idea of them being apart, but then maybe Harp would go too. The thought of it filled her with pain. But perhaps it would be safer.

On she walked, and she shrieked as something horribly furry brushed off her arm. The freezing sludge beneath her feet had made them numb and the smell was lodged in her nostrils, but she was free. Liz Devlin was a wily old bird, there was no doubt about it. She and Cissy looked every inch the old spinster shopkeepers, but there was so much more to them than that.

It felt like miles. She tried to visualise the town above her. She knew Queenstown like the back of her hand, so long she'd lived there, but in many ways it felt strange now, with the Crown forces' omniscient and threatening presence.

Then she saw it, the light up ahead. There was weak torchlight shining through the hole, and she hurried towards it. She found a rope, knotted at intervals, hanging down, and she grabbed it, ignoring the rat that ran over her foot. She hoisted herself up and hissed, 'I'm here.'

'Righto, up you get.' It was a man's voice she didn't recognise.

She clung on, finding the knots on which to rest her feet, and within seconds she was hauled up.

The two men were not local. Both were young, early twenties, she thought. One was balding already, though he was young, and the other was dark and curly-haired. They winced when they smelled her.

'I'm sorry…' she began, embarrassed. She stank and her nightie was almost see-through.

'Ah, you're grand, love. We've smelled worse.' The taller one laughed, taking off his heavy overcoat and giving it to her. She should have objected, but the coat, warm from his body, permeated the numbing cold, and she couldn't resist allowing it to engulf her thin frame. He then took a cap from the pocket of the coat and tucked her hair up inside it.

'I'm sorry we've no shoes, and mine wouldn't fit you, but we'll get you away now anyway and sort that out later on.'

'Right, let's get you out of here.' The other man grabbed her arm and led her to a boat with a small outboard motor and a sail.

'Where am I going?' she asked. Although she knew it would be much too dangerous for Matt to be seen around the town, part of her hoped they were taking her to him.

'Not sure, but we've orders to bring you out to a bigger boat, moored beyond the harbour. Don't worry, though, we know who you are, and you're in good hands.'

They were reassuring, and she instinctively knew they were to be trusted. She allowed herself to be helped into a small fishing boat, mercifully with a tiny cabin, and in out of the weather.

There were two other men aboard who, together with her rescuers, set about sailing out into the bay. It was windy, which was to their advantage, and Rose was grateful when the balding man arrived into the cabin to give her a cup of steaming cocoa from a flask. She wrapped her hands gratefully around the cup and sipped the drink.

The taller man, the one who'd given her a coat, arrived back in the cabin then with a sailor's duffel bag and pulled out a navy-blue hand-knitted pullover and some men's work trousers. 'They'll be miles too big, but at least you'll be warm. And here's a pair of socks. There's a pair of boots there you can have, I'm sure.' He pulled a pair of fishermen's boots out from under the seat. 'Too big as well but at least your feet will be dry. Finish your cocoa, Mrs Delaney, and we'll leave you to it to get dressed.'

Her gratitude to these boys threatened to make her cry. She knew better than to ask their names; they would not tell her anyway. 'Thank you, so much... I don't know how to...'

'Don't worry about it. You have very important friends, missus.' The balding man grinned. 'More than my pelt's worth not to take proper care of ya!'

They stood outside the cabin, their backs to the door, smoking a cigarette between them as the boat pushed out against the wind. The vessel lurched and pitched. Rose thought she might be sick, but she was free, and still alive.

In the frosty air, she slipped off the coat and pulled the now filthy and soaking nightdress over her head. Quickly, she pulled on the undershirt that had been in the bottom of the bag, then put on the huge woollen sweater and the trousers. Surprisingly, they all smelled freshly laundered. Her filthy feet had lost all feeling, but she pulled the hand-knit socks over them, and within a few minutes, she had sensation there again. Then she put her feet in the boots. He was right – they were easily three sizes too big – but she pulled the laces as tightly as she could and thought that this was the most comfortable she'd ever felt.

Once she was dressed, the men re-entered.

'Thank you so much. I feel so much better.'

'Good. You look a bit better too.' The taller one grinned.

'So what now?'

'As I said, I'm not sure beyond that we've orders to take you to another vessel. What happens then, I've no idea. This whole thing is on a need-to-know basis, and we don't need to know much, I'm afraid.' He grinned again. 'I think it's not too far out – an hour or so, they reckon. The two lads out there know what they're doing anyway, so try not to worry.'

Their accents were Cork City, and though she'd never laid eyes on them and she was in a boat in the middle of the sea, she felt safe. She'd seen they were armed as well, so in the event they were spotted, they could at least defend the boat. She settled in and tried not to get sick. The ocean was choppy once they got outside of the calmer waters of the harbour. Despite living beside the sea for most of her life, she rarely ventured out onto it.

The men left her alone in the small space, and she watched the sun rising, almost completely obscured by thick cloud, climbing higher in the gunmetal-grey sky. The wind buffeted the boat, and the rain ran in rivulets down the small grimy windows. She was warmer now in the dry clothes but felt queasy, so she tried to focus on the brightening horizon. Harp had told her something about that before. Harp had been reading 'Don Juan' by Lord Byron when she was twelve, a poem Rose had checked herself because she wasn't at all sure that the reading material Harp chose for herself from Henry's library was always that suitable. She remembered how some man was sailing away from his beloved Julia and was in a terrible way, being pitched around on the high seas. This, of course, led Harp to research the physiological reason for seasickness. Rose smiled. Her daughter was the most amazing gift life had ever given her. Harp was not just bright but also so wise. It was as if she were born eighty years old, and since she was little, Rose had sought and listened to her opinions. What was she doing now? Was she safe? Unlike other mothers, Rose's worries were not about boys or falling into bad company; Harp was too sensible for any of that. But she was so brave, and sometimes her mouth got her into trouble. She was a terrible liar, so if she was questioned by police or soldiers, she would give herself away instantly. Liz had said she was with Danny. That gave her comfort. For all his joking about, Danny Coveney was a good man; he'd take care of Harp.

She settled into the corner, wedging her back against the wall of the boat, knees to her chest and her feet on the seat, and tried to rest.

The outboard motor growled as it battled against the choppy sea, but then it stopped.

The tall lad came back in. 'Right you are. I don't know who you are, missus, but you have some connections. 'Tis more than our lives worth not to deliver you safely. We were warned that you were very precious cargo.'

Rose smiled. She'd survived on her own, with Harp to look after, for so long that being taken care of by someone else was a new concept, and she found she liked it. Matt made her feel safe, and despite the inherent danger of what they were doing, she basked in the glow of his protection.

The lad offered her his hand and she took it, coming out onto the deck. It was freezing cold and the rain was lashing both the boat and its inhabitants. To her astonishment, they'd come up alongside a far bigger boat, a yacht really, with a huge sail and sleek dark wood on the deck and rail. On its aft, it was flying the stars and stripes of the United States.

A tall burly man with a beard and a heavy woollen sweater – in his early fifties, she guessed – balanced and threw a rope to one of the men on her boat. They came so close that the vessels bumped off each other. Rose was led to the edge. On the yacht there was a ladder, and with the help of her rescuers, she stood on the side of the little fishing boat and grabbed hold of the rails. Despite the pitching, she managed to climb up and was half dragged aboard the larger vessel.

'Mrs Delaney?' the bearded man asked, grinning.

She nodded. 'Yes.'

'My name is Mike.' His accent was American. 'I was in the area and I was sent by Pat Rafferty to pick you up. Alexander Jackson contacted him, said you might need some help.'

CHAPTER 27

The cottage was smoke-filled and probably not that clean –
it was hard to tell in the dim light – but the stew was
welcome and Harp drank the tea the elderly couple offered. The turf
fire was giving out peat-scented heat, and Harp wondered if she
would ever again be warm. The couple spoke in Irish, and Harp
wondered if they knew she could understand them perfectly. Neither
Danny nor Marianne had an idea what they were saying, and Harp
couldn't help but smile when the couple switched to English to
address the visitors. It made no difference because their accents were
so thick, it was close to impossible to understand them.

The three accepted the offer to dry their clothes around the fire,
and the old couple pulled out a settle bed from the wall. Danny said he
would be fine on the chair and to give Marianne the bed.

'Can you ask them have they had any contact with anyone? How
are we supposed to know what's happening?'

Harp spoke to the man, who she suspected was a little hard of
hearing. 'Should we just wait here to hear what we should do next?'
she asked, but he seemed confused by the question. To his apparent
astonishment, she tried again in Irish, and he answered easily.

He spoke at length – he was quite verbose once he was using his mother tongue – and Harp translated. Once he was finished, he followed his wife to a room off the main one; she assumed it was a bedroom. It was early morning, but at this time of year, it was still quite dark.

'Matt and JohnJoe are with the column now, but they are going to get them away.' She neglected to translate the many curses the old man rained down upon the heads of the English and went on. 'They're safe anyway, for now. Beckett has been told of his wife's kidnapping and the demand has been made, but there's been no further word. So I suppose we just wait.'

Harp caught Danny's eye as Marianne took off her coat and boots. Her fine silk nightgown was ruined. Her hair, always so elegantly coiffed, hung down in tendrils, and her face totally devoid of make-up made her look even more beautiful, if anything. Beautiful and very, very young. Danny's adoration was plain to see.

'Best we take turns to stay awake and keep watch.'

Danny nodded. 'You girls sleep. I'll stay awake.'

Marianne stood with her back to the fire, shivering. Danny removed his sweater, a warm one Kathy had sent, and put it on her. 'Come on, let's get you some rest,' he said gently.

'Can you stay with me?' she asked.

'Of course.'

Harp withdrew, sensing he needed some time with her. This was wrong. Her mother's incarceration was also wrong, but this couldn't be the right thing to do.

Their heads were close together as he helped her to the bed and gently covered her with a rough blanket. He held her hand as she rested on the bundled-up sacking that served as a pillow. Soon she was asleep.

Danny moved to beside the fire, opposite Harp. 'I can't do this,' he said.

Eventually she spoke. 'I know. I don't think I can either.' She exhaled, glad it was out in the open.

'So what now?'

Harp shrugged. 'Hope Beckett agrees and releases my mother?'

211

'And if he doesn't?'

'Then I don't know. But what I do know is that neither of us can shoot that girl.'

Two wrongs never made a right, no matter how justified the cause. Could she shoot Beckett? Or Ralph? She didn't know. Possibly. Probably, if she was honest. But Marianne was just a girl, gambled by her father and taken advantage of by that loathsome man.

'Do you love her, Danny?' she asked quietly.

He smiled sadly and nodded.

'Is the baby yours, do you think?'

He ran his hands through his hair, then lit a cigarette. 'Probably. Marianne told me he's been married three times and has no children. We were careful, most of the time, but…' He shrugged.

They sat in silence, that thought permeating their exhausted minds. They turned as a gentle knock on the door broke the silence. Danny gestured that Harp get behind him and drew his gun. There was another tap. Two knocks, one knock, four knocks. Danny opened the door a crack and then opened it wide, wrapping his arms around JohnJoe as he drew him in, Matt Quinn behind him.

They whispered so as not to wake either Marianne or the old couple. Matt was explaining to Danny what had happened. Harp turned and found JohnJoe standing before her. She was so distraught; the emotions were in a swirl in her head, and she didn't know how to react. Suddenly, more than anything, she wanted to be in her bedroom under the eaves in the Cliff House, alone. It was all too much.

'Harp.' JohnJoe's arms went around her and she felt her body go rigid. 'It's all right. Your mom is free. She's out. They got her away.'

He held her, knowing what she needed more than she did herself, and she felt herself relax against him.

'Rose is fine. She escaped…'

'What? How? Did Beckett release…' She couldn't take it in.

'No, Liz Devlin blew a hole in the RIC barrack wall, we had a few volunteers at strategic locations to return fire once the sound of the

explosion drew the British, and they got her out through the sewer.'
His eyes lit up with glee at the thought of it all.

'Liz did that...'

'She sure did. She and Cissy are tough old birds. They got Matt to
show them all sorts of things since this whole thing started. He said he
was reluctant but they were determined, so he gave them some explo-
sives and showed them how to use them.'

'So she blew up the barracks?' Harp was incredulous.

'No. They knew that the cell they were using – they only have one
under the barracks – had a ventilation grille, and Liz went down, got
some people to create a diversion on the other side of the street and
draw the guys on guard down there. They were short-handed because
of Winters being in town. She blew the hole by putting the explosive
in the grille. Then she pulled Rose out, got her out through a manhole.
Matt was free by then, so he gave the order, and she was taken by boat
from the quay to...'

'To where?' Harp asked.

'This is the best bit – you're not going to believe this. Jackson, the
consul, contacted Uncle Pat after you visited, said we might need
some help. There was a boat dropping cargo due today, so they just
gained some time and arrived a bit earlier. They will have picked Rose
up by now.'

'So now what?' Harp could feel the tears running down her cheeks
from sheer relief.

'Now we get ourselves down to a Cuskinny cove, not far from here
– there'll be a rowboat. We get out and board the same yacht, and we
get outta Dodge.'

'JohnJoe, are you serious?'

'I am. So come on, we gotta go.'

Matt joined them and hugged her. 'Rose is fine,' he said. 'We need
to get going.'

'Where? I don't understand...'

Matt placed his hands on her shoulders, gazing down into her
eyes. 'This war is over for you now, Harp. You, JohnJoe, Danny, you
are all under suspicion now, so we need to get you out. Me too, for the

time being, so we're going to America, all of us, and once I have you all settled in, I'll come back, finish what we started.'

'We can't just leave! Matt, that's insane! The house, my studies...my things...' Harp could hear the horror rise in her voice.

'Staying is what would be insane, pet. Beckett won't rest, not till he has every single one of us in a noose. We have to go.'

'But...' Harp gazed around. Her mother was on a boat; she was safe. JohnJoe, Matt, Kitty, Danny – they were her people. She could hear Henry's voice in her head. *Go, Harp. They're just things. It's just a house. The books aren't going anywhere. Be well. Be happy.*

'All right.' She took her still-wet coat from the back of the *súgán* chair, the old-fashioned type made out of rope and reeds, bound around branches cut to measure.

'What about her?' JohnJoe nodded at the sleeping Marianne.

'She won't be harmed. She'll be returned to him. It will be taken care of.' Matt ushered them all towards the door.

Danny stopped. 'No. I can't leave her, Matt. I promised her I wouldn't. He knows about us...'

'Danny, I'm sorry, son, but I can't allow it...' Matt began.

'Well, I'm not leaving without her, Matt. I can't leave her to him, not now. She told me she thinks that once the child is born, he's going to take it, discard her, and she'll never see the baby again. I can't do it.'

Harp saw the passion burn in his eyes and knew he meant every word. She knew why Matt was reticent – there were so many reasons: Marianne's condition, who she was, the breach of the rules of engagement. But Danny was right; Beckett was a psychopath. She'd read the writings of the German psychiatrist Koch, who identified criminal psychosis, strange and antisocial or criminal behaviour in people who seemed perfectly sane. Beckett was such an individual; she was sure of it.

'He can't leave her,' Harp agreed. 'We have to take her with us.'

CHAPTER 28

*M*att glanced at the now-awake Marianne, sitting on the side of the bed, looking petrified.

'All right.' Matt signed impatiently. 'But we need to go – now.'

The horse and trap they had used to get there were gone, presumably picked up by the Flying Column, so they had to move on foot. It was probably safer if a good deal slower, as they could stay in fields and out of the way of any patrols. Matt handed each of them a pistol from a box beside the hearth.

'It's like Paris stealing Helen from Menelaus,' Harp said to herself. She'd had the habit since she was a child of likening situations to moments in literature. She realised as an adult that she did it to make anxious situations feel less frightening. Something had happened before, and so it would be all right. Though the story of Helen of Troy didn't exactly end well, now that she thought about it.

'What?' Matt had overheard her, and she blushed.

'Nothing. I was just talking to myself, first sign of madness.' She laughed feebly.

'You're a lot of things, Harp Devereaux, but mad isn't one of them.' He gave her shoulder a squeeze.

'Where are we going?' Harp asked as she fell into step beside Matt.

JohnJoe and Danny each held one of Marianne's arms. The little brown bear was tucked into her pocket, helping her along. The early morning was perishing, and their clothing was still damp, though mercifully it had stopped raining. They walked quietly and stayed by the tall hedges.

'There's a small cove at Cuskinny. There'll be a boat there, all going well. We'll row out to it and hopefully get away.'

'And you're sure my mother is on it?' she asked.

'Sure.' He smiled.

Harp dreaded the answer but had to ask. 'Did he hurt her?'

Matt's mouth set in a hard line. 'I don't know. But if he did, I'll come back and kill him with my bare hands.'

She linked his arm as they walked along. The sea was on the horizon. Matt knew this area like the back of his hand, so they took the quickest route. At one point, when they had to cross the road, he raised his hand for them to stop and be silent.

They could hear voices and boots on the road, and they huddled in a ditch, the leaves heavy with fallen rain dripping down their already frozen necks. The patrol of Cameron Highlanders passed so close, they could hear their conversation clearly, their Scots accents commonplace around the town now.

'Better than the bloody trenches anyway, I suppose,' one grumbled.

'I dunno, mate, reckon the French birds were easier on the eye.'

There was a rumble of laughter, followed by a request for a cigarette. They stopped to light them, and Harp counted five heavily armed soldiers. She thought their heavy kilts and white fur *sporrans* looked vaguely ridiculous, but they were very proud of their uniforms.

To the inexperienced eye, they might just look like lads, recruits to the Queen's Own Cameron Highlanders regiment, but Harp and the people of Cobh knew what they were really like. In retaliation for the killing of an RIC constable in an ambush last August, they'd broken out of their barracks and gone on a rampage in the town, breaking shop windows, damaging private houses too, and it wasn't until a detachment of Royal Marines were deployed to prevent further wreckage that the whole town could breathe again.

'I wish I'd a warm wee lassie to curl up with after this, instead of Gordon's farting and snoring.'

'I'm so knackered, I'd not know what to do with one if I ever had a lass in my bed,' another moaned.

'Looks like these bloody night patrols are going to be the way of it while Beckett's in charge anyway.'

'He's right crabbit over his missus, though he doesn't pay her any heed when she's there.'

'I'd pay her plenty of heed if I had her.'

Another burst of ribald laughter. Harp saw Danny hold Marianne to his chest.

'That Yank got there before ye! Too late, sunshine...'

'And ye better not let the gaffer hear ye – he's just up ahead – or ye'll face a worse fate than that Yank...' They moved on.

So Danny and Marianne's affair was common knowledge. That would stoke the flames of Beckett's ire to have the lower ranks joking about him being cuckolded. Did 'gaffer' mean Beckett? Or another of their superiors?

They walked on, the dawn trying valiantly to cut through the grey mist rolling in off the sea. This time of year the sun didn't rise until after eight in the morning, so they had the cover of darkness to protect them.

They began the descent down a steep field to the small secluded beach. It was rough underfoot, but with the men's help, Marianne made it. She never once complained or made any remark, quietly doing all they asked of her. As Harp had always suspected, Marianne had inner depths she did not allow the world to see.

They dropped down onto a small pebble beach, and to their immense relief, there was a dark-green boat with two sturdy oars. Matt and JohnJoe dragged it down the pebbles, Harp keeping watch, her pistol cocked and ready.

'Halt!' The whistle came first, then the gunshots. Matt reacted, as did Harp, Danny and JohnJoe, all returning fire. Getting into the boat would be suicide – there was no way they could row fast enough to get away. They had no choice but fight it out.

'Harp, stay down,' JohnJoe shouted, dragging her behind a rock and taking aim in the direction of the gunshots. Then they saw them, the Highlanders they'd seen earlier, and with them was Beckett.

One of the Highlanders fell instantly; Matt got a direct hit. Then a second fell; Harp got him in the chest. The other two took cover, and Matt shouted for everyone to get in the boat while he provided covering fire.

JohnJoe half-pulled Harp towards the shore, both of them abreast of Matt, all three of them firing constantly. Danny and Marianne were further up the beach, taking shelter behind another rock. The two Highlanders taking cover went down, dead from direct headshots fired either by JohnJoe or Matt, leaving only Beckett. Matt cursed as his pistol ran out of bullets; JohnJoe's did too.

Beckett kept firing while taking strategic cover as he advanced towards Danny and Marianne.

'Get to the boat!' Matt shouted at JohnJoe, and JohnJoe pulled Harp after him. Danny was clearly out of ammunition; there was no firing now from where he and Marianne were hiding.

Beckett stood before the rock, his pistol cocked and ready, and pulled Marianne out from behind it. JohnJoe, Harp and Matt took cover, knowing there was nothing they could do. Beckett had two pistols.

'Kneel down, you slut!' he roared at Marianne, who slid to her knees. Then he pointed the gun at Danny. 'You too, get out here. Kneel beside her.'

Beckett took the second pistol from his holster and handed it to a trembling Marianne. 'Shoot him,' he commanded.

'No!' Marianne wailed.

'Shoot him or I shoot you,' Beckett barked.

'You won't – I'm carrying your child,' she begged.

'That bastard isn't mine – I know that for a fact – so shoot your baby's father or I shoot you.'

'Do it, Marianne,' Danny said. 'Save yourself and the baby. He's going to hang me anyway...'

'You'd do well to listen to your lover, Marianne dear,' Beckett spat.

'Please, Marianne, do it.' Danny's eyes begged her.

With trembling hands, she took the gun from Beckett, cocked it and aimed at Danny's temple. Before anyone had time to register what was happening, she spun and shot Beckett.

He reeled back, blood spurting from his shoulder. Danny surged forward, grabbing the gun the brigadier dropped, and finished him off with a bullet to the head. His body fell, lifeless, on the pebbles.

'Come on.' Danny grabbed Marianne by the hand and ran to the shore. Matt and JohnJoe were already in the process of shoving the boat into the water. Harp helped Marianne wade in and climb aboard. The boat wobbled dangerously as the men got in too. Matt and JohnJoe grabbed an oar each, pulling with powerful strokes away from the beach strewn with dead British soldiers.

They rowed around the corner and then they saw it, the gleaming white hull and enormous sails of the yacht, moored no more than a hundred yards away. Within moments, two crew helped them aboard.

'Harp!' Rose threw her arms around her daughter, and then around Matt. Warm blankets and hot drinks appeared as they were led below deck. Marianne clung to Danny, who never left her side.

CHAPTER 29

*T*he Le Havre port was busy, but Matt tried to get enough taxis to take them all to a hotel in the town centre. Despite the luxury conditions on the yacht, they were exhausted and upset by the events of recent days. The yacht was not an ocean-going one, so they were catching a liner from the port to Boston. Kathy Rafferty had booked it all and sent word of the details.

Harp and JohnJoe opted to walk, leaving the others to travel by car.

'But you don't know the way?' Rose was worried.

'We'll find it, Mammy, I promise. The hotel is called Le Clef d'Or. We can ask, and the town is that way.' She pointed at the mass of buildings ahead.

A purser approached them and addressed them in French, and to everyone's astonishment, Matt answered fluently.

'You're a dark horse.' Danny grinned. 'How come you can speak French? Like we all expect Harp to be able to do things like that, but you never struck me as the Francophile type.'

Matt smiled. 'A Frenchman called Jean-Claude Bellac worked in the dockyard. He taught me a lot of things as a young fella.'

'Where is he now?' JohnJoe asked, fascinated.

'Ah, he died a few years back. He had no family that I knew of, so I buried him in the old graveyard out at Cuskinny.'

Rose slipped her hand in his. Harp knew he'd taken Rose there to see the grave, beautifully tended by Matt all these years. It seemed Jean-Claude was the closest thing to a father Matt had ever had.

'And I suppose you're fluent too?' Danny teased Harp. 'So you and Napoléon here, making the rest of us look like dunces?'

'*Mon français est plutôt bon, mais je ne l'ai pas mis en pratique depuis un long moment.*'

'See?' Danny turned to Rose, grinning. 'You ain't gotta worry about her. She'll run rings around anyone, that girl of yours.'

Harp and JohnJoe set off on foot, hand in hand, glad to be alone at last.

'I'm so relieved things worked out as they did. I could never have hurt Marianne and neither could Danny,' Harp said.

'I know. He got involved with her because he was told to, but he never expected to fall for her. And then when she became pregnant, he was so worried about her and fearful of what Beckett might do.'

They stopped at a café and Harp suggested they go inside. The waiter, a tiny officious man in his fifties with a pencil-thin moustache, looked disapprovingly at them as they entered speaking English, but his face changed immediately when they took a seat and Harp ordered.

'*Bonjour, deux café au lait et un croissant et un pain aux raisin s'il vous plait.*'

'*Certainement, Mademoiselle.*' He nodded and minced away, his mirror-polished shoes dazzling in the bright French sunshine.

It wasn't exactly warm, but the damp cold of Ireland was becoming a dim memory. France was somewhere Harp had always imagined she would get to – she and Henry would discuss it often – but she couldn't have anticipated the circumstances.

'I know we're lucky to get out with our lives, but I can't stop thinking of my books, my harp, letters, photographs, the painting you did of me and Mammy and Henry. I…' Harp felt selfish and silly.

JohnJoe didn't dismiss her misgivings; he knew what her things meant to her. 'I know, Harp, it's hard. But we'll go back soon. I really think it's close.'

Their coffees and pastries arrived, and she knew she should savour her first coffee and croissant in France. She'd read enough Proust and Baudelaire to appreciate it, but her heart was heavy.

'Do you really, JohnJoe? How can you think that? They won't ever give up, go home, let us live in peace. When will it ever end? We kill theirs, they kill us, civilians, women, children. The whole horrible cycle never ends.'

'It feels like that, I guess, and I know sometimes I think that too. And Winters might have been a disaster, but the ambush at Kilmichael last week, that was such a success, it rattled them. They've closed all of the small barracks – it's too dangerous. The people are with us and they know that. They can't stop us when we're all on the same side.'

'"No man has the right to fix a boundary to the march of a nation…"' she said as she stirred her coffee.

'Don't tell me.' JohnJoe wrinkled his brow in concentration. 'Parnell?' he asked triumphantly.

'The uncrowned king of Ireland, yes, in the aftermath of the Land War. You see? It never ends. Parnell thought he could end it, so did Daniel O'Connell, Wolfe Tone, Robert Emmet, the French, the Spanish, Hugh O'Neill, Red Hugh O'Donnell – the list goes on and on. Men and women through eight centuries, trying to repel the English from our country, using the ballot box, the pulpit, the pitchfork, now the bomb and the bullet, but nothing ever works. Will this time be just the one for our generation? End result just the same? Britain tightening its grip, forcing us to bow down again?'

JohnJoe leaned over and took her hands. 'I'll never promise something I can't deliver, Harp, but I don't think it will end like that, I honestly don't. But you know something? If it does, I'm going to be proud, and glad I was involved in some small way, because without people like us in each generation, the flame of passion for freedom would flicker and die. We have it because of them, because of the people who went before. We took up the cause in our time. I think we'll win, but even if we don't, then maybe our children will, or their children, because one thing is certain – for as long as Irish blood runs in Irish veins, we will never give up.'

'I know, and I agree, but it's just so hard... And then there's...' Harp wasn't usually so despondent, but it was as if a huge weight were bearing down on her.

'Ralph Devereaux? It's knowing he's still out there, isn't it?' JohnJoe knew what was at the root of her worries.

She had not yet spoken to him about that day on the train four years ago. She wished with all of her heart she'd never asked him and Danny not to kill Ralph. If only they had, he would be gone now; the lingering malevolence of his presence wouldn't exist. But now that she knew he was alive and intent on her downfall, it felt oppressive. She nodded.

'Danny told you about the day on the train?'

'He did.'

'I should have been honest. I...I hated lying to you and I swear I've never lied to you about anything else before, but... And I know you asked us not to...'

'I wish you'd have killed him. I should not have tried to stop you. He hates me and my mother and now you two, but me especially with such loathing, just because I exist. I don't think it's even the fact that Henry left me the house – that's only a part of it. He thinks he should have this lord-of-the-manor life, this position in society. He's not had it and I'm the reason.'

'He's deluded. But yes, I can see you're right. He will have to be dealt with. But this time, I think it will be taken out of our hands. He's a known informer, working with Crown forces, and you know what Collins thinks about that.'

Harp shrugged. 'He'll wriggle off that hook too. He always does.'

'Maybe, but maybe not. Matt would happily put a bullet in him himself for all the grief he's caused you and your mother.'

'Well, he'll hardly be able to do that all the way over in Boston, will he?'

'I guess not.' JohnJoe smiled. 'I know you're leaving your home and all of that, but it will be nice to be in America, away from it all for a while anyway, won't it?'

Harp knew he was relieved and happy to be going back, but she didn't feel the same way; she loved her home. But on one level he was right. It would be nice to live in peace, and at twenty years old, she was tired. 'I doubt Matt will stay,' she said. 'He probably doesn't even want to leave, but he's had orders from the top to get out. It's too risky now, especially after Beckett and Marianne. He's one of the most wanted men in the country.'

'Your first Boston Christmas. We'll be home by the twelfth of December.' JohnJoe smiled and she tried to match it.

They finished their drinks and the delicious buttery pastries and walked outside again. The striped canopies and the tables and chairs on the footpaths full of men drinking coffee from tiny cups and ladies wrapped in furs with miniature dogs on their laps were so exotic. It was chilly but the bright sun warmed them enough to make it comfortable. She tried to soak it all in.

JohnJoe bought a bunch of anemones from a street vendor, presenting them to Harp with a kiss. 'I know Boston's not home for you, but I'll try to make it the best it can be.'

'You make everything the best it can be. I love you.' She took the flowers and buried her face in their delicate heads, inhaling the slight fragrance. Only in France, she thought, would you be able to buy flowers in December. She felt him take her hand and insert both their hands in his coat pocket. Though it was bright and sunny, there was a chill in the air.

'I love you too.' He smiled. 'What will happen now, do you think?' he asked as they strolled along.

'There are no witnesses, so they can't charge Matt or anyone else with the shootings. Danny was released but they'll know you and Matt broke out of Spike. And now there's no sign of you, so they'll charge you in your absence. You'll never be able to go back – none of us will.'

'We will when Ireland is free.' JohnJoe put his arm around her shoulder and kissed her head. 'We'll go back, Harp. It might be next year or in ten years or fifty, but we will repel them and we will go home, I promise.'

'I thought you said you wouldn't make any promises you can't keep?' She smiled sadly.

'I just know, one day, we'll go home.'

CHAPTER 30

*H*arp had never seen such splendour. Christmas in Ireland was a warm cosy season. Children made home-made garlands, and there was always a tree and a cake and a fine goose dinner with clove-studded ham and all the trimmings. But America was a whole other level.

She, Kathy, Kitty and Rose had been shopping for gifts, decorations and more food than it seemed possible for an army to eat, but Kathy insisted it would be the best Christmas ever. The O'Dwyer sisters were overjoyed to be reunited with everyone again, and it was shaping up to be a very jolly Christmas indeed.

They'd read with horror the news from home that the Devlins wrote. The city of Cork had been burned the second week of December, and the Tans had taken great delight in looting and setting fire to all they could, then cutting the hoses of the firemen who tried to battle the blaze. Morale was high, though, despite the deprivations and hardship. The country was almost completely under martial law, but each new measure gave people courage. The British were panicking. The losses they were sustaining were relentless, small effective cells wreaking havoc up and down the country with the support of the people. Collins had even infiltrated Dublin Castle, rumour had it, and the IRA knew what the British were doing at every single juncture. The assassination of fifteen intelligence officers, the famous Cairo Gang, was met with approval. They were supposedly a crack team of G-men who would sort the Irish out once and for all, but Collins sent out his squad and executed them all simultaneously one Sunday morning. The action sent every officer in the city scurrying in behind the walls of Dublin Castle for safety. His army of waitresses, chambermaids, postmen and shopkeepers all conspired together to ensure there was nowhere for the agents of the Crown to hide. Ireland was a very dangerous place to be for anyone doing the work of the king, and that was exactly the way Collins planned it.

The reprisal was swift and horrific. Later that same day, an armoured tank drove into Croke Park, where a football match was going on. It was an important game, and the crowd was big. They opened fire, and fourteen were killed, including two children, and sixty were wounded. Later that night, three men were rounded up and beaten to death in Dublin Castle. The British said the men were trying to escape, but that was a lie. They hanged another two.

Though the reprisals were vicious, they served to galvanise the public support for the IRA still further. Nobody saw or heard anything when the police did searches or interrogated civilians. IRA operatives could melt into the crowd, and weapons were hidden in prams, under babies, in women's underskirts. The rebels were mercurial and seemingly unstoppable, and it was as plain as the noses on their faces, according to the Devlins, that the British were losing. They were on the back foot now, and all they had to do was keep up the pressure a little while longer.

Pat and Matt were working tirelessly. Matt was such an asset and was in much demand as a speaker at rallies. A section commander, who until recently was in the thick of it, had a purse-loosening effect on the diaspora, and Harp and Rose were so proud of him. He spoke calmly and with such conviction, never glamorising violence or taking any personal credit. He actively refused to tell of personal encounters with the Crown forces, but he left his audience in no doubt that their contributions mattered and were helping turn the tide of the war, and that their dollars were now and in the future going to provide the cornerstones of the new Republic. Their contributions were righting the wrongs that saw their ancestors board ships, hungry and dispossessed.

Rose, Kitty and Harp too addressed the wives of Clan na Gael members, knowing that in many cases the true decision makers of the biggest financiers of the war were the women. They were, like Matt, clear in their delivery, explaining the terror of Irishwomen, fearing for their sons and husbands but also for themselves. They didn't shy away from telling of the use of rape as a weapon by the Black and Tans, the cutting of women's hair, the tarring and feathering. They explained how boys and men were selected for execution arbitrarily, how the reprisals for all rebel activity were swift and entirely disproportionate. They delivered the reality with dignity and courage, and it made them feel at least less like they'd abandoned their fellow countrypeople.

Rose had written to the Devlins, asking the fate of their house, and they'd replied to say they'd seen to it to lock it up, cleaned it out of any foodstuffs and so on, and that they were keeping an eye on it. Brian had come down from Dublin and had closed up his father's house and had confided to Matt in a letter that he was relieved that Matt and Rose and Harp were in America; it gave him one less thing to worry about. Brian had never been told outright the nature of his father's republican activities, for his own protection, but he was not blind and could guess.

Brian tried to stay apolitical, but Matt knew that Brian had become known as a doctor you could take an injured Volunteer to in the safe knowledge that he would do his best to patch him up without involving the authorities. All injuries now had to be reported to the police, so it meant treating any injury had to be covert. Brian worked in St James's Hospital, but he saw people in his home too, under cover of darkness, and was always on hand. Harp knew the risk Brian was taking and was worried but proud of him.

Matt had had correspondence from the top echelons of the IRA to remain in the United States until further notice. Beckett's death had stirred up a hornets' nest, and Cork was already on high alert. The shooting of the Lord Mayor earlier in the year, the death of his successor, Terence MacSwiney, as a result of a hunger strike in a British jail, the ambush at Kilmichael, the burning of Cork, all made the place as explosive as a tinderbox.

As 1920 was fast approaching its close and 1921 awaited, Harp began to feel a little more optimistic. She missed home so much, but JohnJoe had confided to her that Pat and Kathy had bought her a harp for Christmas, and she couldn't wait to play it.

The four women had stopped the shopping for a break and were seated in the elegant foyer of a beautiful hotel on Copley Square. Kathy ordered coffee and sandwiches, and they took it all in. Marianne would have loved to come, but she got tired easily and decided to skip the trip. She and Danny had found a little apartment near the Raffertys' house and were inseparable. She'd gone to the hospital and been checked out, and everything was well with both mother and baby.

Harp was still astounded by the scale, the wealth, the mix of people.

'So what do we still need?' Kathy asked.

'Well, I just needed a gift for Celia, and I got her this.' Harp showed them a beautiful illustrated book of Irish fairy stories she'd bought for the Rafferty's maid. Harp and the coloured girl had become friendly when she first visited in 1916 and had remained in touch by letter ever since. Celia loved mythology, and she and Harp had enjoyed many conversations about the similarities between the stories her mother told her, that had been passed down through generations of slaves, and the ones of Irish mythology. There was a recurring theme of the child hero or the mother goddess, but the African tradition focused more heavily on animals. Harp assumed it was because animals were so much more part of the tapestry of life on that continent. She and Celia enjoyed an easy friendship together.

Harp was delighted to hear that her friend was doing a night course in dressmaking. She was a gifted seamstress and had plans to leave service once she qualified and set up a little business with the help of the Raffertys. Celia was quick to point out that they were unusual in their benevolence; the owners of most homes who employed coloured help cared nothing for their staff's personal advancement – in fact it was actively discouraged, so difficult was it to get good servants. But the Raffertys were good employers. Their butler, Clayton, a tall, imposing man with dark skin and silver curls, had been with them for over twenty years, and Mrs Dennis, the housekeeper, even longer. They were a formidable team and the house ran like clockwork, but they enjoyed the greatest respect from the family.

Kitty had tried to help around the house when she first arrived but Kathy was having none of it, so Kitty had spent the time grieving for her husband and taking care of her sister. She looked so much better than she did when Harp and JohnJoe put her on the boat in Cork all those months ago. Pat asked about Seamus all the time, mentioning his heroic contribution often and saying how proud he was of his family, Harp and Rose included, for their selfless bravery. Ever so slowly they began to hear that sound they'd missed for so long – Kitty's infectious laugh.

Rose too found the adjustment from staff to gentlewoman a bit unsettling and kept trying to help Mrs Dennis, offers which were politely and kindly rebuffed. The Rafferty house was large and there was enough room for everyone, but Harp knew Rose and Matt felt in the way. They were used to living under their own terms, and while Harp thought her mother was enjoying being open about her relationship with Matt, she knew Rose found living in the Raffertys' house rather strange. Rose and Matt had been given a large double room when they arrived, and nobody had remarked upon it. Harp didn't care, but she knew her mother was a little embarrassed about sharing a bed so openly with a man she wasn't married to. But this was Boston, not Cobh, and people didn't care too much about other people's business as far as Harp could tell.

'Oh, that's beautiful! She'll love that.' Kathy admired the book. 'That reminds me, she's making a new Christmas tablecloth and I need to get some embroidery thread for it. How about I go off and do that and you ladies carry on shopping and I'll see you at home?'

Kitty got up too. 'And I promised Jane I'd get her some dark-blue ribbon, so I'll come with you, Aunt Kathy, if that's all right?'

Harp smiled to see the beam on Kathy Rafferty's face. All she'd ever wanted was a family of her own, and now she had it. Her beloved boys were home, bringing the Irish entourage with them, not to mention that she was soon to become a grandmother to all intents and purposes as well.

Rose and Harp were grateful for the opportunity to be alone together; solitude was a rare commodity in Boston. JohnJoe and Danny had returned to work for Pat so were out most of the day. Matt had offered his carpentry services too, but Pat preferred to use Matt's talents in meeting influential people and encouraging support for the Irish cause. While he saw the benefits, Rose had confided to Harp that Matt would rather be doing manual work. He was good at bolstering nationalism in the sons and grandsons of immigrants, but it wasn't his natural environment.

They finished their coffees and Kathy bid them goodbye.

'Alone at last.' Rose smiled. 'They are so lovely – Kathy is every bit as nice as I knew she would be from her letters – but I feel like we have no time together, just us two.'

'Yes, they're so kind and welcoming, but it feels a bit intense, doesn't it?'

Her mother nodded. 'Kitty and Jane are very happy there, but they're family. I'm delighted for them, and I know there's lots of space, but I do wish we had a little place of our own. I cringe as Clayton calls me "ma'am" and waits on me. Once a servant, always a servant, I suppose.'

'Do you miss the Cliff House very much?'

'I really do. I know the Devlins are taking care of it, but some days I wonder if we'll ever get home again. Matt would be picked up the moment he set foot on Irish soil. I know everyone keeps saying we just need to persevere, but I do sometimes wonder, will we ever go home again?' Rose's eyes glittered with unshed tears. 'I know we should be grateful, and I am, so much, for the Raffertys. Goodness knows what would have happened if they'd not sent the boat for us. But I just want to live a peaceful life in Cobh.'

Harp smiled at her mother's use of the new name. It was yet another thing that was infuriating the British in the town, how the locals refused to call it Queenstown any more.

'I remember sitting in the window of the upstairs library, on that little seat Henry made for me. I must have only been five or six, and I was painting. He told me about Queen Victoria, and how she visited in 1849 with her husband. He said that she painted a landscape of the islands and the harbour from the deck of the royal yacht, and behind her, on the quayside, the hungry, ragged masses who were lucky enough to scrape together the price of a steerage ticket, were making their way to the coffin ships. She was the reason it happened. She allowed the shipping of grain and meat and butter from that exact same harbour while the people starved.'

'I'm glad we don't call it Queenstown any more, though it feels odd.'

Harp stood. 'Will we walk some more?'

She and her mother had had enough shopping, being naturally much more frugal than their munificent American hostess, whose lavish and open-hearted gifts had embarrassed Rose. They were happy just to stroll and soak up the atmosphere. It hadn't snowed yet, but it was bitingly cold. Kathy made sure that they were all adequately dressed for the weather, and Celia and a local seamstress had worked tirelessly on a wardrobe for each of them.

They passed a beautiful red-bricked church, its façade opening onto the street. In the doorway were a bride and her new husband. Their family and friends threw rice, and the church bells rang.

'Why don't you and Matt get married here?' Harp suddenly asked.

'What?' Rose was bemused.

'Well, you want to marry, don't you? And the only reason you didn't was because it would have been dangerous for anyone to be Matt's family because of what he was doing. But that doesn't matter now, and at least you could live as man and wife.'

Rose coloured. 'I'm sorry, Harp, does it embarrass you that Matt and I...'

Harp laughed. 'Mammy, you're the prim and proper one of the two of us. I couldn't care less. I am a liberal young woman with a mind and body of her own. I read D. H. Lawrence and James Joyce, so I have no such qualms. But I know you'd rather be respectable, so why not marry him? You love him, he loves you, so what's stopping you?'

Rose laughed, a sound that Harp had loved since she was a child. 'Please tell me that you'd rather be respectable too,' her mother said, her eyebrow arched reproachfully.

Harp suspected Rose knew that her and JohnJoe's relationship was more physical than was proper for a girl and her beau. Harp winked. 'I care nothing for respectability, honestly I don't. I never fitted in anyway, so it's utterly pointless to try. I'm reading a wonderful American essayist at the moment – Pat had his book in the library – Ralph Waldo Emerson. And he said to be yourself in a world that is constantly trying to make you something else is the greatest accomplishment.'

'So is this your way of telling me that you and young Mr O'Dwyer are not adhering to the rules of engagement for young courting couples?' Rose asked.

Harp smiled. She and JohnJoe had a wonderful connection, mental, emotional and physical, and she refused to be made to feel bad about it. They were careful to ensure no baby arrived as a result, but she saw her body, and his, as wondrous things of joy and pleasure.

'Say no more,' her mother admonished. 'I should berate you, I suppose, and give JohnJoe a stern talking-to, but given my history, what I'm doing now and after everything we've endured, that seems silly. Be very careful, though, won't you? Life is still hard for a girl on her own with a child and no husband. I should know.'

'We are. Don't worry. Do you wish things had been different?' Harp asked as they passed the wedding party and linked arms as they strolled along, the bright lights of shops selling unimaginable treasures illuminating the darkening day.

'In what way?'

'Having me, staying single, Ralph, Henry, all of it.'

Rose stopped and turned to face her daughter as the first fluttering of dry snow began to fall silently. Harp thought she looked like an angel, with her dark-blue coat with the fur collar framing her face, the dark hair and expressive eyes that had made many more men than Henry Devereaux and Matt Quinn fall for her, though she never knew it.

'Harp Devereaux, I can't believe you could ever ask me that. Having you in my life as my daughter has been the greatest privilege, and I am so lucky to have you. This whole thing, Ralph, the British, Pennington – the only thing that truly terrifies me is the idea of anything happening to you. So no, I regret nothing, and if I had my time to do over, I would do it exactly the same way, because to do anything different would have meant you would not be the you I know and love so much.'

Harp gazed at her mother. 'I love you too. Now, will you please marry Matt Quinn rather than behaving like some kind of Madame Bovary?'

Rose rolled her eyes. 'I haven't read that, but I assume she's some kind of a harlot?'

Harp chuckled. 'She's not really, but she does cause scandal.'

'Anyway, I can't marry him even if I wanted to.'

'Why not, for goodness' sake?' Harp found her mother so intractable sometimes.

'Because he hasn't officially asked me.' Rose smiled triumphantly.

'Pah, and we're supposed to sit around like wallflowers at a dance, waiting to be asked, is that it? Why don't you ask him?'

That laugh again. 'I might be from a different century to you, but there's no way I would ever do that, however modern you might want me to be.'

Harp knew her mother was right. Falling pregnant at seventeen gave her two routes: live as would be expected of a girl of low moral character, shunned and despised, or rise so far above the sneers and the underhanded comments as to force people to accept her respectability. Rose had chosen the much more difficult road, and through her sheer determination to be respected, she was. The price for this was to live an exemplary life in that community, above moral reproach.

Though they were thousands of miles away and nobody knew the sleeping arrangements of the Rafferty household anyway except the inhabitants and staff, who couldn't care less, Harp knew the impropriety weighed on her mother. But so too would asking a man to marry her.

'I suppose so,' Harp agreed with a sigh.

'Maybe you and JohnJoe will tie the knot instead?' Rose asked.

'No.' Harp was decisive. 'I have no need of a husband. Marriage enslaves women. Now I need no permission from anyone to live my life as I choose. I'm a adult and I can make my own decisions. If I marry, I suddenly lose that autonomy and become the property of my husband. I could never agree to that. JohnJoe and I are together because we choose to be, not because some law dictates it. Or because we have bent to the laws of polite society. We're equals and that's the only way I could be with him.'

'And what about what JohnJoe wishes?' Rose asked quietly.

'He feels the same way.'

'Hmm. Does he, I wonder?' Rose wasn't convinced.

CHAPTER 31

*P*at Rafferty sat at the head of the huge table and caught Harp's eye. She knew he was delighted to have them there. Danny and JohnJoe were back, so both he and Kathy were relieved. He'd confided to her just how much they'd missed them in the four years they'd been away. Kitty and Jane were settling in so well, and though Jane still didn't say much, she was growing into a confident, calm young lady. Kathy had arranged for her to go to school when she arrived, and she loved it; Jane was by far the most intellectual of the O'Dwyer children. Pat had even brokered a kind of peace with their aunt in England and her vicar husband, so while relations would never be described as warm or cordial, at least there was a thaw.

Kitty was very active in the Clan na Gael women's branch now, and kept in touch with her former Cumann na mBan sisters at home.

Matt sat beside Rose, and while Harp knew he was itching to get back to Ireland, he was relieved the people he cared about were safe. They spoke often and he told her that Brian was always on his mind, but he was confident his son was intelligent enough to stay out of trouble, and besides, Matt had people keeping an eye on him in Dublin.

Attempts were being made at a truce, and the rumour and counter-rumour mill was in full flow. Matt had it on good authority that the British were anxious to make peace, that they'd had enough. And the only peace that would be tolerated from the Irish side was a complete and immediate withdrawal of all Crown forces from Irish soil, permanently.

Pat tapped the side of his glass to get a bit of quiet. 'Hey, you two, pipe down.' He pointed at Danny and Marianne, who were laughing at a joke JohnJoe had told them. It was good to see them so happy.

Everyone was dressed in their finery, and Harp noticed what a handsome bunch they made. She still didn't believe her mother's and JohnJoe's assertions that she was beautiful, but the others certainly were. JohnJoe's arrival home had caused a flurry of invitations from the ladies of Boston, and Harp could sense their disappointment when they discovered that he was spoken for. If Kathy or Pat harboured dreams that he'd settle down with a nice local girl, they never showed it.

She knew JohnJoe had no regrets, and when she arrived downstairs in the scarlet-red dress Celia had made for her, his eyes told her all she needed to know. He looked very handsome, and she felt proud to be his girl.

She sometimes wondered if it would have been better to meet him later in her life, to sow their wild oats first, but he laughed when she suggested it, claiming she was wild enough for him.

'Family, friends, I just want to say a few words.' Pat's resonant voice filled the now-silent room. 'I would like, on behalf of Kathy and myself, to welcome you to our home, and to assure you that there is no time limit on the invitation. We're delighted to have you all. We've had four lonely Christmases here since the boys left for Ireland, and while we are inordinately proud of them and all they achieved over there, I would be lying if I said I wasn't thrilled they are home safe and sound.'

Kathy was seated between JohnJoe and Danny, and she held their hands, one either side.

'Thank you as always to Clayton, Mrs Dennis and all of the staff for taking such good care of us, and you'll find some gifts downstairs under the tree for you all to open after your own Christmas feast.'

Celia had explained to Harp how the servants' Christmas dinner was served after the family's and how once they'd eaten, the family usually came downstairs and there was dancing and fun. Harp couldn't wait; it sounded marvellous and egalitarian and typical of the Raffertys.

'Thanks to my wife, the beautiful Mrs Katherine Rafferty, who has the light put back in her eyes now by not one but two other men.'

There was a rumble of laugher around the table.

'I know I was a very poor substitute for her boys all these years. Kathy, you're the reason I've lived and continue to live the life of the happiest man on earth. And all of this' – he waved around the beautifully decorated room and at the sumptuous feast – 'is her doing too. If it was left to me, we'd be having hot dogs and French fries.'

'Was that an option?' JohnJoe quipped, and Kathy swiped him playfully. She was always trying to broaden their palates, but the Rafferty men preferred plain food. It was a running joke.

'And finally I want to raise a toast to a very special young woman who showed such bravery and intelligence. If Miss Harp Devereaux had not visited Alexander Jackson that day in Cobh, and impressed upon him the parallels between the Founding Fathers of this great American nation and those patriots who are trying to do the same job in Ireland, he might never have contacted me and this could be a very different Christmas. But she did, and her words saved lives, no doubt about it. To Harp.' He raised his glass.

The entire table chorused, 'To Harp.'

'So here's to a merry Christmas. May 1921 bring us health and happiness and, with the help of the Almighty, our dearest and most fervent wish, to see our homeland free.'

'To Ireland free,' they all chorused and clinked their glasses.

Harp saw her mother glance at Matt, and an unspoken conversation passed between them. Then she noticed it, the glint on her mother's hand.

Matt stood up. 'On behalf of the Cobh contingent, I can't thank you enough, Pat and Kathy, for all you've done for us. If you'd not come to our rescue when you did, well, I doubt that some of us at least would be alive now, and that's the truth. The importance of your support throughout the struggle can't ever be underestimated. And the Irish Americans of the future will know how much their fathers and mothers have contributed to the freedom of Ireland. It will happen…' His eyes burned with intensity.

Harp realised she loved him. His gentle presence, his wry humour, his capable ways had been a feature of her life since Henry's death when she was twelve. It occurred to her that while her natural father was an appalling man, life had seen fit to offer her not one but two exceptional men as father figures, and she was truly blessed to have them both.

'Have no doubt, capitulation of the Crown forces in Ireland is imminent. And while it is frustrating to wait and watch from the sidelines, it is the only option for us right now.' He glanced at Rose, who gave him a smile; it visibly relaxed him.

'Now if you'll indulge me for a moment more. In 1912, a young woman and her daughter engaged me to attend on the funeral of Mr Henry Devereaux. It was a cold day, despite it being springtime, and as they stood by the graveside of a man that few people knew at all, and only two knew well, I watched them and something happened inside of me.'

Harp was astonished. Matt held the table enthralled. He was not a man to openly discuss anything personal, so everyone was intrigued.

'My wife died when Brian was a boy and so it was just my son and me all those years. But watching Rose that day, so dignified in her grief – well, I don't know. Something happened.' He smiled. 'We became friends, and I tried to help her as best I could. That draughty, leaky old house was in a bad way, but through sheer hard work and determination, she turned it around, and with it, her own and Harp's futures. Despite the fact that I had fallen deeply in love with her, I never imagined we could ever be more than friends. I wasn't in a position to offer her anything, and my position within the Volunteers would make her vulnerable should I be captured.'

Everyone's eyes were on him. The tension of living under British rule had etched deep lines on his handsome face, but today he looked relaxed and happy.

He turned to gaze at Rose. 'I love this woman, and I have done for eight years. I will love her to the day I draw my last breath, and so when I asked her to marry me last night, it was to my supreme relief she agreed.'

The table erupted, and soon Rose and Matt were caught up in a series of hugs and handshakes. Clayton was instructed to pop the champagne, and soon everyone was toasting the happy couple.

'Congratulations, Mammy,' Harp whispered, hugging her mother. 'Who did the asking?'

Rose laughed and kissed Harp's cheek. 'We asked each other. Is that good enough for you?'

'It is for now.' Harp grinned. '"Now all we need is to continue to speak the truth fearlessly, and we shall add to our number those who will turn the scale to the side of equal and full justice in all things,"' she quoted.

'I know that one. It's Lucy Stone,' Matt said from behind her.

'It is.' Harp turned and hugged the man who would become her stepfather. 'Welcome to the family, Matt,' she said, and he held her in a tight hug. 'I wish Brian could be here.'

'I do too,' Matt said. 'I sent him a telegram yesterday, when we decided, and he replied that it was about time for us, so I think he's happy.'

The meal continued in high merriment, and everyone was in great spirits. Kitty and Jane were a little more subdued than the others, but they managed to get into the spirit of things.

'So are we talking about a Boston wedding?' Kathy asked, topping up everyone's glass. 'Because I have some great ideas.'

Pat rolled his eyes in mock despair. 'There goes this year's profit.'

'I think we will get married here. Matt and I have talked about it, and we'd like to marry as soon as possible. But really a low-key, no-fuss wedding is what we'd like. You've all done so much for us already...'

'Absolutely, low-key, for sure.' Kathy winked. Her lustrous red bobbed hair and perfect make-up made her look like something from a magazine, but Rose and Harp both knew that behind the façade, she was an extremely kind person.

'How about we make it a double wedding?' Danny asked.

Marianne's face lit up.

'Have you asked her?' Pat asked with a grin.

Danny turned to Marianne. 'What do ya say, Marianne? You wanna get hitched?'

'Danny Coveney, I did not raise you to propose like that!' Kathy announced indignantly, much to everyone's delight.

'OK, OK...' Danny took a piece of tinsel from the table setting and knelt before Marianne. 'Will you marry me, please?'

'We'd love to.' Marianne giggled, one hand on her rapidly swelling abdomen. Danny tied the piece of tinsel around her finger, and the entire table burst into applause.

JohnJoe's hand found Harp's under the table. 'How about us, since everyone else is doing it?' he joked, knowing her feelings very well.

'"Men marry because they are tired; women because they are curious: both are disappointed."'

'And we're taking marriage advice from Oscar Wilde now, are we?' He chuckled.

'Fair point,' Harp conceded. 'Maybe someday, when we're old and grey, we'll surprise everyone and get married.'

'I'll wait,' JohnJoe said, his eyes locked with hers.

EPILOGUE

*T*o his astonishment, the key still worked. He was sure that conniving wretch Rose would have changed the locks, but then she was probably quite certain her hired thugs had seen him off for good.

The house was clean and smelled quite pleasant considering it had been empty for a while. Someone had been in and covered the furniture and closed the shutters. It was dark at this time of the evening, and he found a box of matches and lit the gas lamps. The tiled floor of the hallway had not changed since the house was built, and the bannister of the large winding staircase gleamed from years of beeswax polish.

'It could be rather lovely, I suppose, in time,' Pamela remarked as she followed him through to the dining room, her heels clicking on the ceramic tiles. 'It is exciting, though, to finally be in your family seat.'

The first thing he saw when he entered was a hideous portrait of Rose, Harp and his brother, Henry. They must have sat for it at some stage or something. Well, that would be the first thing to go, followed closely by all signs of the previous inhabitants and the remains of the house as a guest house. His mother would be turning in her grave to see all sorts of riffraff paying to sleep under her roof. His eyes fell on the harp, standing in the bay window. He would take great pleasure in taking an axe to it, though he should probably sell it. Knowing that fool Henry bought it for Harp meant it was most likely valuable. Either way, it wasn't staying; none of it was. He would keep the books, or possibly have a dealer come and make him an offer on the most valuable ones and he could pocket that privately. Pam insisted that he control their finances, but it was good to have a little put by for emergencies all the same.

Pamela knew that his origins, while illustrious, were not as grand as she was used to, but she loved him hopelessly and so was clearly trying her best to sound enthusiastic. He could have sold her on the house more easily if it had been summer and five years ago. But this wondrous opportunity had landed in his lap now, and the opportunity of a lifetime had to be taken in the lifetime of the opportunity. Admittedly Ireland at this juncture in history was an unpleasant, dangerous place, but surely it was just a matter of time before Lloyd George really got serious about crushing the rabble and sorted the place out for once and for all. Still, the unrest had brought about his good fortune, so the whole thing was ideal really. Once he heard that Rose and her vulgar, working-class entourage had scuttled off to America, he thought there was only one thing to do: press his advantage. Beckett was dead and of Marianne there was no sign. Possession was nine tenths of the law, and he now possessed the Cliff House. Never again would that treacherous witch or her peculiar brat cross the threshold. This was a Devereaux house and a Devereaux house it would remain.

To his delight, Quinn and the Americans were getting the blame for Beckett's murder and that of a patrol of Cameron Highlanders. Rose, Harp and Quinn were also firmly back in the frame for the murder of Pennington, so they could never set foot in Ireland again if they valued their necks. It had all turned out so much better than he could even have hoped.

He and Pamela had married in the registry office in London, thus securing him financially, and now he had his home back as well.

Pamela had not been keen on the Ireland idea, but he gave her a load of old guff about his parents and feeling close to them. He said it was the only place he could truly be happy and that it was just a quick visit, and of course she'd succumbed.

'And the woman who lived here...?' Pamela asked again. He'd always been deliberately vague on the subject.

'Has left, for America, I believe. She was just a servant who was taking care of the place for me.' He dismissed her with a wave of his hand. 'Anyway, it doesn't matter. We're here and we're going to live happily ever after in my family home. What a spectacular view.' He opened the shutters.

The rising moon illuminated the harbour below as the stars twinkled overhead. Despite the cold, he felt a thrill of delight. He was back where he belonged, in the house that should have been his all along, not in the hands of that tart and her bastard child, with enough money to fund the lifestyle he wanted, in a place where his name meant something. Where *he* meant something.

Since his mother sent him away as a boy of twenty for some silly indiscretion with a married woman and a few guineas of debt – she was always one for overreacting – he'd wandered the world, barely getting by, enduring all manner of humiliations. His mother had never intended that for him. She loved him, so much more than Henry. His papa did too, though Henry was such an oddball that it wouldn't have been hard. But his parents loved him, and this was the life they wanted for him. They were kindhearted and resisted putting his brother in an institution where he belonged, but it was Ralph who'd paid the price. Finally justice was done and he was where he should be.

The winter sun had set, and the garden glistened with the frost that had not melted all day. They could see their breath on the air. Winter-flowering witch hazel and clematis grew in profusion, and he was glad that the garden had been so well tended over the years. It would be an easy job for someone to bring it back under control.

'Well, we'll need to get it warmed up if we're going to stay here for a while.' Pamela hugged herself through her long fur coat he'd bought her, with her money obviously. She had travelled to Ireland on the premise of a short trip, but the sooner she realised it was going to be extended, the better. He didn't need her constantly carping about going back to India. If he never set foot in that hellhole for the rest of his life, it would be too soon. Ralph had no intention of ever leaving Queenstown.

'Indeed we will, my love.' He put his arms around her and kissed her.

'Should we not stay in the hotel in town until we can get this house open and running? I thought we were only making a flying visit, but if it means that much to you to stay for a few weeks, then that's what we shall do. But we will need somebody. I mean, we have no staff even...'

'We certainly will, and I know you'll be such an asset to me in that regard – you know about such matters so much better than I do. I could book you into the Queen's. Bridges, the manager, is a friend of mine actually. We'll do that, my darling, if it's what you really want.' Ralph always spoke as if the money he spent were his own. 'I'll stay here. It would feel too strange to be here in this town and not sleep in my own house, but I completely understand that it might be too cold for you. I couldn't bear for you to be uncomfortable, so I'll manage alone.'

He saw her weigh it up. Since hearing of her daughter's disappearance, Pamela had been distraught and needy. It was ideal really, because now that she was free of Alfie and his debt, she could become prey for fortune hunters, and he had to make sure he gave her enough affection to stick around but not enough for her to become complacent. The restoration of this house to the manner he wanted it would be costly, and staffing it appropriately too would not be cheap, but Pamela could more than afford it.

'No, of course I'll stay with you.' She sighed.

'Oh, my dear, will you?' He infused his voice with loving gratitude and was rewarded with her indulgent smile. 'You're so kind. I know it's not as we'd want it just yet. There's a terrible pall of commerciality over it all. Do you know she used to keep it as a boarding house?' He shuddered distastefully.

'Yes, Marianne stayed here and was very happy. Everyone was kind to her here.'

Ralph felt that familiar dread. Another sobbing fit, no doubt. Honestly, the woman was tedious. The girl was gone, sure, but these things happened. Could she not just get on with it?

'Of course, I had forgotten.' He drew her in for a hug and kissed the top of her head. 'I'm glad the staff of my home were kind to dear Marianne. She deserved every consideration. I...I'm sure you'll hear from her one of these days...' His voice cracked a little.

'I know, and it means so much to me that you miss her too. But what if she's dead?'

'We'd have heard, wouldn't we?' Ralph said for the hundredth time. 'Beckett's body was found, but hers never was.'

'But what if those rebels took her and she was never heard from again...'

'She's a force of nature, Marianne Pascoe – I'll always think of her as a Pascoe, and how you and she could arrive to any event in Shimla and turn every head in the room. The Pascoe ladies were legendary for their beauty, their charm and their wit. Marianne was one of the funniest women I ever met.' In this instance he wasn't actually lying; Marianne had a very funny way of seeing the world and could be quite acidic on occasion, which he always enjoyed. 'I'm sure she's fine, and when she's ready, she will make contact.' He used this line of chat sparingly, but it was a dead cert every time.

'I just love her. She's my daughter and carrying my grandchild. I adore her, Ralph. I think I'm going out of my mind with worry.'

'I know you do. She's adored,' he soothed. *So much so that you shipped her out to boarding school as fast as it was decent, her father gambled her in a card game, and you talked her into marrying some cretin because you didn't want her around, getting in your way.*

'I miss her so much, Ralph. It's like a physical pain, the loss of her,' Pamela whined. 'If I didn't have you, I would be so adrift in the world, so alone.'

'You'll never be alone, my love. I will always be here.'

'She did love it here, the garden especially. She spoke about it often in her letters.'

Of course he'd not forgotten the connection between the Becketts and this house, and if there was any way he could foster a love in Pamela of the place, it would be through the possibility of Marianne turning up again. 'Perhaps we could ask around, maybe even get a private detective to look for her...'

Pamela's eyes welled. Honestly the woman was like a leaky tap these days.

'Ralph, you are one of the kindest, most generous, most thoughtful men I ever met. How did I get so lucky as to have you?'

'I feel like I'm the one that won the prize.' He kissed her damp eyes, wiping the tears with his thumbs. She loved that and was like putty in his hands then.

'You are so decent and honourable. You're not like anyone I've ever met.'

'Well, you're the heiress who took on half a man.' He nodded ruefully at his leg with the prosthetic strapped on.

'You are not half a man. I won't ever listen to you say that. You're a war hero, dedicated to serving king and country, and a wonderful man to boot.' She snuggled into his chest, placing her hands inside his jacket. 'I can think of a way to warm up,' she murmured. 'We can set about getting staff and so on tomorrow. The brigadier they've sent to replace Oliver here is an old friend of Papa's and was there when he met Mama. Lady Ardington told me last week when I took tea with her at Claridge's. I'm sure he'll help us.'

'Of course. And you'll soon get to know the wives of the officers and the local families of our class, and you'll have this place running like clockwork in no time.'

'But is it not frightfully dangerous, Ralph? I know we said we'd visit, and we will of course, but perhaps we should not be making any permanent plans just for now. Then we could go home to Shimla, let everything settle down here, and come back for visits.'

It was time for Ralph to show his hand, the final stroke. 'Of course we can, my darling, if that is what you wish, but I have had it from

some of my connections here, old army chaps, that they might be able
to track Marianne down.'

Pamela deliberated and looked around the cold house.

He suppressed an inner sigh of exasperation. Marianne was a
trollop who had her way with that slimy Yank and expected her
husband to accept the consequences. She played with fire and got
burned, simple as that. Perhaps the IRA had done away with her.
Frankly he couldn't care less, but it was good leverage with Pamela so
he'd feign concern for as long as it suited him.

He was almost there, he could feel it, but there was a slight hesita-
tion still. He played his last card. 'Marianne loves you, she knows
you're with me, and she loves this house, my house. Where else would
she turn up if she decides she wants to?'

'I suppose you're right. I told her I was selling the Shimla house to
pay off Alfie's debts, so that's gone.'

'So we're home?' He used his best pleading smile, head to one side,
vulnerable puppy eyes. It had taken years to perfect but worked every
time.

Her face melted as it always did. 'Yes, my darling Ralph, we're
home.'

* * *

THE END.

I SINCERELY HOPE you enjoyed this book. If you did I would delighted
if you would leave me a review.

In which case you might be happy to know that the fourth book in
this series, *Roaring Liberty*, is now available now:

Roaring Liberty

HERE'S a sneak preview of the first two chapters....

. . .

Chapter 1

JUNE 1921, BOSTON, MASSACHUSETTS

'What is it?' Matt said as Harp looked up from her book and watched the colour drain from her mother's face and knew instantly something was very wrong. Outside, the bustle of activity as the city came to life on Shore Road, Boston, was loud despite the early hour.

Rose dropped the letter on her plate, right on top of her scrambled eggs and toast. She gazed at Matt and opened her mouth as if to speak, but no words came out.

'Rose, what is it?' he urged.

The bright morning sun shone through the window of their first-floor apartment over O'Malley's Boots and Shoes. They'd moved in the day before St Patrick's Day, finally leaving the hospitality of the Raffertys in favour of a modest yet comfortable home of their own.

It was nothing like the Cliff House, their home in Cobh, County Cork, and it was a far cry from the sumptuous surroundings of the Raffertys, but their two-bedroomed place, with a large kitchen and living room combined, was pleasant and cheerful and served their purposes perfectly.

'Mammy?' Even from across the table, Harp could see the letter was in Liz Devlin's handwriting, a sloping copperplate. But a letter from the Devlin sisters wasn't unusual. 'Mammy, what's the matter?'

Rose swallowed, visibly steadying herself. 'Ralph Devereaux and Marianne's mother have moved into the Cliff House. They're behaving as if they own it. Pamela's redecorating the whole place, and they're hobnobbing with the gentry and the British as if they have every right in the world to be in our home.'

'What?' Harp was shocked. 'Is Liz sure? I thought Ralph and Pamela were in India? That's where Marianne has been sending her letters. No wonder she's heard nothing back. I can't believe this!'

Grimly, Rose passed Liz's missive to her daughter, the pale-blue notepaper now stained with eggs and butter. Harp scanned the neatly written words. Liz was brief and to the point. Ralph had turned up one night, not long after Harp and Rose made a speedy getaway from Ireland in a hail of gunfire, and installed himself in their house. He was telling everyone that it had always been his and that he had only allowed them to stay on out of the goodness of his heart. When he was challenged by Mr Bridges in the hotel, who mentioned that Harp had been bequeathed the house by the late Henry Devereaux when he named her as his daughter and heir, Ralph had scoffed and said in the hotel bar for all to hear, 'If you recall my poor departed brother, he was hardly capable of a coherent sentence, let alone a romantic tryst with the maid. No, he was soft in the heart as well as the head, and his housekeeper clearly tricked him. But it's all been sorted out by the legal chaps now and I'm home in my family's house, so all is as it should be.' The crowd, apart from Bridges, had been receptive to him. They were British officers and Protestant gentry, and it seemed they accepted his version of events.

Matt, who had been sitting in furious silence, pounded his fist on the table. 'The sheer gall of that man! How dare he!'

'And there's nothing we can do.' Rose tried to fight back the tears, but her voice was choked.

'There is,' Matt said darkly. 'I could go back to Ireland to sort him out for once and for all.'

Rose's eyes blazed. 'We've talked about this, Matt. You are *not* going back. You have orders to remain here, you know you have, and surely you're not going to defy Collins himself? You would be a very valuable prize to the British, and they'd take great pleasure in extracting whatever information they could from you under torture before they hang you, so you have to stay. You know too much.'

'Mammy's right, Matt,' Harp said kindly. She was furious herself but was doing her best not to show it, not wanting to make matters worse. 'I know how frustrating it is to have to sit it out here in America when you want to be back there, in the thick of it, but you're doing valuable work, talking to the Irish here, ensuring they know

how their dollars are being spent. Pat Rafferty says the take of dona-
tions is double what it was before you came, so you're not doing nothing, you know.'

Matt ran his hands through his once sandy now mostly silver hair
in frustration. To go from being the commander of a squadron of the
IRA, engaging and winning against the Crown forces every day, to
making fundraising speeches in Boston was not what he wanted, they
all knew that, but lives depended on him staying where he was.

'But to think of him, in your house, Rose and Harp... I... It makes
me so angry. He was the one that told Beckett about that night with
Pennington, he's the reason I'm exiled, and now he gets to play lord of
the manor...'

'I know.' Rose placed her hand on her husband's. 'I can't bear it
either, but bear it we must, it seems. And it won't be forever. The war
with the British is surely coming to an end, and when we win, Ralph
Devereaux and his kind will find life very uncomfortable indeed.
People have long memories, and those that made Irish lives hell
when they had the British to back them up will suddenly find themselves alone and vulnerable. Ralph is a coward at heart, so he'll leave
soon enough. Harp will get her house back. We just have to be
patient.'

Harp thought her mother had blossomed in the months they'd
been in Boston. She had always been a beautiful woman, there was no
doubting that, but her dark-brown hair seemed more luxuriant of late
and her skin was glowing. She did have deepening lines on her face –
she was thirty-nine years old, and the last few years had taken their
toll. Still, her eyes were the same, warm and brown, even if there were
signs of crow's feet around them.

'I just want to go back alone, deal with him myself.' Matt spoke
quietly.

Rose sighed. 'I can't have this out again. Matt, please. I know
you're angry – so am I – but we're under orders to remain here. We
have to do as we've been instructed. I want to go home as much as you
do, but we have to wait it out.'

'So we just let him grab everything that Henry left to you and

Harp, let him walk in and take it over after all your hard work?' A vein in his temple pulsed.

Harp and Rose exchanged a glance that spoke volumes. Matt was upset about the house, but there was more. He hated Devereaux for all he'd done. It was personal.

'What choice have we, Matt?' asked Rose gently. 'He's clearly in with the British, he's well known to all the local gentry families, so they'll welcome him with open arms, and you know the IRA doesn't want to touch Ralph Devereaux for now. He's not a military target, and no one has ever proved he's a spy. He's just an evil, selfish individual. We have to be patient.'

'It's hard to be patient, Rose. I know you're confident of a truce, or some end to hostilities, but what if that's just wishful thinking? They've had us in their grip for eight hundred years – maybe they won't ever give us up.'

'They will, Matt. You know yourself the losses they are suffering aren't sustainable. Public opinion is turning over there and Britain has had enough of war and death and destruction, so it's just a matter of time. But until it happens, you must carry on as you are – and Harp and JohnJoe as well. They've raised so much money for the cause, with their beautiful singing and Harp's playing. The three of you are in more demand than ever. Wait until the truce, and then we can all go home to where we belong.'

Boston was a beautiful city, and it was a joy to live in peace after all they'd endured – and the Raffertys had been so welcoming, nothing was a problem – but Harp knew her mother and Matt were just filling in time. They had physically moved to the United States, but their hearts were still in Ireland and always would be.

Harp didn't say it, but she felt differently. America was rapidly becoming home to her, and she loved the freedom and forward thinking of her new adopted country. Compared with Ireland, she found people were less judgemental, less interested in the doings of their neighbours, and it was a refreshing change. The control of society that was wielded by the Catholic Church in Ireland was something she'd always found suffocating, and there was no space in Irish society for people who were outside of their influence. The Protestants were allowed to live alongside them, but she and Henry Devereaux – one born Catholic, the other Protestant, but neither a believer – were seen as misfits, yet another reason she never felt like she belonged in Cobh. Here, many people were religious, but there was such a broad spectrum of churches and belief systems that none felt as if it had a monopoly. And even the Irish she knew were not as subjugated as Catholics back at home. The Raffertys, for example, went to Mass at Easter and Christmas, and funerals and weddings were held in a church, but the Church didn't seem to impact anyone's daily life. Harp thought back to the days in Cobh, when the priest would rant on a Sunday morning about people being drunk, even going so far as to name names, denouncing anyone who stood outside the church at Mass, or who was not following the 'fish on Fridays' rule. Girls wearing the latest fashions of shorter skirts, common now after the war, were told their mortal souls were in danger, and that they were deliberately tempting men with their harlot-like ways. No blame was laid at the door of men on that subject either – it was always the woman's fault. Every word, thought and action of the people of Ireland were monitored and commented upon by the clergy, and Harp was glad to be out of their oppressive grasp.

She was also enjoying her music. For her, it wasn't only about the fundraising, although she realised how important that was. Playing her harp and singing were also deeply fulfilling on a personal level. She and JohnJoe were so happy when they were performing together. The truth was, she and JohnJoe were blissfully happy when they were doing anything together.

She knew Matt and Rose were anxious to make a home of their own back in Ireland, but she also realised Rose wasn't ready to let her daughter go just yet. Harp had tried a few times to raise the topic, but her mother just assumed Harp would go back with them when the time came.

The horn of the lorry beeped outside. It was JohnJoe, Danny and the others picking Matt up for his new day job. Pat Rafferty had won a contract to restore a beautiful old hotel and had been having trouble finding enough skilled carpenters, so Matt had offered his services. The fundraisers and speeches were usually at night or on the week-ends, so working for Pat filled the days. Now Matt stood, gathered his tobacco and matches and took his cap and jacket from the hook by the door. 'This is too much, Rose, too much by far.' He kissed her cheek and left.

Harp waited until he was gone before speaking. For Matt's sake, she had been holding back her anger, but now she felt free to express it. 'Can you stomach the idea of that man in the Cliff House, lording it over everyone, Marianne's stupid mother on his arm?'

She hated Ralph even though he was her biological father, not Henry. Thank goodness the awful man had no idea that his brief dalliance twenty-two years ago with the maid, a very young and impressionable Rose, had resulted in Harp. Only those closest to her knew the truth. And that was exactly how Harp wanted it to stay. Ralph meant nothing to her but trouble. She took a fierce bite of her toast.

Rose shook her head. 'You shouldn't say that about Marianne's mother, Harp. Pamela might not be stupid –'

'She married Ralph – need we have further proof?' Harp replied sardonically. She knew from Marianne that Pamela was mad for Ralph and would do anything to marry him. She'd obviously got her wish, though Harp was sure Ralph just saw a wealthy widow. Taking over the Cliff House was one thing, but a house like that cost money to run and Ralph was totally work-shy, so he'd need to find the funds somewhere. Harp was fairly sure Pamela Pascoe, with her Pascoe family trust fund, was his meal ticket. 'I suppose she's letting him have all Marianne's inheritance. Her father might have been a hopeless gambler, but her grandfather was the one who made that money, and by all accounts he was a shrewd businessman. And Pamela has money of her own as well, according to Marianne, more inheritance. But if Ralph gets his greedy paws on any of it, she can kiss it all goodbye. Thank goodness Marianne and Danny are doing well enough for it not to matter.'

'The whole thing makes my blood boil too,' admitted Rose. 'But you'll get your house back when the war ends. He's made too many enemies to stay in Ireland. I know Matt finds it hard to believe, after all the endless fighting, but I can't help hoping they will come to some arrangement soon. It's hurting everyone too much.'

Harp wasn't sure Ralph would let go of the house so easily, but she thought her mother was right about the end being in sight. King George V had addressed the opening of the Parliament of Northern Ireland in the Belfast City Hall ten days ago. The Unionists were delighted to have him there, but his speech was targeted at those republicans in the audience, men who were in no way loyal to him. It had been a brave move and could have been met with derision and violence – indeed in some quarters it was – but Harp felt it was the beginning of the end of hostilities. She had read the full account of his speech in the newspaper, and now she quoted, "'I appeal to all Irishmen to pause, to stretch out the hand of forbearance and concili-ation, to forgive and to forget, and to join in making for the land which they love a new era of peace, contentment and goodwill.'"

Rose smiled at her daughter's ability to recall the king's exact words. Speeches, poems, songs or whole paragraphs from books, many of them obscure, had been quoted verbatim by Harp since childhood. Others found her ability either impressive or odd, but Rose was used to it. The strange thing was that Ralph had the exact same ability. He was extraordinarily clever and had used that intellect to manipulate and cheat his whole life.

Not that Rose had ever mentioned that to Harp. She knew her daughter regarded Henry Devereaux as her real father, not Ralph, and Harp wouldn't want to hear about any likeness between her and the man she thought of as her wicked uncle. And Rose felt the same way. Gentle, kind Henry Devereaux had been the one who raised Harp to be the young woman she was today: beautiful, quirky, talented and amazingly knowledgeable – at least about the things that could be learned from books.

'Do you really think so, Harp? Really?' Despite her earlier opti-mism, Rose was suddenly doubtful. 'Matt thinks they won't ever let us go, not really. Britain has ruled Ireland since 1169, and look at all the efforts made over the years – rebellions, invasions, wars, negotiations – but nothing ever worked. Maybe some hodgepodge version of home rule will be offered at best, and that will set the whole thing off again.'

'No. This time it's different. We fought for a republic, and we declared a republic in 1916, remember? And then Collins took over, and he knows how to fight them – he gets under their skin in a way nobody else ever did. We had them running wrong, Mam, remember? They were terrified to come out of their barracks in the end, and they know in London that we can keep that up indefinitely. We have the people behind us, we have right on our side, and we have Mick Collins. I believe in him, and if anyone can get us free, it is him. The British are making conciliatory noises for the first time in eight hundred years.'

'I know what they say, but Matt says that saying something and doing it are two different things, and there's been so much loss and destruction, so much hardship and pain... I don't know any more, I really don't. The likes of Ralph Devereaux always get their way in the end. He could never bear the idea that Henry left you the house. It rankled with him so much, not just the house, but the idea that an upstart servant like me would have such notions. That's how Ralph and those like him see us, Harp, as inferior.'

Harp leaned over and took her mother's hand, gazing deeply into her dark-brown eyes. She recited the most wonderful words she knew by heart. '"We declare the right of the people of Ireland to the owner-ship of Ireland, and to the unfettered control of Irish destinies, to be sovereign and indefeasible. The long usurpation of that right by a foreign people and government has not extinguished the right, nor can it ever be extinguished except by the destruction of the Irish people."'

The lines of the Proclamation of Independence that was read by Pádraig Pearce outside the GPO on Easter Monday in 1916 hung between her and her mother for a moment.

Then she added, 'They have tried to destroy us, Mam, there's no denying it, but they have not brought about our destruction, and so we fight on and we'll never give up, never. They will be repelled from our country, and Ralph will be repelled from our house. I don't know how or when, but I think what you said to Matt is right. It will happen soon.'

Chapter 2

JohnJoe gazed in astonishment at his friend Jerry Gallagher. 'You're not serious?'

'Deadly serious.' Jerry was planing the door they were working on with gusto, feeling the smooth wood with his hand every few strokes to make sure it had the right finish. 'You and Harp are amazing musicians. And when the war is over, there'll be fewer fundraisers to take up your time. You two are getting quite the reputation – it would be a shame to let that all disappear when the cause is no longer the pressing thing it is now. You need to think about going professional.'

JohnJoe went back to sanding. They were preparing the ballroom door together, getting it ready for hanging. The huge restoration project on the Criterion Hotel had everyone on the Rafferty crews working to get it ready in time. Matt was supervising the team fitting the windows, while JohnJoe and his crew were on doors and architraves. Danny was overseeing all the plastering and blockwork, and Pat was working with the architect, who seemed pleased with how everything was going. Between all the teams, they employed fifty men. They'd had to subcontract the painters, and JohnJoe was in charge of keeping them on task as well. Jerry was his very reliable second in command.

The hotel was due to open amid much fanfare the week after next, and the opening night was to be a celebration of Irish culture. Musicians, dancers, a storyteller and the finest of Boston-Irish cuisine would be on offer. The ballroom, one of the largest in the city, was going to be a huge draw, as concerts and performances of all kinds were lining up to book the venue. Pat Rafferty normally didn't bother with restoration – he was more interested in construction – but something about this hotel had taken his fancy and it had become a labour of love. His wife Kathy had teased him that he was having a crisis about getting old and creating his legacy, but behind it all, she was proud of him, and she and Rose had worked very hard at the décor, making sure the whole experience of staying at the Criterion would be one guests would never forget. Rose's considerable experience in the industry had proved invaluable.

'I can't just walk away and let Uncle Pat down, even if I wanted to,' JohnJoe pointed out. 'He's got another contract for building a street of stores and houses, and we'll be starting on that as soon as we've finished here. Pat relies on me. Besides, even if Harp and I wanted to be musicians, we wouldn't know where to start.'

Jerry made one last pass with his plane. 'That's OK, because I'll do all that for you. I've decided I want to be a promoter, someone who books entertainment acts to play at venues like this place when it opens, music, theatre, dancers, all that sort of thing. People love to go out to see a show, and for example, here at the Criterion Hotel, we could do a dinner and a show ticket combined. I'd make the arrangements with the venue, book the acts and take a cut. Simple really.'

JohnJoe was intrigued. 'And that's a real job, like you can make a living at it?'

'Maybe not a proper living at first. I'd have to advertise and hold auditions and build up a portfolio of acts to begin with, but eventually I think I can. A venue owner could ask for a jazz band, or a showtunes singing and dancing act, or a dancing dog, whatever he wanted, and I'd supply it.'

'But you already have a well-paid job. You're a carpenter, and a good one, and you've enough work to keep you going forever. Uncle Pat says you're one of the best he's ever seen, so I don't get it. Why would you leave it for something that might not work out?'

Jerry shrugged and grinned. 'I came over here for adventure, and because the British would have put my neck in a noose if I hadn't, but if I'm going to spend my life laying floors and sanding architraves, then what's the point? I'd have been doing that back in Ballyfermot. I'm only a carpenter because my old man did it before me and his before him – it wasn't my choice.'

Jerry Gallagher was a small dark-haired man in his early thirties. He had sleek hair brushed back from his high forehead and hazel eyes set in a face that was well constructed and symmetrical. Harp had put her finger on it: He wasn't good-looking in any conventional sense, and he was short and slight, but there was something compelling about him, a kind of energy, like he was always thinking ahead to the next thing. He was sociable and friendly, but there was something secretive about him too. You got the impression that what you saw was not really who he was. And you'd be right.

Jerry had been an infamous member of the IRA back in Ireland, mainly for the brazenness of the ambushes and attacks on the British that he led. He orchestrated in particular a very successful attack on a Dublin Metropolitan Police barracks, executing the chief, a known torturer, from four hundred yards away with a single shot to the head. The word was that if Jerry Gallagher chose a mark, he would hit it every single time and the enemy would never know from where the fatal bullet came. That night, with Jerry providing covering fire, the police had been relieved of their weapons and the barracks burned to the ground. The officers were found tied up in their underwear on a nearby bridge in the freezing night air. The photograph of them, half-naked, humiliated and freezing, had circulated widely in republican circles, and the word was that the Royal Irish Constabulary chief had made the arrest of Jerry Gallagher a personal vendetta.

Jerry had to be removed out of the clutches of the British immediately, and like many of his comrades before him, found himself on a boat to Boston, with Pat Rafferty waiting there to give him a job and set him up. Jerry was an unusual character and an unlikely person to have left such a string of audacious attacks in his wake, as he was quietly spoken and gentle and kept himself to himself. He lived in two rooms over a butcher shop on East 4th Street on Telegraph Hill and never went to the bars or out dancing with the other guys who worked for Pat Rafferty. Despite that, he wasn't stand-offish, and JohnJoe liked him.

'So explain to me again what you're thinking?' JohnJoe said.

Jerry nodded. 'I met this guy, Leo Cohen is his name. He's a singer. I heard him at a little bar down in Roxbury, and we got talking. He was telling me how he was signed with some agencies that got him places to perform – gigs, he called them.'

'Wouldn't it be more fun to be on the stage yourself?' JohnJoe helped Jerry right the heavy ballroom door and hang it on the hinges before returning to the second one and placing it on the makeshift bench they'd built for the purpose of preparing the doors, architraves and skirting.

'Couldn't carry a tune in a bucket.' Jerry grinned as JohnJoe screwed the ornate brass handles to the door. 'No, but I'd love to break into that world. It's hard, though. The Irish aren't really big in theatre circles – it's more the Jews run that. Although this Leo says I don't look Irish.' He cast a sidelong grin at big Mick Boyle, who was pushing a heavily loaded wheelbarrow of sand past them. Mick was a block layer from West Kerry who had a florid complexion, wide features and a beer belly.

'Hey, there's more than one kind of Irishman, y'know!' JohnJoe winked.

'And that's another reason for me to sign up you and Harp. You're both gorgeous to look at, and that's a great help.'

JohnJoe laughed uncomfortably. 'Well, Harp is, anyway, that's for sure. And she loves the theatre, and she's a great musician. But going professional? I've never thought about it, and I'm sure she hasn't either. I don't know anyone in the proper music business, but then maybe that's because I don't know any Jews...'

That was the way of it in Boston. The Italians did their thing, restaurants and things like that, the Irish were builders, the Chinese did laundry and had shops – every group of immigrants had their niche and stuck to themselves.

'And so,' continued Jerry, as he stood back and cast a critical eye over the first door to ensure it was perfectly hung, 'if I want to crack that business, I need an act to get started. You just play the music, and I'll be your manager. You'll need a fiddle player as well if we're going to extend your repertoire, but I think I have that sorted.'

'Oh, you do, do you?' JohnJoe thought it was comical how certain Jerry was that he and Harp would go along with his plan.

'Yep, got it all arranged.'

'Hey, do I pay you two old ladies to be gas-baggin' all day?' Pat passed them by with the architect and cuffed JohnJoe playfully on the head. 'This is the future, Eugene. What you think, eh? Is my empire gonna be in safe hands with him and Dannyboy over there?' Pat gestured to Danny, who was smoking a cigarette while plastering a wall expertly.

Eugene Kent had known Pat Rafferty for years and everyone understood that despite his jocular manner, he loved his nephews like his own sons. 'It will go from strength to strength, I'm sure, but we're not ready to be rid of you yet, Pat.'

'Too right, and you won't be. My old lady would throw me out by the weekend if I was under her feet all day, so I'll be brought off a building site feet first,' Pat joked. 'But yeah, we got good boys with these two, and they got themselves two nice ladies too. Behind every successful man is a good woman, and we got the best, right, JJ?'

JohnJoe smiled. He would have loved Harp whatever anyone thought, but it was an added bonus that his uncle did too. Marianne and Danny were married and had a baby girl earlier in the year, a sweet little thing called Katherine after their beloved Aunt Kathy, although to avoid confusion, she was always called Katie. He and Harp enjoyed visiting them, and secretly it was the life he longed for, but convincing his stubborn girlfriend to allow him to propose, get them a nice place, settle down and have some babies was a whole other matter. She loved Katie and was very good friends with Marianne, but she had no desire whatsoever to follow her lead into matrimony. He knew better than to raise the topic, since she shut him down each time he even hinted at it. She was more interested in education and a career than being a wife and mother.

'We sure do have the best,' JohnJoe agreed.

After the two men moved on, he returned to the conversation with Jerry. 'But *why* do you want to do it? Be a promoter, I mean? I understand why people would want to be on stage, but doing all the bookings and making the arrangements... I don't know – it doesn't sound like much fun.'

261

The other man shrugged. 'When I was a kid, my ma saved up and brought me and my brother to the Gaiety to see the pantomime. My da thought she was cracked as the crows to be wasting money on stuff like that, but Ma loved it too, and so we went. I'll never forget it. The place was magic, you know? All gold balconies and red velvet seats. And when we sat there in the dark with a bag of toffees between us and they were all up on stage, singing and dancing, I don't know, I just... I loved it.' The way he spoke, without shame or embarrassment, made him unusual. He was not like other men, especially those in the building trade, gruff and unemotional.

'And so then I left school, of course, and served my time as an apprentice with my da and my brother in the family business. But every chance I got, I was at a show or a concert or something. My da never understood it, and he was a bit mortified really, I think, but then I joined the Volunteers and he was proud of me.'

The second door was ready for hanging now, and together they lifted it into place beside its partner, screwing and fixing as they went. JohnJoe offered his friend a cigarette as they stood back and admired their handiwork. The doors were six feet wide each and ornately carved; the two of them hung perfectly.

Jerry leaned against the wall as he smoked. 'Being a promoter is a good fit for me, I think. I'm a good talker, and I'm honest and trustworthy. And even if I'm not a singer or a dancer myself, I can tell a good one from a dud every day of the week.' He exhaled a long plume of smoke. 'I used to play a little game with myself, back at home – which acts I saw that would go on to make it, play in the bigger places or go over to England or even over here, and which wouldn't. I had a kind of a knack for picking winners. I'd love you to be my first act, but I guess I'm going ahead with this anyway.'

JohnJoe sighed. 'So you'll be telling my uncle any day that he's losing the best carpenter he's had in years, will you?'

'Well, that's show business, JohnJoe my friend, just show business.' Jerry winked and grinned.

ABOUT THE AUTHOR

Jean Grainger is a USA Today bestselling Irish author. She writes historical and contemporary Irish fiction and her work has very flatteringly been compared to the late great Maeve Binchy.

She lives in a two hundred year old stone cottage in County Cork with her husband Diarmuid and the youngest two of her four children. The older two show up occasionally with laundry and to raid the fridge. There are a variety of animals there too, all led by two cute but clueless micro-dogs called Scrappy and Scoobi.

The Harp and the Rose is her twenty-fourth novel

ALSO BY JEAN GRAINGER

To get a free novel and to join my readers club (100% free and always will be)

Go to www.jeangrainger.com

The Tour Series

The Tour

Safe at the Edge of the World

The Story of Grenville King

The Homecoming of Bubbles O'Leary

Finding Billie Romano

Kayla's Trick

The Carmel Sheehan Story

Letters of Freedom

The Future's Not Ours To See

What Will Be

The Robinswood Story

What Once Was True

Return To Robinswood

Trials and Tribulations

The Star and the Shamrock Series

The Star and the Shamrock

The Emerald Horizon

The Hard Way Home

The World Starts Anew